DEDICATION

To Jessica Gibson: Thank you for always having faith in me and my writing.

Chapter 1

PEYTON

"So, this bitch gets in my face and demands I tell her what the *fuck* I'm doing with her man. *Demands*! Who the fuck is she, thinking she can demand I tell her shit?"

"And let me guess. You need an attorney now?" I took a sip of my cosmo.

My best friend Lorelei, and I had gone to the bar down the street from our work that we frequented almost every Friday night and sometimes for happy hour during the week. Rick's was everything you would expect from a bar in Beverly Hills. The food was great, the atmosphere was on point, and the drinks were always perfect and made with the best liquors. But what set Rick's apart from other bars in the area, and what kept Lorelei and I coming back, was the vodka tasting room.

It wasn't just a room. It was a walk-in glass freezer designed solely for vodka in its purest form. They gave out faux fur coats to wear in the twenty-eight degree box, and a vodka expert spent around fifteen minutes giving tastings and information regarding the hundred or so different vodkas that were lined along white leathered shelves. It was a neat experience. Lore and I had only done it once, but since it was a glass case, we watched people do it all the time.

Lorelei waved me off. "No, I don't need an attorney. Before I could do anything, Tom got in her face and told her to back the fuck up."

"Oh. Does *he* need a lawyer now?"

"No." She rolled her chocolate brown eyes. "You don't even practice criminal defense."

"Fine," I agreed. "Continue."

"This chick burst into tears. *Tears*! In the middle of the club."

"Wow ..." I breathed, flipping my long, dark hair over my shoulder. "Why did she cry?"

Lore shrugged. "I guess they recently broke up and she's still in love with him. Funny thing, I don't care. I'm never going out with that dude again. I don't need that shit in my life."

I chuckled. "Gotta love online dating."

"Right?" She took a sip of her cosmo. "And what guy takes a girl to a club on their first date? I mean, I like to dance and drink as much as the next girl, but I'm not putting out unless they at least feed me."

"You're too much." I laughed.

"That's why you love me." She grinned and smoothed her hair down.

"I love you because you save my ass on a daily basis."

"I do save your ass daily," she agreed with a laugh.

We had been working for a family law firm in Beverly Hills for over five years. We met the day she was hired by Chandler & Patterson, LLP as my paralegal. She was my eyes to make sure I didn't screw up any pleadings, and my paper pusher, making sure my client files are in date order and pristine—among other things. And she's my best friend. Some firms frowned upon attorneys friending "lower" colleagues, but not C&P. When an assistant worked well with the person they were assisting, it was like a well-oiled machine.

Chandler and Patterson was a high-profile law firm that represented well-known famous actors/actresses, directors, musicians or other people in the limelight getting divorced and/or had custody issues. Given our clientele, we also specialized in prenuptial agreements and tried to do mediation when we could. Most of our clients didn't want the public to know what was going on in their marital lives.

I got into law because of my father. Before he retired, he was a criminal defense attorney for twenty plus years, and then a judge in Los Angeles. I wanted to follow in his footsteps, and while I didn't practice criminal defense, my ultimate goal was to become a family law judge one day.

"So, did the chick leave or what?" I was interested in hearing the end of the story since my dating life was shit. Shit meaning I went on dates that never led anywhere. I either didn't like the dude, or once he found out what I did for a living, it turned him off because he assumed I'd take him for all he was worth if we ever got a divorce in the end. Sure I knew what to do and what not to do when it came to the financial aspects of a marriage, but not all marriages ended in divorce. Needless to say, those guys weren't the right ones for me.

Lorelei snorted. "I don't know. She ran off crying, and I didn't see where she went. Tom bought me a few more drinks, we danced, and then I went home."

"Alone?" I smirked.

She furrowed her eyebrows. "Yes, *alone*. The guy had no potential. He was cute and all, but I don't have time for girlfriend drama. I'm too old for that shit." I was two years older than her thirty, so I was too old for that shit too.

"At least you have men interested in you."

"Pey," Lorelei leaned forward and grabbed my hand, "you have men interested in you. You're just not interested in them."

It was my turn for my eyebrows to raise. "No, I don't." I knew that wasn't exactly true. I was picky.

She blinked slowly, shaking her head as if she couldn't believe what I'd said. "See that guy over there?" She nudged her head at the bar.

I turned and saw a guy with a buzzed head of brunette hair, dressed in jeans and a button-down blue shirt, looking our way. "Yeah?"

"He's been staring at you for the last twenty minutes."

"He's staring at you," I argued.

"Um, no."

I looked at the guy again, and he raised his tumbler. I turned back

3

to Lorelei. "Okay, so maybe he *is* looking at me, but only because it's a Friday night and he wants to get laid."

"And?" She chuckled.

"I'm not into that kinda thing. I want to be fed, too."

We both started laughing, and I turned to look at the guy again to see if he was still looking at me. He was, but he scowled then looked away.

"Aw, he thinks we're laughing at him."

I shrugged. "Good, he'll stop staring."

"We're fucking bitches."

I nodded. "We are. But I came to have a drink with my friend after work. I didn't come here to have a one-night stand."

"Maybe you need one."

I turned my head slightly and narrowed my eyes. "What?"

"You're so wound up because of work. I get it, it's stressful, but that's more of a reason to get laid."

"Well, not with *that* guy." I waved my hand in the direction of the poor dude.

A smile spread across her ruby lips. "Well, let's find you one."

My Uber driver dropped me off at the front door of my building, and after taking the elevator up to my floor, I stumbled out three sheets to the wind. Lorelei and I had drunk one too many cosmos —*five if I remember correctly*. And because we were in our own world, gossiping and people watching, we didn't find me a guy to go home with. That wasn't really my thing, though. Plus a lot of the men who frequented Rick's were lawyers, and I didn't want to get involved with someone I had cases against. That could get messy, and it was unethical. If attorneys did get involved with each other, they needed to inform their clients, and then one of the attorneys would need to withdraw from the case so it wasn't a conflict. Who wanted to do that for a one-night stand? Not me.

As I passed my neighbor's place, I placed my hand on the door wishing he'd open it, pull me in and fuck me. *If* I were to have a one-night stand, I wanted it to be with my sexy neighbor. Apparently, a lot of women had lived out that fantasy. I heard him all the time enjoying the company of those women, and each of them sounded different. I giggled to myself as I stood outside his door, remembering some of the things I'd heard.

"Did you get that lamp at Target?" one woman had asked between moans. "I'm gonna fuck you hard!" another woman had shouted. At first, I'd thought it was Sam shouting because it sounded like Batman's deep growl. And another that had me laughing so hard was, "You like that, you saucy biscuit?" Where Sam found these women was beyond me. And the ones who moaned over and over *and over* annoyed the fuck out of me. I wasn't sure if it was because he was that good in bed or they thought their screams were sexy.

And every time I wished it were me.

Since I was buzzed, I wanted more than just a quickie with my vibrator tonight, but my neighbor didn't open his door, so I carried my drunk self to my condo. Thinking about it, I should have had that guy with the shaved head at Rick's buy me my drinks and take me home. At least I wouldn't be pining over my neighbor, who didn't even know I existed.

That wasn't true.

Sam knew I existed, but only that I was the girl next door. We'd never said more than two words to each other in the three years that we'd been neighbors. Maybe he had a rule about not eating where he shits or, in this case, fucking his neighbors. Maybe he thought I had a man. Or maybe he thought I was ugly. I never saw the women he brought home (only heard them), so maybe he only screwed supermodels who talked like superheroes or had a thing for comfort food.

After stripping my clothes and leaving a trail back to the door, I stood in front of the floor-length mirror in my bedroom. No, I definitely wasn't a supermodel. For one, I wasn't tall and all legs. I was five-five, and I only had normal-sized breasts. Not the ones that spilled over the cups of bras or the ones that needed a push-up bra to even look like boobs. I'd heard the saying that a man really only needed a handful. I had that covered, but no more than that. I wasn't fat, but I wasn't runway material either. I was *normal*. I weighed what was right for my frame.

My desire to be with Sam started to fizzle out as I continued to stare at myself, thinking of all the reasons why he never gave me a second look. And then it happened ...

"Yes!" the woman screamed. "Yes! Right there!"

I knew what she was referring to behind my bedroom wall. I'd never seen it, but if the banging was any indication, I knew he was fucking her hard because his headboard was hitting the wall next to mine.

Bam.

Bam.

"Yes! Fuck yes!"

Bam.

Bam.

"Well, son of a bitch," I muttered to myself. My buzz was definitely wearing off, and my hatred for Sam was rising. "You've got to be kidding me!"

"You like that, Nikki?"

"Yes!" Nikki screamed *again*.

I rolled my eyes. *Well, I could have answered that question.*

Sam started to groan, Nikki started to moan, and I'd had it. Before I knew what I was doing, my butt-ass-naked-self was banging on the wall between our condos. "Stop!" I shouted. "Some of us are trying to sleep!"

I was such a loser. Sure it was late, but it was a Friday night, and I'd just let my hot ass neighbor know I had no life because I was "sleeping" at three in the morning and not getting my brains fucked out like Nikki.

The banging of the headboard stopped, and I sighed. It worked. If only I'd done that years ago, Sam might have realized I could hear him and maybe he'd pick a different place to screw them. Like the couch or the kitchen counter. Hell, maybe even the floor.

I started to walk toward my attached bathroom when there was a knock on my front door. I stopped mid-step and didn't move hoping *he'd* leave. There was only one person it could be, and apparently, I'd pissed him off. More knocks came, and I held my breath. If he couldn't hear me breathing, he'd assume I was sleeping.

And more knocks.

"Open the door, Peyton."

He knew my name? I mean, I knew his name because I was a woman and we did that shit. As soon as I'd seen him when he moved in, I wanted to know his name, but of course, I couldn't ask him. That would be crazy.

I wasn't shy. I had to present cases in a courtroom, and all eyes would be on me as I spoke. I also met with strangers every day, from new clients to attorneys I'd never worked with before. But this was different. This was Sam. This was the hot neighbor whose name I knew only because I'd heard a chick screaming it. Of course, that was when I had a glass to the wall and my ear pressed against it, trying to hear what was happening in his bedroom. *Little had I known I didn't need the glass.* But I had no idea he knew my name.

"Peyton, open the door."

I sighed and closed my eyes. Sam had said more than two words to me now. Granted it wasn't face-to-face, but if I opened the door, it would be more than the eight he'd already said.

"I'm not going away until you answer the door."

I wasn't sure how our neighbors were feeling about Sam yelling at my door. It was late—or early. However you wanted to look at it.

Sam knocked again. "Damn it, Peyton. Open the fucking door."

Before he caused more of a scene, I snagged my robe from the back of my bathroom door and threw it on as I made my way to the front door. Thankfully I wasn't sleeping. My hair and make-up were still intact and gave me a little more confidence when I swung the door open.

"What?" I hissed.

He opened his mouth to speak, and then I watched as his eyes traveled down my body and then back up. "I thought you were sleeping?"

"I said I was trying to," I clarified.

"You sleep in full makeup?"

I scowled. *Who was this guy?* "No, I just got home and was getting ready for bed until I heard you—"

"Do you want to join us?"

I opened my mouth to speak, but no words came out. Sam smiled, and then I remembered why I was infatuated with him. He was tall, dark and handsome: the perfect combination. His white teeth shined against his olive skin, and I swallowed. My gaze then traveled down his bare torso, and my eyes widened. I'd never seen him shirtless, *and fuck me*, he was perfect. Washboard abs, a trim waist that connected to that V that drove women crazy, and not a lick of hair on his chest. His lower stomach was a different story, and I knew exactly where the light dusting of hair went.

"Do you want to join us?" he asked again.

"How do you know my name?" I blurted.

"What?" He chuckled.

"How do you know my name?" I repeated.

"Because we've lived side-by-side for three years."

I crossed my arms over my chest. "But we've never said more than hello to each other."

"Do you know mine?" he asked.

I snorted. "Kinda hard not to when the women scream it nightly."

"Does it turn you on?"

"I ... What is this?" I asked, moving my hand back and forth between us.

Sam placed a hand on the doorjamb then moved in closer as he whispered, "You weren't sleeping, and are dressed only in a black robe, which leads me to believe hearing me fucking a chick was turning you on. So I want to know if you want to join us."

"But when you came over here, you didn't know I was only in a robe and *not* sleeping," I corrected.

With his free hand, he ran his fingers along the silk collar of my robe. "I've seen how your eyes drop when you see me, and a tint of red spreads across your cheeks. I know you want me, and I figured hearing me turns you on. I want to get you in my bed."

I stepped back, and his hand fell away from my clothes. "You think that I'd want to share you?"

Sam cracked another smile. "Have you ever had a threesome?"

"That's none of your business."

"That's a no. In that case, I'll kick Nikki out and it can just be us."

What the hell was happening? "I'll pass," I stated, and reached for my door to close it.

Sam grabbed it. "You sure?"

I was starting to realize that my fantasy with this jerk was only that—a *fantasy*. He wasn't who I thought he was. I mean, he did sleep with a lot of women, but I just thought...

I thought he'd one day realize the girl he wanted lived next door to him.

I was totally a loser.

"I'm not into that."

He smiled again. "Into what?"

I waved my hand in the direction of his condo. "Being another notch on your bedpost."

He laughed. "Peyton, we've been neighbors for a while. I *know* you want to be another notch, and I'm giving you the chance."

"You're such an asshole."

"But you've thought about it, right?" he asked, totally ignoring the fact I was pissed and had just called him an asshole.

Not wanting to give him even more of a bigger head, I said, "I thought that you were a nice guy."

"I am a nice guy. When I want something, I go after it. Doesn't mean I'm an asshole."

I crossed my arms over my chest again. "Why now? Why are you willing to kick that poor girl out?"

"When you banged on my wall, I realized that I could be fucking *you*, so I came over here to get you. Nikki is down for whatever. If I can only have you alone, then I'll kick her out."

"Have you ever heard the saying too little too late?"

"Don't be like this, Peyton. You know we both want each other. I'm sorry I waited until now."

I rolled my eyes. "Wanted."

"What?" He tilted his head.

"I'll admit that I thought you were cute. But now I know you're a sleazeball, and I don't want to catch anything. Have a good night." I pushed him back and closed the door in his face. I was definitely no longer drunk or horny. In fact, I wanted to move right then and there. *What had I'd been thinking?* He'd been with countless women. *Countless!*

I picked up my discarded jeans and blouse as I walked back to my room and went to take a shower. I felt dirty just being in the same space as Sam. When I got out of the shower, it sounded as though he was literally screwing Nikki against the wall. I heard what I assumed was her body moving up and down the wall as he thrust into her. Sam was trying to torture me.

There was no way I'd be able to sleep with my head next to all the moaning. Therefore, I grabbed a pillow off my bed and went and slept on my couch.

Chapter 2

PEYTON

I didn't see Sam the rest of the weekend. Granted, it was probably because I didn't leave my condo except to go to my parents' for our weekly Sunday night dinner. I wasn't sure if I was doing it on purpose or if my brain was conveniently making up stuff for me to do instead of leaving, but I'd cleaned my entire place top to bottom, put some old clothes in a garbage bag to donate to Goodwill, and caught up on a lot of TV shows on my DVR. It was a productive weekend, and I didn't hear a peep from Sam's side.

No thumps.

No moans.

No screams.

And he never came back to my door.

Monday started like a lot of them did. I had to be in court first thing before heading into the office. I had a Settlement Conference on the docket, and luckily opposing counsel and I had come up with an agreement. No trial would need to be set, and it would save time and money for the clients. But I had another hearing that I knew wouldn't be so easy. It was against an attorney who liked to drag issues out.

Dressed in a black pantsuit with a white blouse, I went through the metal detector and then made my way to the courtroom where my first hearing was scheduled. There were three different courtrooms that heard various family law cases throughout the day. When I entered the room with no windows, I took a seat in the back row next to my client who was already there.

"Morning, Derek. How are you?"

He turned his head to me. "I'll be better once this shit is over with. Paps are following me around more than usual."

A warm smile spread across my face. "That explains the few in the parking lot."

Derek was an A-list actor. It also helped that he was easy on the eyes. He had a scruffy vibe going with shaggy brunette hair and a beard the ladies went crazy for. He was getting divorced from another actress because they'd each found other people they wanted to be with.

"I guess I should be used to it, though."

"Living in the limelight does have their perks. That's how you met Maggie, right?" Derek was already engaged to another actress, Maggie Sharp.

"Yeah, we met on the set of Manmade," he confirmed.

I'd seen the blockbuster hit about a synthetic drug that burned one-percent of body fat with every dose. Derek played a doctor, and Maggie was his patient who didn't follow the correct dosage. The premise was he had to save her before side effects killed her. Then, of course, the characters fell in love—apparently on and off screen.

The judge entered the courtroom, and we stood, waiting for him to take his seat before returning to ours. The bailiff called the Judge's first case, and I watched as Booker Jameson (who I had my second case against) and Regina Rinks approached the designated tables in front of the judge with each of their clients.

I had a good rapport with Regina. We had the same way of doing things. We both wanted to get everything filed timely and have the cases settled in the six months it took for a divorce to finalize in the state of California.

Booker, on the other hand, liked to be difficult. He represented a lot of female clients, and I was almost positive they retained him because of his British accent, dreamy blue eyes, short blond hair that spiked up as if he just fixed it real quick after fucking a chick and, of course, his beard. A lot of women liked beards, and I did have to admit Booker looked sexy with his. When I first met him, I'd swooned at those features too. It was hard not to.

Until I realized how cocky he was.

He didn't have a bad reputation, but I was positive he and Sam shared the same nightly extracurricular activities. He just had that way about him. His panty-melting smile didn't help either.

I grabbed my phone from my purse to check emails and pass the time as I waited for my case to be called.

"We're unable to come up with a Settlement Agreement, Your Honor," Booker stated.

I tried to tune him out, I really did, but his accent was like silk moving across my skin. I looked up briefly, rolled my eyes, and returned back to my phone. After a few more minutes, the bailiff called my case. Derek and I stood, and we started walking down the middle aisle. Booker and Regina were gathering their belongings, so we waited for them to leave. I turned at the sound of the wood door opening to see Ernie Berg and Derek's wife walk in the doors.

Regina left first, and we smiled at each other, and then Booker turned. His blue eyes met my brown ones, and he winked. He winked!

Jackass.

I stilled as he passed me. Instantly, the scent of sandalwood and musk hit me. *Damnit! He smelled good too.*

I did my best not to look at him as I moved around him so I could start my hearing.

My first hearing was short and sweet. We settled the case, and I had an hour or so before my next one against Booker. I decided to go outside to soak up some sun. Every day that I had court, I took the stairs. It was my thing. I didn't go to the gym or anything of that nature, so I figured taking the stairs justified my laziness. At least that was what I told myself.

As I made my way down the stairwell from the third-floor courtrooms, I heard the door behind me open and then footsteps descend. I didn't think anything of it until my name was called.

"Hey, Peyton."

I turned to see Clint Davis from Booker's firm coming down the stairs. Their firm was mostly male attorneys, and they all seemed to think their shit didn't stink. His slicked back blond hair was perfectly in place, his suit had no wrinkles, and he smelled like *Old Spice*.

"Hey, Clint."

"Your case, Marriage of Waterford?"

"Yeah?" I responded as I stopped with one leg on a lower step than my other.

"I was just retained by the husband."

"Great. It will be lovely to work with you again." Really it wasn't, but I was being nice. Clint had a sleazeball vibe to him. "I look forward to it." I went to continue down the stairs, but his words halted me.

"Do you want to go get a drink? Talk about the case?"

It was not my practice to go get drinks with opposing counsels and talk about any cases. When I left the office, I left my work there. Sure I thought about cases, but I didn't think it was fair to bill my client for happy hour.

"I haven't received the sub of attorney yet, Clint," I said, trying to deflect his question.

He dug in the brown, expanding file folder he was holding. "I actually just had it filed."

Well, fuck.

He handed me the filed copy, and I took it, trying to think of something quick to say. "I can't, Clint. I have a client meeting."

"Tonight then. I need to get caught up on the case."

Read the file! "I'm sorry, I have plans. Why don't you set a meeting with my assistant and we can discuss things?"

"It's a harmless drink."

This guy didn't quit. Just as I was about to respond, Booker, of all people, walked up the stairs. Our eyes met, and there was disgust in his eyes as he passed, though the disgust was directed at his co-worker. *Interesting.*

"I didn't say getting a drink wouldn't be harmless. You're married anyway." Out of the corner of my eye, I saw Booker's steps falter as he chuckled. "I'm just really busy and think it's best we set a meeting in my office—or your office. Whatever works." As I turned to leave, I called over my shoulder, "Have a nice day."

"So you and Clint, huh?"

I jolted at Booker's question as he sat next to me in the back of the courtroom. I turned and rolled my eyes at him. "Um, no."

"That wanker wants to get in your knickers."

I furrowed my eyebrows at him. That would *never* happen. "Do you talk about all your co-workers like that?" I didn't know the British language all that well, but I knew wanker wasn't a good term.

Booker smirked. "Only the ones who deserve it."

We sat in silence as I watched my client walk in and find a seat on the opposite side from me. Usually, I would sit next to my client, but being next to Booker was doing *things* to me. My run in with Sam on Friday night must have had my brain thinking of sex because I started thinking about giving Booker a blow job. A blow job *in the middle of court* to Booker, who was gorgeous on the outside, but nasty on the inside.

Okay, to be fair I didn't know if Booker was nasty on the inside. I'd only ever talked to him about cases, and I knew of his reputation. I just assumed since he liked to poke the bear in a sense, that he was that way in and out of court. So why the hell my brain was envisioning myself giving him a BJ was beyond me.

I was trying not to be turned on even more by Booker's scent of sandalwood and musk when the bailiff finally called our case. We stood, and Booker motioned for me to go before him. As I made my way up the center, the Bailiff instructed everyone who wasn't a party to the case or an attorney to leave the courtroom. Because it was a custody case, and all child custody cases were confidential, the courtroom needed to be empty. It wasn't your typical child custody case where the parents were fighting over who would get the child. No, Booker's client wanted grandparent rights. The grandmother wanted custody of the little girl based on bullshit she thought was true.

We all walked up to the two tables before the judge, Booker and his client on the left, my client and I on the right. We sat and waited for the judge to begin.

The judge read a file on his desk as he spoke, "We're here on the motion from attorney Jameson for modification of child custody. I've reviewed the motion. Counsel, do you have anything to add?"

"Yes, thank you, Your Honor." Booker stood, buttoned his black suit jacket and started speaking again. "My client is the grandmother to Ms. Winter's client's ten-year-old daughter, and it has come to my client's attention that Ms. Alexander is going to clubs almost every night and leaving her daughter, Carly, at home by herself."

That wasn't true.

Booker continued. "Mrs. Vogel was also told that there are drugs in the home."

That wasn't true either.

"And who has told these accusations to your client, Mr. Jameson?"

"Mrs. Vogel's friend who lives in the same complex as Ms. Alexander."

"Ms. Winters?" the judge looked to me.

I stood. "Yes, good morning, Your Honor." I looked to Booker for a brief second before turning my attention back to Judge Walters. "Mr. Jameson's client has no personal knowledge of what goes on behind my client's door. It's only speculation and hearsay. My client is a single mother due to Mrs. Vogel's son being incarcerated, and she is doing her best as a young, single mother. There are no drugs in the home, and when Ms. Alexander needs to go out, she hires her neighbor's sixteen-year-old daughter to watch Carly."

"Your Honor," Booker cut in, and I started to get agitated. This was typical Booker. He knew this case was shit. There was no proof of anything he accused my client of, and to be honest, I had no idea why he would take the case in the first place. "My client requests a drug test be ordered as well as a psych eval for Ms. Alexander."

I shook my head at the ridiculous request. "Your Honor, Mr. Jameson's requests are preposterous. My client is of sane mind, and Carly's a solid B student. Given what Carly has endured with her father going to jail, Ms. Alexander is doing a fantastic job raising her."

"Mr. Vogel is in prison for selling drugs, Your Honor," Booker retorted.

"My client had nothing to do with his dealings and was never charged," I countered.

"I'm going to stop you both right there," Judge Walters stated, holding his hand up. "Ms. Winters is correct, Mr. Jameson. Your motion is based solely on speculation and hearsay. I'll dismiss this case without prejudice, Mr. Jameson, and if you'd like to file another motion with more proof, we can revisit this matter. As for now, you simply don't have enough proof."

Booker's client groaned, and I tried to hide my smile. Booker always assumed he'd get what he wanted, but in this case, he hadn't. My client hugged me to thank me, and then turned to leave. As I exited the courtroom, Booker started walking next to me.

"You know what this means right?"

I turned and looked up at him as we kept walking. "You're going to file another motion?"

"Yes, but also my client wants to get CPS involved."

"You think Child Protective Services will find anything?"

He grinned. "Doesn't matter if they do. Just means I get to see your lovely face more."

I stopped walking. Booker didn't.

Was he flirting with me?

I made it back to the office a little before noon. As I walked through the double glass doors of C&P, I waved to the receptionist. Maria was around Lorelei's age, had long black hair, spoke with a Hispanic accent, and was living the fantasy we all dreamed about— the perfect marriage with two perfect kids. Maria waved back, and I continued down the hall toward my office.

"How was your weekend?" Lorelei asked as I stopped at her desk for my phone messages.

I shrugged. "Uneventful."

"You should have taken me up on my offer from last week. The lake was awesome."

"Lore," I smiled, "my idea of fun doesn't involve not showering for two days."

"Technically, it was one day, and you just wash off in the lake."

I shivered. "Gross."

"So, how many chicks did Sam bang this weekend?" She leaned toward me as though she was waiting for the latest gossip.

Lorelei knew all about Sam. She'd seen him, she'd lusted over him herself, and she'd once heard him fucking. She quickly left to go home after, and I knew we'd both used our trusty vibrators thinking about what we'd heard. Now, the thought made me want to punch him in the face.

I shrugged. "Just one on Friday night."

"Sounds like he's slowing down." She smirked.

I blew out a breath. I hadn't had enough coffee for the conversation. Instead, I changed the subject. "What does my calendar look like this afternoon?"

"Ava Ashley is coming at one to go over her disso packet." A disso packet was a dissolution packet of all the documents one files with the court for a divorce. I'd already met with Ava when she hired me to represent her as her attorney for her divorce. She was an actress who had been nominated for a few Emmys, and she was my age. And she was *stunning*.

"Great. Let's take lunch now so we can be back before one."

I was engrossed in surfing the internet when Lorelei stuck her head in my door and informed me Ava was waiting.

"Perfect." I stood and made my way down the hall to the reception area. I hated keeping clients waiting. Everyone had somewhere to be, and not particularly in their attorney's office.

"Ava." I smiled my greeting. She looked up from her phone, and I waved her over. "Let's head back." She smiled, and when we rounded the corner, I asked, "Would you like something to drink?"

"Wine?" She laughed.

"Bad day?"

"Just nervous."

I nodded as we approached my office. "No need to be nervous. That's why you hired me. I'll make this process as smooth as possible. But I'm sure we can find you something *after* you sign all the papers for court. After you," I gestured for Ava to enter my office. It wasn't a corner office. It was ten by ten with a glass wall overlooking the skyscrapers of downtown LA in the far distance. The opposite side had a glass wall as well that gave me a view of Lorelei's desk.

After Ava and I had sat at my mahogany desk, she handed me her packet that consisted of her Schedule of Assets and Debts and Income and Expense Declaration. Lorelei would prepare the Petition, Summons and Proof of Service based on the information I gathered in my consultation with Ava. "Do you have any questions regarding these?"

Ava sighed. "I don't know ..."

Lorelei walked in with two glasses of water. I smiled at her as she set them on my desk then turned to leave.

"Let's go over your I&E first," I suggested. "It's not required to file with the Petition for Dissolution, but I like to have all my ducks in order to get the ball rolling."

Ava nodded, and I began to skim the form she had written her answers on. When I'd first started working on high profile cases, I was shocked by how much our clients made. It shouldn't have been a surprise given that they were Hollywood's A-List, but it was a lot more than I made. Granted, at the time I had only been an attorney for two years. Now I was working my way up, and in the last five years, I'd gotten several raises, but it was still nowhere near the millions Ava indicated she made.

When I got to her monthly expenses, one thing, in particular, stuck out to me. "You spend over thirty-thousand a month on entertainment, gifts, and vacations?" It wasn't unusual, per se, but we were talking a month, not a year. Usually, the number was half that amount.

Ava chuckled. "I think it might be more."

My eyes widened. "On entertainment? Maybe we need to count some for another category?"

She shrugged sheepishly. "Well, will the court know what the expenses are for?"

I leaned back in my chair. "Not exactly, but if you're saying that you spend thirty grand on entertainment, and you're including eating out as that expense, it needs to be broken up because there's a place for that."

Ava shook her head of long blonde hair. "I wouldn't call it eating out."

"Is it hookers or something?" I laughed, but I was kind of serious. I'd seen it before.

"Well ..." she trailed off. "Not really."

I leaned forward and rested my elbows on the wood surface and crossed my hands in front of my chin. "Whatever you tell me will stay between us. You know that. Attorney/Client confidentiality."

She sighed and then blurted, "It's a sex club."

My eyes widened. I wasn't expecting that answer. "You spend thirty-thousand on a sex club?"

She took a deep breath. "No, but whatever I tell you must stay between us. It's highly confidential."

I nodded my agreement. "Of course."

"Trent and I are members of a high-end sex club. It meets once a month in Beverly Hills. You have to be a member to attend, or be invited by a member, because it's highly exclusive. The cost is dependent on which membership you purchase. And I have the highest membership which is twenty-thousand a month."

I was silent as I soaked in the information. I had so many questions, and none of them had anything to do with Ava's divorce—*or maybe it did.* "When we met for your consultation, you said that you were getting divorced for irreconcilable difference. California is a no-fault state, which means cheating can't be the cause of divorce."

That wasn't entirely true. When someone cheats, and the other doesn't approve, that was an irreconcilable difference—*technically.* However, I knew judges who wouldn't grant divorces for that reason. Instead, the parties were sent to counseling to try to make their marriage work.

Ava shook her head. "Cheating isn't a factor. It's honestly our work. He's away on set, or I'm away on set. We don't see each other except at Sensation and ..."

I watched as she took long sips of her water before speaking again. "Okay, maybe it is cheating. I mean, I don't know for sure, but like I said, we don't see each other except for at the club."

I nodded. "So you both have other partners, and you're not into that anymore?"

She sighed. "I love the club. A lot of people I know go to it, and it's safe. No crazy fans or anything like that. I just needed more out of my marriage, and Trent isn't willing to give it to me. It's like he wants his cake and to eat it too."

"Did you tell him you're filing for divorce? I remember you said you were thinking about not springing it on him."

"I did." Ava nodded.

"What did he say?"

She shrugged. "He didn't really say anything except he wasn't surprised. He also said he was hiring an attorney we both know."

"Who's that?" I questioned and took a sip of my water.

"Booker Jameson."

I started to choke on the liquid as it went down my throat.

"You've heard of him?" Ava asked.

I snorted. "Yeah, we work with his firm a lot."

"He's a nice guy."

I chuckled. "Maybe, but not when it comes to working with opposing counsels."

Ava took another sip of water. "Why's that?"

"He has a reputation of making people produce a lot of discovery, and is known to request ex parte hearings like they're nothing."

"What does that mean?"

I took a deep breath. "He has a way of spinning things to make judges schedule emergency hearings. Usually, it's with custody or domestic abuse. Luckily, you don't have children, and you haven't told me about any abuse."

Ava shook her head. "No, no children and no abuse."

"Well, I wouldn't put it past him to ask for you to provide every bit of email or anything that could look good for Trent." I started to skim the file Lorelei had put together of my notes and client intake from when I'd first met with Ava. "If I remember correctly, your prenup is pretty cut and dry. Given that you both have separate incomes and have been living as though you are single, there shouldn't be an issue with spousal support. The only thing we really need to determine is any property you purchased together."

"He wants it all."

I sighed again. "Figures. And Booker will try to make that happen."

"He'll get all the houses?"

"I won't let him and neither will a judge." I grabbed Ava's Schedule of Assets and Debts and scanned it quickly. "You indicated that all these properties are shared. Does that mean you purchased them fifty/fifty?"

"Give or take. We had our accountants work it out."

"Well, let's get all the paperwork from them so we know exactly how much each of you put in, and we'll need to get the properties appraised."

"Can we avoid all of that?"

"Only if you two agree on what to split."

Ava chugged the rest of her water. "He'll never go for that. He thinks he makes more money than me."

"Doesn't matter if he makes more money. If anything, the judge might award you spousal support because of it. We'll find out. I'll get everything filed today before the court closes. I'll also get a process server to serve him."

"Trent knows it's coming soon, and he won't open the security gate for anyone. He'll wait until they prepare his papers before he does anything."

"There's no reason for him to avoid service if he knows it's coming."

She shrugged. "He thinks that if he's first, he'll get everything."

I laughed. "Doesn't work that way, and if Booker tells him it does, he has another thing coming."

"Can I serve him? I still need to pack a bag before I stay with my friend while we figure all this out."

I shook my head. "No, parties can't serve each other." I'd dealt with people avoiding service before, but this was different. Celebrities had extra security, so you had to be sneaky. If Trent wasn't leaving his mansion until Booker told him to, I had to come up with a plan.

"Does Trent know where you are now?" I asked.

"No." She shook her head. "I just told him last night that I wanted a divorce. I don't think he's aware I've already started the process."

"Do you know if he called Booker?"

"Probably not. I think he was going to wait until the next club night."

My mouth dropped open. "Booker's a member?"

Ava looked down at her lap, took a deep breath, and then looked back to me. "Yes, but you don't know that. It's how we know him."

I smirked. I thought Mr. Cocky could get any woman he wanted. He sure acted as such. "When's the next party?"

"Saturday night."

I was still smirking. "And you said it was by invitation only? Meaning *I* could be invited?"

Ava grinned. "Yes, but I'd need to submit the paperwork today so it can be approved by then."

"What do we need to do?" I asked, still smiling.

"You'll need to fill out a guest form and also get tested for any STD. But if you come, I don't want people to know you're serving Trent with divorce papers."

I smiled warmly at her. "No one will know and I'll leave afterward."

Ava was silent for a few beats and then she asked, "Peyton, would you like to come with me to Sensation?"

I smiled. "Are you inviting me?"

She grinned in return. "Yes."

I chuckled. "I accept your invitation. Now, what do we need to do to get me in?" I couldn't believe I was going to serve a client's husband at a sex club.

Sometimes you had to do what you had to do.

Chapter 3

PEYTON

T hat night, after my meeting with Ava, I went home to submit the form to become a guest. I didn't want to do it at work and have the IT department see that I'd searched a sex club even if it was for a case. As I pulled up the website, I read on the home page:

Sensation.

A sacred place free from judgement or inhibitions.

The only rule: Ask before you touch.

Sensation is an exclusive black-tie party attended by at least one hundred and fifty of the clubs most privileged members, and held once a month at an undisclosed mansion in Beverly Hills.

You may watch.

You may interact.

You can come together or you can choose to come alone.

The choice is yours.

Would you like it rough?

Would you like to be caressed and worshipped?

Or would you simply like to observe?

What do you desire?

What did I desire? It wasn't some guy I hooked up with at a bar or my neighbor that only wanted me for sex. I wanted something *more*. Someone who didn't care what I did for a living and wanted more than one night with me. I hadn't been with a man in a few months. I went on dates that never led anywhere because I either didn't like them or they got turned off because of my profession.

Immediately after I submitted the form, an email arrived in my inbox, letting me know where I had to go to be tested for sexually transmitted diseases. Before I could read more about Sensation—though I didn't think a sex club was my cup of tea either—Sam had a visitor. There was no way that I could read about how to become a member (even if I wanted to) or anything of that nature while Sam was screwing some chick right behind my bedroom wall. So, I closed my laptop, turned up the TV and watched my favorite comedy *How to Get the Girl* with the drop dead hunk Jason Black. He was *definitely* on my celebrity fuck list.

"I can't believe you're going to a sex club tonight," Lorelei exclaimed. "And without me."

I laughed. The entire week she'd been bitching about how I was going and she wasn't, and now that I was getting ready to leave, her bitching was a million times worse. "You act like I'm going to get my freak on."

She chortled. "You think you're just going to walk in, find Trent, serve him and leave?"

"Um, yeah," I stated as I swiped *MAC* Shroom eyeshadow along the brow bone of each eye.

"Peyton." Lorelei cocked her hip, placing her hands on either side. "You are not, and I repeat, *not* going to let this opportunity slip by."

I set my eyeshadow brush on my bathroom counter. It clicked against the granite as it settled. "This is for work."

Lorelei threw her hands in the air. "Oh my God! You're going to an elite sex club where there are famous people. Famous people who want to fuck, and you aren't even going to cross a name off your celebrity fuck list?"

I looked down at the floor, thinking about what she was saying. I honestly hadn't thought about it before now. "You think they'd want to do a no-name like me?"

Her eyes bugged out. "Um yeah! I've been telling you for years that you're hot as fuck. You don't listen to me."

"But I'm not like Ava. Jason Black isn't going to look twice at me."

Her mouth dropped open. "Jason Black is a member?"

I rolled my eyes and reached for my eyebrow brush again. "I don't know. But I'm saying that a celebrity like Jason will be all over other celebrities. Not some chick who has had him on her celebrity fuck list for four years."

"I thought it wasn't only celebrities that are a part of this club?"

I swiped a shade of Copperplate in the crease of my eyelid as I spoke. "It isn't. I'm just giving an example."

"As your best friend, I'm telling you that you can't let this opportunity pass. Get in there, find Trent and serve him, and then at least *watch* people get their freak on. Maybe that will loosen you up, and you'll find a hot guy to be with. Even if it's only for one night. Live a little."

I paused, applying a shade of Silver Fog on the inner corner of my lid, and looked at Lore in the reflection of the mirror. "I'll think about it."

I had to admit that going to this elite sex club was a rare opportunity. In my head, I'd pictured a free-for-all of people screwing on every piece of furniture. I'd imagined whips, chains, floggers, gags, Doms and Dommes. I had no idea what to expect. What I did know was that I was to dress in cocktail attire. Ava had told me that women didn't wear panties to the club—*for easy access*. I chose to wear a thong because going commando was too ballsy for me.

"You better," Lore responded. "And I want details."

"I can't give you details. It's confidential, remember?" It wasn't confidential that Lorelei or anyone knew about the sex club, but it *was* confidential to discuss or expose who and what went on in the mansion.

"Okay, I don't need to know who was there. I just want to know what *you* see and what *you* do."

I rolled my eyes and shut the bathroom door in her face. I had to finish getting ready for the party, and I was tired of arguing with my best friend.

My black Louboutins with silver spikes across the heel clicked on my hardwood floor as I made my way from my bedroom to the living room. Lorelei looked up from a magazine she was reading at my breakfast bar as soon as I came into view.

She was speechless.

"Well?" I snapped. If I looked like shit, I needed to know. I was dressed in a sleeveless black dress that hugged every curve. My hair was pulled back in a loose Chignon at the nape of my neck, and dangly, black-beaded earrings hung from each ear. But what made my look were the shoes. You could never go wrong with a pair of thousand dollar Louboutins.

"If I saw you at a sex club, I'd be all over that." She waved her hand up and down.

"So I look okay?"

"Honey, you look better than okay. If Jason Black is there, he will definitely be all up on you."

I shook my head and chuckled under my breath. "Okay. Well, Ava is picking me up in a few minutes. We should walk down so I'm ready."

Lorelei handed me my black clutch. "The Petition and Summons are in here with the blank response papers for you to serve Trent."

I smiled. "You're the best assistant ever."

"Best assistant as in once you become a member of Sensation you'll bring me as your guest?"

I chuckled. "Yeah. If that ever happens, you'll be my plus one."

"The perks of this job keep getting better and better." She laughed.

We made our way out my front door. As I was locking it, I heard Lorelei speak.

"Hi, Sam."

My hand stilled on the key in the top lock.

"Hey, ladies," he responded.

I looked over and saw his gaze on me. I glared.

"Peyton, I have to say you're looking good enough to fuck."

Lorelei gasped. I'd never told her about my altercation with him from a week ago. I knew I was going to be interrogated for hours. Luckily, I didn't have that long. I pulled the key from the lock and started walking toward him because, unfortunately, it was on the way to the elevator. Lorelei didn't move a muscle. Her eyes were the size of silver dollars as she watched, waiting to see what I was going to do.

I stopped right in front of Sam and looked up at him. I was so close that I could feel the heat from his chest seeping into my bare shoulders. "Lucky for me, you'll never get the chance." I stepped back to walk away, but he grabbed my wrist to halt me.

"You're still pissed about last week?"

"I'm pissed that you're not a better man."

"Peyton, we've been over this—"

"We haven't been over shit." I broke free from his grasp and started to walk away. "You're an asshole. End of story."

He smirked, and I rolled my eyes, still walking away. Lorelei started to follow me, but she was looking back and forth between us as she walked.

"Where are you going dressed like that?" Sam inquired.

I turned around, walking backward. "To have a threesome."

Lorelei sucked in a breath again, and I grinned at Sam then turned around to continue to the elevator. I could feel Sam looking at me as we stood, waiting for the car to arrive. I knew he was there because I hadn't heard him go inside his condo. Once Lore and I were in the elevator, and the doors started to close, my eyes met his. The look he gave me told me that what we were doing wasn't over. I was a challenge for him, and he obviously wasn't used to one.

Once we were out of sight from Sam, Lorelei turned to me. "If you don't tell me what the hell that was about, I will quit C&P on Monday."

I looked up at the lighted panel ceiling. "We don't have time to get into it."

"Pey, you better make time. That shit was intense. Fuck, I didn't even know you'd ever talked to him except for hello."

Once we were on the ground floor, the doors opened. I saw Ava's limo parked on the street in front of my building as we exited. "I promise to tell you everything tomorrow. Ava's here."

"Give me the *Cliff Notes* version for now."

I stopped walking before we exited to go outside. I didn't want Ava to hear anything to do with my personal life. "Sam was being Sam and screwing some chick on Friday like I'd told you. I got fed up, banged on his wall to stop, and then he showed up at my door and asked me to join them."

Lorelei's mouth dropped open. She was speechless again.

"I turned him down because I wasn't going to be involved in that shit, and he obviously can't take no for an answer."

"But ... But you've thought he was hot for three years," she stammered.

I shrugged. "That was before I knew he only thought with his dick."

She sucked in a deep breath as if to calm her excitement. "Okay. We have a lot to talk about. Therefore, I'm coming over for lunch tomorrow, and you're telling me *everything*."

I smiled. "All right, but don't forget I have dinner with my folks tomorrow night," I reminded her. Once Lorelei started to gossip, it could last for hours and I really did have to be at my parents by five for dinner.

"I also want you to text me when you're home tonight."

"What if I don't come home?" I smirked.

She grinned, a look of approval in her eye. "Fine. Be safe, and I want *all* the details tomorrow. And I mean *all* of them."

We said our goodbyes as the limo driver opened the back door for me to slide in.

"Hey," Ava greeted.

I smiled back. "Hi."

She handed me a glass of bubbly champagne. "Love the shoes."

I took the glass from her. "How can you see them?" I laughed and looked down at the dark floor.

"I saw them while you were talking to Lorelei. I might need to steal them." She grinned.

"Over my dead body." I took a sip of the tart goodness. "Do I look okay, though?"

Ava was dressed in a red, halter top dress. Her blonde hair was down and curled, and her shoes were black Louboutins without the spikes on the back.

I felt the car moving as she spoke. "You're perfect. Some girls wear corsets with skirts. Some wear bras with skirts. Really, you can wear whatever you feel sexy in."

"So I should have only worn the heels?" I joked.

Ava burst out laughing. "Well, it is a sex club."

"Is there anything I need to know before we get there?" I asked, changing the subject.

"Not unless you plan to stay longer than serving Trent."

I bit my lower lip. A part of me wanted to stay. Again, it was a once in a lifetime thing, and like Lorelei had said, I shouldn't let the opportunity pass. Plus, if Jason Black happened to be a member and he did want to sleep with me, I was all for it.

"Do you want to stay?" Ava asked. "I can have my driver bring you home whenever you want."

"He doesn't need to do that. I can Uber it when I'm ready to leave."

"Nonsense. He gets paid big bucks, and I'd rather pay him for doing something other than sitting in his car playing *Candy Crush*."

I chuckled. "We'll see. I still don't know what I'm getting into. My priority is finding Trent, though."

A frown formed on Ava's face. "This is the first time we've come to the club separately."

I reached out and placed my free hand on hers, giving it a light squeeze. "I'm sorry. But you are certain he's coming?"

"He'd never miss it. Even when he's filming, he always comes back even if it's just for the night."

"Do you mind if I ask what you two did together there?"

Ava sighed as though remembering her time together with her ex. "A lot of threesomes. He also likes to watch me with a woman."

"Oh ..." I breathed. "What do you think he'll do tonight?"

She shrugged. "Usually he gets a drink or two, and then we find someone to join us. Tonight, since we aren't together, he'll probably find two women to be with, but he likes to watch first to get more in the mood."

"Watch?" I asked.

Ava smiled tightly. "Not everyone can go into a private room. There are people all around ... enjoying themselves."

Images of my daydreams flashed in my head of people screwing on all the furniture. Seems I might be right about that one. "Okay, so I should find Trent at the bar?" I assumed there was a bar of some sort since she'd indicated he gets a drink or two.

"There are a few bars set-up, but he likes the one by the pool so he can smoke."

"Great, I'll start there." I was thinking about my plan of attack when another thought came to me. My head twisted sharply back at Ava. "Bookers going to be there tonight, huh?"

"Yeah. He comes every time too."

My stomach dropped. The possibility of seeing Booker at a sex club made me nervous. I wasn't nervous because I thought he might tell people he saw me (if he did see me). What made me nervous was potentially seeing him engaging in sexual acts. I wasn't sure if I could ever forget that image. A part of me did want to see it, though. There was no denying I found him attractive. Plus, knowing he was a ladies man, I kind of wanted to see it in action. Then I'd know what all the fuss was about. Seeing him in court would be awkward, but it would probably make him nicer since I knew his secret.

I bit my lip to try and hide the smile that formed on my face as I pictured Booker fucking a chick doggie style. I cleared my throat. "Okay. Just curious what to expect."

"Everything will be fine. I mean, on your end. I might just hide in the shadows or if I find someone, go upstairs with them for the night. Trent might flip. He won't cause a scene, but he might come looking for me after you serve him."

"Everything *will* be fine," I agreed. "Booker's not stupid. Given that Trent knows you want a divorce, he shouldn't be that surprised. He'll more than likely seek out Booker, and then Booker will calm him down. I'm sure he'll feed him bullshit, but I'm not worried."

"I hope you're right. I'd hate to leave early."

I turned toward her. "You will not leave early. Trent doesn't have the upper hand here, Ava. But if you do want to leave early, don't worry about me. I'm totally okay with Uber. What I want you to do, though, is find the guy you've always wanted to sleep with and bring him upstairs, or whatever, and forget all about what I'm doing and how Trent is going to react."

"Okay," she agreed. "I have been eyeing Michael Zapino."

I sucked in a sharp breath. "Michael Zapino from *How to Get the Girl*?"

"Yeah." She beamed.

"Please. Pa-lease tell me Jason Black is a member?" My excitement was through the roof as I pictured finally meeting Jason. Lorelei would flip—if I could tell her, which I couldn't. When we were talking about me hooking up with Jason, I was totally joking.

She laughed. "He is. Are you a fan?"

Was I a fan? I didn't miss an episode. "Fan isn't the right word."

"I'll introduce you."

My heart began to beat faster. "For real?"

"Gives me an excuse to talk to Michael." She winked.

How was I going to meet my crush and not be able to tell my best friend in the morning?

Chapter 4

PEYTON

The limo pulled to a stop, and I turned my head, looking out the tinted window. Two women and a man were walking up the red carpeted stairs. The two women were dressed in skimpy but elegant dresses, and the guy was in a black and white tuxedo. It looked as though we were attending a black-tie affair.

As I waited for the driver to come around to open my door, I turned my attention to Ava. "This place is spectacular." There were no other words to describe the stucco house with pillars and topiary placed along the twelve or so steps. I couldn't imagine what it would look like in the light of day.

Ava smiled. "It is. Are you ready?"

Before I could respond, the door opened and we slid out the back. Once we'd both adjusted our dresses, we began to ascend the stairs. Ava reached in her clutch and pulled out what looked like a black credit card with the word "SENSATION" written in silver. The O of the word was a 3D dodecahedron. Only six of the twelve sides showed with the center blank while the five remaining sides that attached were white, red, green, blue, and a silvery white.

"Black card status?" I teased.

"It's so security knows I'm a current member. We all get them. And if we cancel our membership, they take the card away."

"Are they all black?"

She shook her head. "No, it depends on what level you are. I'm Diamond."

"And that's the highest?"

"Yeah." She smiled and flashed the tall, bulky, and quite handsome man the card. He was dressed in black slacks and a black polo shirt with an earpiece in his ear. He smiled at her and then looked at his clipboard.

"What are the other levels?" I asked, watching the man scan the clipboard.

"Pearl, Ruby, Emerald, Sapphire, then Diamond."

I nodded. There were so many questions I wanted to ask, but we were on a mission. Or at least I was. This was for business and not pleasure. Though I was curious what each level meant, it didn't matter since this was for one night only.

"Thank you, Ms. Ashley. You and Ms. Winters can go on inside." I balked at him knowing my name, but then remembered I'd submitted my info to be her guest and I had to be listed on the guest list.

Before we stepped inside, I looked over my shoulder to see a line of limos and town cars lining the circular driveway and continuing down the street. It had just turned ten o'clock, and it seemed everyone wanted to be inside when the party started.

Two men each pulled the double wrought iron doors with frosted glass open as we approached. They were smaller than the bouncer and were dressed more as butlers. They smiled and nodded at us as we stepped over the threshold and into the marble entryway.

Ava walked to what looked like a coat check area. I followed even though neither one of us had jackets. "We have to leave all of our belongings here. They don't allow cell phones, cameras or anything of that nature. I usually slip my lipstick in the front of my dress with my membership card."

"Why do you need your membership card?"

"There are things not everyone can do." She smiled.

"Oh?"

"If you see something you like, just let me know and I'll get you in."

I was intrigued but didn't press her more as more people walked in the doors. She motioned for me to set my purse on the counter for the coat check person to take it.

"But your divorce papers are in here," I whispered.

"Right ..." she trailed off, biting the corner of her lip as she thought for a moment. "Can you fold it and stick it in your dress?"

I looked down at my sleeveless, barely there dress that hugged every inch of my torso. A dress that had no room for a single piece of paper let alone ten plus an envelope. "Um ..." I hesitated, trying to think of a plan just as the attendant reached her hand out for me to hand over my belongings. "Guess I'll make it work." I dug in the black clutch and pulled out the legal sized envelope. We each handed over our purses, and the attendant put them under Ava's last name.

"Just remember that there's no pressure for you to do anything you don't want to do. If you aren't comfortable, go outside and tell Luke to call my driver. They know his number—it's in my file. They'll call Steve, and he'll come get you."

I nodded as I folded the envelope and stuffed it in the inside of my dress. It made my left boob a little bigger, but luckily I had an agenda, and the papers wouldn't cling to me for long. "Okay. I'm sure I'll be fine."

Her smile brightened. "You will be. Are you ready?"

"You already asked me that," I teased because I wasn't sure if I was ready. I didn't have a choice, though.

"I know, but this is it. Once we go behind this black curtain, you'll see things."

I looked to the curtain that separated the entryway from the rest of the house, swallowed hard and then nodded. "Let's do it."

We each pulled a corner back then stepped through. It felt as though we'd entered another realm. The lighting changed from neutral to shades of reds and pinks. Music you'd hear at a nightclub instantly got louder, but not so loud that you had to scream to talk to the person next to you. It was as if they played it to drown out the moans of ecstasy.

"People don't wait around do they?" I asked.

"Regulars, and those wanting more than one partner, don't. Some come in, get it out of the way, and then watch for most of the night. Then they do it again and go home at three when the party ends."

"Interesting," I commented as my gaze landed on two women kissing near a fireplace. The blonde had her hand up the other woman's dress, caressing her ass as they moaned into each other's mouths.

"Let's go get a drink and find Michael. Then you can look for Trent, and you'll know where I am so you can find me after you serve him."

"Perfect."

I was trying to keep my cool as we maneuvered through the vast space. From what I could see, the furniture cost a month of my mortgage payment, but it was hard to tell exactly what color anything was because everything was a shade of red or pink. Plus, it was hard to look at the furniture with everything that was happening live in front of me. I tried to take everything in since I wouldn't be back.

We rounded a corner and walked into a room with ceiling-high bookshelves and glass windows that overlooked a glowing swimming pool. I could faintly see people standing near it as we walked farther into the room and directly to the bar.

"Trent should be out there, right?" I pointed to the pool.

Ava turned her gaze toward the blue water, and took a deep breath. "Yeah."

I reached up and placed my hand on her shoulder. "Relax. Everything will be fine." Fine was definitely the word of the day. It wasn't an ideal situation to be in. Usually, the party that was serving the other party wasn't in the same vicinity, let alone at the same house party. Granted, it appeared this mansion was on a massive lot, and Ava could hide if she wanted to.

We each ordered vodka cranberries, and then we left the room and headed in another direction. I wasn't certain where we were going, and I was convinced I was going to get lost at some point—it was a given. We took turn after turn and peeked into room after room with open doors until Ava stopped abruptly.

"There he is." She nudged her head, and I followed with my eyes. The room was almost the same as the one where we'd gotten our drinks. People stood around talking—watching—touching.

"Looks like he's only watching a guy with ..."

All words left my brain. Next to Michael was Jason. They were both staring at a guy groping a chick while she rubbed the front of his pants. Jason's piercing green eyes never left the couple as we stood and watched them. He was more gorgeous in person even with a tint of red lacing his features. His dark hair was slicked back, and his arms bulged in his tux. Instantly, I felt like a giddy high school girl who had a crush on the quarterback. It didn't matter that I was over thirty. What mattered was the hottest guy I'd ever seen was only ten feet away from me.

"Let's go talk to them," Ava said and took a step, but then stopped as two women approached Michael and Jason.

I watched as the blonde sat in Jason's lap. His hand skimmed up her bare thigh and cupped her ass as she leaned into him. I had no idea what the redhead was doing to Michael. My gaze was on Jason. I wished his hands were all over my body.

"Yeah, let's go talk to them," I said in agreement, my gaze not faltering.

"He's with a girl now."

I turned my head to Ava. "So? Is there a rule that you can't interrupt? I thought you were into threesomes?"

"But I was always with Trent."

"You gotta start somewhere, right?" *And I don't want to miss my chance of meeting Jason.* I took a sip of the cool cranberry drink. I didn't taste the vodka though I knew it was in there because I saw the bartender pour it.

"Right," she agreed and started toward the high back chairs where they were sitting.

Taking deep calming breaths with each step, I tried to relax so I didn't make a fool of myself. What if I said something stupid? What if I had something on my face? I instantly started brushing imaginary shit from my face.

And now I look like a spaz.

I stopped my movements, hanging back a few steps as Ava greeted Michael.

"Hey, Mike," she purred.

My head turned to face her as the words left her mouth. I wasn't expecting the sultry tone of her voice to leave her lips. Now I was positive I was out of my element.

Michael's eyes moved from the redhead to Ava. "Hey, A. Where's Trent?"

She paused for a moment before answering. Clearly no one knew she wanted a divorce. I didn't blame her. "I think by the pool." She shrugged.

"Who's your friend?" Jason asked.

My gaze turned back to him, and he looked me up and down. *Me!* No-name Peyton Winters.

"This is Peyton," Ava responded.

"Never seen you here before, Peyton," Jason rumbled.

"It's my first time," I replied. I had no idea how I got the words out of my mouth. The sound of my heart pounding in my chest was drowning out the thump of the music.

"What are you into?" Jason leaned forward, and the blonde slid from his lap. She cut her eyes to me and glared.

My cheeks heated at his question. "What do you mean?"

He smirked and stood only a foot or so from me. "Do you like to only watch? Are you looking to interact? Do you like it rough, or do you like to be caressed and worshipped?"

"I ..." I stuttered. *Did he seriously just ask me the questions that were listed on the website?* "I'm not sure."

"Well, why did you come to Sensation if you're not sure what you're looking for?" Jason reached up and ran a finger over my pink lips.

Before I could respond—hell, who was I kidding? I was about to faint like a crazy fan—Ava spoke.

"Actually, Peyton needs to do me a favor before she does anything with you, Jay."

Jay. I wanted to call him Jay.

I snapped out of my daze and muttered a quick, "Right. It was nice to meet you. If you're still here when I get back, I'll have an answer for you." I smiled sweetly at him. Or at least I hoped.

Jason's eyes turned to Ava. "What do you mean she has to do you a favor?"

I spoke before Ava could. "I just need to go do something real quick, and then I'll be back." I smiled and turned before they could ask again.

Walking back in the direction of the room with the bar, I looked for an exit to go to the pool. People were all around doing their *thing*. One couple was on a chair, the woman bouncing on the guy's cock. I wanted to stop and watch because it was my first time seeing someone other than myself having sex in person, but I was on a mission. I needed to find Trent, serve him and then get back to *Jay* and tell him ...

I wasn't sure what I was going to tell him because before I could come to a conclusion, I spotted Trent. He wasn't alone, though. He was standing with *the* man himself.

Booker Jameson.

My feet faltered as I stepped outside the door and onto the stone walkway that led to the pool. It wasn't because I was hesitant to speak to Booker. I just wasn't prepared to see him yet. My thoughts were on finding Trent, and then finding Jason, but now the side profile of Booker had me stopping in my tracks as though he was the one I wanted.

He was dressed in a black tuxedo. I'd seen him in suits, but there was something about the way the elegant tux formed around his frame that made me see him in a different light. *It could also be that I was reveling from Jason hitting on me.*

I chugged my watered down cocktail back and then set the empty glass on a tray. I grabbed the envelope from my dress, unfolded it, straightened my shoulders, and stood tall as I walked over to the two men. Trent's gaze hit me first, and he stopped talking as a smile spread across his lips. Booker turned in my direction, and the moment he realized it was me, he narrowed his eyes as though he was wondering why I was there. I didn't give him much time to ponder any questions he might be thinking. I nudged the envelope toward Trent, and the moment he took it from my hands, I said, "Trent Inglewood, you've been served."

Trent's smile faltered, and Booker hissed a "fuck" under his breath.

"Have a good evening." I winked at Booker and walked away.

No one got the upper hand when it came to Booker. Granted, it didn't matter that Trent was served first. It was the fact that I took Booker by surprise. If I had to bet money, I'd bet that he and Trent were just talking about Ava wanting a divorce and what Booker needed Trent to do for him to represent him.

The couple having sex on the chair were still going at it as I passed them on my way back to Ava and Jason, but now they were in a different position. The woman was bent over the side of the cream-colored, high-back, cloth chair, and the man was fucking her from behind. Her boobs bounced with each thrust, her moans piercing the air.

I looked around at the crowd. Some were feeling each other up as they watched. I wanted to stop and watch like others were because it was turning me on, but I needed to get back to Ava—back to Jason. I felt as though if I left Jason for too long, he'd return to the blonde, forgetting I ever existed. If I did one thing tonight, I would try to see what I could do with Jason Black. There was no chance I'd ever have this opportunity again.

I entered the room where I'd left Ava. She and Michael were

sitting on a couch with her legs bent over his lap as their mouths were locked. Jason wasn't with the blonde that I'd feared he would be. He was with both girls. Of course he was. *Why would he wait for no-name Peyton?*

Needing to tell Ava the job was done, I walked up and tapped her on the shoulder. "Sorry to interrupt," I said. "It's done."

She broke her lips from Michael's and her eyes widened as she looked up at me. "It is?"

"Yeah," I replied, looking around for a clock. I needed to remember what time it was so I could put it on the Proof of Service I was filing on Monday.

"Peyton." My attention turned when I heard my name. It was Jason. "You're back," he continued.

I nodded. "I am and you're—"

"Passing the time until you returned." He smiled.

I swallowed—hard. "Really?"

"Really. It's not every day a pure fox like you comes to Sensation."

"Pure fox?" I asked.

"He means virgin," Ava cut in.

"I'm ... I'm not a virgin." I laughed awkwardly.

"You're a sex club virgin," Jason countered and stood.

"Well, yeah," I confirmed, and bit my lip.

"And I want to show you the ropes."

I was going to faint for sure this time. Or drop dead. Yes, I was going to drop dead in front of my celebrity crush because I was that much of a spaz. I turned my eyes to Ava. Why? I had no idea. I was a big girl, and I was used to being around celebrities, but I'd seen every movie and TV show Jason had been in, and I owned them all on DVD.

Ava nodded her head as if telling me it was okay and I should go for it.

"What did you have in mind?" I asked as I turned back to Jason.

His eyes looked behind me, and before I could turn to see what or who he was looking at, a warm body pressed against my back. I instantly knew who it belonged to because his scent of sandalwood and musk swarmed around me.

"Now that you've fucked Trent, how about we talk about me?"

Chapter 5

PEYTON

My body became tight as I felt Booker's warm breath against my neck. I didn't know how to respond to him. He was clearly pissed, but did he mean what I thought he meant?

"What the fuck, Book—" Jason dared.

"Piss off, mate," Booker spat back.

I slowly turned my head toward Ava and mouthed, "What the fuck?" Her eyes were wide. Michael stood to stand next to Jason.

What is going on?

Jason moved his gaze back to me. "Did I hear him correctly? You went to fuck Trent Inglewood?"

I opened my mouth to respond, but instead, Booker did. "Choose your words wisely, *love*."

I knew what Booker meant. Ava filing for divorce wasn't public knowledge per se. It was, in fact, public record if anyone were to look at the court records since we had already started her divorce proceedings. But here, now, there were only four people who knew what was going on, and I knew Ava wanted to keep things under wrap.

"No." I shook my head, still not turning around to face Booker. "I just needed to speak with him for a few minutes." I mean, really, I wasn't gone more than five minutes.

"Then why are you all up on her, Booker? We were clearly getting somewhere, and from what Peyton has told me, she isn't an *adventurist*."

Adventurist? What did he mean by that?

"I should go," I said to Ava who was still sitting on the couch she and Michael were making out on only moments ago. I took a step to do just that, but Booker grabbed my arm and started to steer me away from the group. "What are you doing?" I hissed, trying to free my arm from his grasp.

He didn't speak.

"Booker!" I heard Jason yell.

Booker still didn't say a word as he led me through the house, destination unknown.

"Seriously, let me go!" I tried to wiggle my arm free, but his grip was firm and there was no use.

He stopped just as we turned a corner. Before I realized it, he'd pushed me against a wall and once again his warm body was pressed into me. This time it was his hard front on mine.

"Aren't you supposed to ask before you touch?"

He looked down at where he held my wrist. "If I would have asked, you would have said no. I'm not into being told no."

"So you think the solution is to manhandle me?"

"Fight it all you want, *love*, but people will just think we're role playing."

I looked into his blue eyes that were burning with the hottest of fire. "What do you want from me?"

He licked his lips, and my traitor stomach dipped. "You don't want me to answer that."

I rolled my eyes and sighed. "Stop playing games. I know you're pissed that I served Trent here, and I know he's retaining you."

The irritation rolled off of him as he growled. "You know nothing."

I blinked. "What does that mean?"

He stepped even closer, and I immediately *felt* what he meant. "Ever since you first rolled your stunning, brown eyes at me in court four years ago, I've wanted to bend you over my knee."

I laughed. There was no other response that I could come up with.

"Your laugh only makes me harder."

Say what? "You're kidding," I whispered.

47

"I'm not. And now that you're here and we can—"

"We can't do anything," I stated. "First of all, our clients are here, and second of all, they aren't the only clients we have together. It's unethical, and we could get in *a lot* of trouble."

Attorneys could date each other, but they couldn't be opposing counsels and there were steps they needed to do like tell the judge and withdraw from the cases they were on together.

"That's where you're wrong. We're in a different world here. Anything that happens behind these walls is confidential. Nothing leaves this house. *Ever.*"

Was he serious? Being at this elite party was definitely a different world. A world where no one had inhibitions. A world where no one cared if people stopped and watched, and where no one cared if you had a crazy fetish. Everything was *normal*.

"I don't know what I want," I confessed, thinking about what Jason had asked me. Jason, the man I'd lusted after for years because he was the hot, untouchable celebrity. Now he wasn't so unobtainable, and I also had a man who irritated me to no end wanting me. There was also the guy at home who only wanted me for sex. And Clint probably wanted me for sex too. Thinking about it, they all did. I was *not* telling Lorelei she was right and I had men fawning over me.

Which one did *I* want, though?

It seemed I would have to make a decision quickly. I turned my head to see Jason walking toward us. I swallowed. Booker turned in the same direction, and I waited for the pissing contest to re-commence.

Do I stay?

Do I go?

Do I run far, far away?

Jason was within a few feet of us when Booker grabbed my chin, turned it back to face him, and then his lips crashed upon mine. I stopped breathing, not believing what was happening. His hand skimmed down the front of my neck slowly—like a drop of water sliding down a window. The light touch caused goosebumps to rise on my silky skin, and a shiver went through my entire body. His tongue traced my lower lip, and I opened for him. I didn't know why. I thought I'd be against this man *ever* touching me, let alone kissing me.

But I wasn't.

His tongue slid in ...

Tasting.

Sucking.

Savoring.

As he started to suck on my tongue, a fire erupted from within. Before I knew what was happening, my arms wrapped around his neck and I pulled him tighter. We were flush. No air could get between us. His short beard rubbed against my cheek as our mouths fused together. I wanted more.

So much more.

"Christ," he muttered as he pulled his head back after long seconds. "I thought you'd be as cold as your last name, but I was wrong. You're hot like a fucking devil."

My eyes fluttered open at his words. "You think I'm the devil?" I asked, and then noticed Jason was staring at us.

Booker either didn't see or didn't care because he didn't look at him. "Yeah, I do. A devil that has tempted me for so long. And now that I've had a taste, I'm not going to stop."

My eyes cut to Jason. *Should I choose the one who tempts my body, or the one who tempts my soul?*

Booker turned his head finally. "Do you want him too?"

"I ... I—"

"I don't like the way he looks at you, and I'm not into the same things as he."

What the hell did that mean?

"What things?" I asked, looking at Jason as he leaned against the wall, arms crossed across his chest about ten feet from us. "And how does he look at me? I just met him."

"For starters, if you want to be with two men, I'm not the one to join you."

My eyes slid back to Booker. "He's ... gay?" I whispered as I instantly pictured Jason *with* another guy.

"Not sure. But I know he likes threesomes, and I'm not into sharing."

Was I? I'd never been in one (even though Sam propositioned me a week ago to join in on one), but at Sensation it seemed you could have anything you wanted for a night. "I need another drink," I stated and slid around Booker. I still wasn't sure *how* Jason looked at me. Sure he was showing me interest, but I thought he was only being polite or playing a game.

Booker didn't follow me, and neither did Jason. I didn't care if they stood there and had a stare down. I had to get out of there, and I needed another drink so I could wrap my head around the situation. Booker, of all people, had just confessed he'd wanted me for years. What did I do with that information?

The bartender remembered me, and after I had grabbed another drink from the bar near the pool, I ventured around, taking in what I saw. I didn't know where Ava was, but I hoped she was enjoying herself and Trent wasn't harassing her. I had no clue where Booker or Jason went. They were probably still trying to decide who was going to be with the "pure fox." It made me feel like a virgin. This time, though, I knew what I was getting into. Or did I? If Booker was correct, I could be with Jason and another man. That would be new for me. Being with another woman would be new to me as well. If I went with Booker, there was no telling how my night would turn out.

Rounding a corner, I spotted a large crowd in a semi-circle looking at something. It was hard to see even in my four-inch heels, so I stepped forward and slid in between a couple. Once I was in front of them, I turned to say thank you for letting me through, but the woman's eyes were closed, and the man's hand was up her dress. She was lightly moaning as his hand thrust in and out of her. My pleasantry died in my throat because instantly my pussy became wet and I was jealous of the pleasure she was receiving. It had been months since I'd been with a man. Months since one had touched me like that—made me come—made me feel.

I felt weird staring at them even though it was *allowed*, so I turned around to finally see what the crowd was looking at. While sipping my drink, I saw that a man was sitting in a red, high-backed chair. He had a mask on that covered his eyes and nose. His mouth was still exposed, and from what I could tell, he was handsome. He had a strong jaw and defined lips. He was also dressed in a black and white tux, but what set him apart was that he held a leather leash in his hand.

My eyes traveled down the black rope, and it stopped on a blonde at the other end. She, too, had on a mask, but hers was only covering her eyes. It was lace, and therefore, see-through, and she was dressed in a black leotard with a collar around her neck. The leash attached to her collar, and she was sitting at the side of him like a house pet would.

"That's Savior."

I jumped at the voice—the voice with the accent that was starting to do things to me. Or maybe it was because I was already humming from everything around me. Booker was once again behind me. I could feel his heat against my back. It was like a hundred candles trying to burn my skin, but I didn't turn to face him.

"Savior?" I asked.

"He's a Dom."

"Why is his name Savior? Did he save someone?"

"Everyone needs saving. Savior does so in a way that one's demons can no longer haunt them."

I stared at Savior and his pet. "How does putting a leash on a woman save her?"

"Some people who have experienced trauma in the past find a certain peace in relinquishing control, almost a trance. I've heard rumors that a state of mind known as subspace is unlike anything anyone has experienced."

"Are you into that?" I gestured to Savior.

"You mean BDSM?"

"Yeah." I nodded.

"Not like Savior."

"What do you mean?"

"I don't mind a little bondage, but I'm not looking for a pet or to cause anyone pain."

But he'd told me that for four years he wanted to bend me over his knee. That meant spanking, and to me, spanking would hurt.

We were silent as we stared at the scene and I thought about what he'd said. Savior's pet started to lick his hand and my eyebrows arched. *How was this saving her?* I had no idea what BDSM was all about, and thankfully Booker wasn't into ... *that.* I couldn't imagine a woman licking his hand like she was a puppy.

I finished my drink, brain freeze tempting to cause me pain as it quickly went down my throat. It didn't, and I set the glass on an empty tray that was next to me.

"Savior does demonstrations and provides hands-on training if you're interested. Or," he stepped closer and whispered into my ear, "I could show you what *I'm* into."

My body shivered again as it reacted to the thought of Booker *showing* me. I didn't respond. Instead, I stepped back and pressed into him. His lips immediately went to my neck, and he trailed light kisses down the slope and across my bare shoulder. My body hummed, and I made my decision. Even though I could get my law license suspended for what we were doing, I still wanted it. I wanted *him.* Even if it was for one night in a confidential mansion. Lorelei had told me to not let this opportunity pass, and even though it was Booker, who I'd see in court, I trusted him. He could get in trouble too, so I was certain he wouldn't run off and tell anyone at his firm that we had sex.

Booker's hand wrapped around my waist, and he pulled me closer to him. His erection was unmistakable as it pressed into my backside. My head tilted back and rested on his chest, savoring the feel of him licking up my neck and making the moisture between my legs thicken. I was so turned on that I was tempted to kneel at his feet and take him in my mouth like I'd envisioned in court the other day. All my worries disappeared as I felt his hand descend down my thigh and then up under my dress. *Christ!*

I *knew* what he was going to do.

I *wanted* what he was going to do.

I *needed* what he was going to do.

Then he stopped.

"You're wearing knickers." It wasn't a question.

I nodded slowly, still in my lust haze.

"Why?"

My eyes opened. *What kind of question was that?* "Because I wear panties." My words came out as a pant. I wanted him to continue the torture on my body.

"But you came to Sensation," he stated.

I nodded again.

He turned me so I was looking up into his cornflower eyes. "You only came here to serve Trent?"

Again, I nodded.

"What about that bloke Jason?"

I looked down at Booker's chest. I couldn't look him in the eyes any longer. How did I tell him that if he hadn't shown up when he did, I would be with another man? A man who lived in my fantasies nonetheless.

"He's my celebrity crush," I confessed.

Booker snickered. "Your celebrity crush? That nutter?"

"Nutter?" I looked back up.

"Jeez, he's just a pretty boy who can't please a woman by himself."

"How would you know?" I challenged.

He smiled. "Honestly, we've both tagged some of the same birds, and they've told me he doesn't do the pleasing."

"Are you jealous?"

He paused for a moment, looking directly into the depths of my soul. "Should I be?"

"No." I shook my head. I was done playing around. The moment he first pressed his mouth to mine, my body made my decision. Now the rest of me was agreeing. I just hoped it was the right one.

Booker pressed his lips to mine again. The kiss started off slow, building as we tried to convey what we wanted. At that moment, we wanted each other. Tomorrow would be a different day.

"Take your knickers off," he said against my lips.

"Here?" I asked, and looked around as I pulled my head back. No one was watching us. Savior was probably doing something because everyone was facing in that direction.

"Either you take them off here, or we go upstairs to a room."

I didn't care that there was sex all around me. I was new to this, and even though I wanted to let Booker fuck me right here and now, I couldn't.

"Up—"

Booker grabbed my hand and dragged me through the crowd. I had no idea where we were going or where the stairs were. Before I knew it, we were at the front entrance and hurrying up the stairs. He tried the first door, but it was locked. He tried the second, but it was locked as well.

"Are they all occupied?"

"They better not be or I'm fucking you right here."

My belly got tight at the image. I would be okay with a quick fuck against the wall since it seemed secluded up here. I stepped back on my heel to stop him from walking. "It's okay."

"What's okay?"

"I want it now. I want *you* now."

He smiled and cupped the side of my face with his hand. "While it's tempting, I have other plans for us."

I grinned. "You do?"

"I told you I was going to show you what I was into. At least partially."

"Partially?"

"There's one thing I can't get out of my head, and since we have this opportunity, I'm taking full advantage of it."

"Okay," I breathed.

Booker kissed my lips softly and then returned to checking the doors. They weren't all locked, but all were occupied. "Fuck," he groaned and tried the last knob. It opened. Booker turned to me and smirked. "Last chance to change your mind. Once we cross the threshold, there's no turning back."

I swallowed. "I'm sure."

The light was already on as he tugged me into the room, and I felt as though I'd walked into a magazine. The first thing I noticed was the panoramic skyline view. It was breathtaking as city lights twinkled in the distance in the dark of night. My gaze then came back to the room as we stepped farther in. A giant pop-culture painting of a woman hung above the fireplace. I didn't recognize her, and that was probably for the best. Two white plush chairs sat in front of the fireplace, and a table with a bowl of condoms was placed between them.

"This room isn't red," I stated as I looked around.

Booker laughed. "No, gorgeous, it's not. That's only downstairs."

"Have you been in this room before?" *Why was I asking him this?*

"Does it matter?" he asked, loosening his black bow tie.

"I guess not. It's beautiful, though." I needed to talk about the room and not his past *adventures* at Sensation. He was a member of the club, and there was no telling what he'd done in any of the rooms. My gaze dropped to the floor because I couldn't bear to look at him as I thought about his past. Alternatively, I focused on my exploration of the room. I expected a bear skin rug to be in front of the fireplace. Instead, it looked like a brown and white cowhide rug.

"Come over here."

I turned and saw Booker standing next to a king size bed. The linens were white and crisp. "Doesn't look like anyone has used the bed tonight."

"Why are you stalling?"

I shrugged. "I'm new to this."

"Sex?"

"No." I wasn't new to sex. It had just been a while.

Booker took a few steps then tugged me to the bed. Nerves washed over me like an electric current. Was I about to have sex with Booker Jameson? Sober?

"You look fucking lush tonight. Beyond fit."

What the hell was he talking about? Lush and fit didn't go together in the American language. "Is that a compliment?" I asked.

He chuckled. "Yes, and your tits are lovely in this dress."

I blushed. "Thank you."

"Now, it's time to lose your knickers because it's time to fuck."

My belly clenched at his words, and I was unable to respond. He walked around me and began to unzip the back of my dress. Once the zipper was down, the dress slid off my body and into a pool of black at my feet. Booker's finger ran along my spine, and once again goosebumps rose from my skin. His touch was like electricity being plugged into a socket, and my body was that socket.

"Stunning," he murmured.

My head hung as Booker continued his exploration of my backside. Then his hands hooked into the straps of my lace thong and down my legs.

"Step out," he ordered.

I did. My kick ass Louboutins were the only thing left, and when I looked up to meet his eyes, he was staring at my center. I blushed under his gaze and waited.

"Lie on the bed."

This was it. I'd already had his mouth on me, but we were about to explore another level. A level we would have to pretend didn't happen. I turned and then started to crawl up the bed.

"On your back, gorgeous."

I looked over my shoulder at him as he spoke and then I turned to lie in the center of the soft mattress. The white comforter hugged my bare skin as I watched Booker discard his tie and then his shirt. What

I saw was something unexpected. His left pec and left arm were both covered in black ink. From what I could tell, it looked like roses scattered in clouds. There was also Chinese script over his heart mixed in to the design.

I didn't speak, even though I wanted to ask what the script said and what his tattoos meant. He was fit—and probably not in the same way he meant I was. His chest and abs were chiseled, and I itched to reach up and touch him. My gaze traveled down his chest and stopped at the cut hips that started to reveal the V that led to his cock.

He bent and picked up my thong. "I think I'll keep these."

"What?" I laughed. "You can't keep my panties."

"Want to bet? Something to remember this night by."

A sinking feeling descended on my heart as I remembered that this was only going to be one night. "Okay," I whispered, and he stuck my panties in his pants that were now on the floor.

"I never thought I'd get this night." He started to walk around the side of the bed as he spoke. "I always thought you'd be cold like your last name and brush me off. I also didn't know you were into coming to a sex party, or I would have invited you a long time ago."

"I'm not."

"But you're here in this bed at a sex party," he stated.

"I never planned to be in this position. I came to serve Trent and I was only going to watch because my assistant told me I shouldn't let this opportunity pass."

He reached down and picked something up off the floor. "You would have joined Jason."

My eyes moved to see what he'd picked up off the floor and they widened. "What is that?" I asked, forgetting about Jason.

Booker smirked. "This is what I'm into."

"I thought you weren't a Dom?"

He pulled the Velcro apart and reached for my wrist. "I'm not."

"But you're into bondage?"

"You've never been tied up before?"

I shook my head and smiled. "No, can't say that I have."

He took the black cuff and fastened it around my left wrist. The other side was attached below the bed. "I know you like to be in control. You're feisty in court. But, when you're tied up and let someone else take over your body, you'll submit." I watched as he moved to the foot of the bed and pulled another cuff from the floor. "And when you don't need to make a decision on what to do or what needs to come next, you can simply enjoy yourself."

"Who said I don't enjoy regular sex?" I asked as he cuffed my left ankle.

"Just a hunch. There's only one way to find out." Booker walked to the other side of the foot of the bed and picked up another black cuff. "The only thing you need to focus on is how I'm going to make you feel."

He grabbed my right ankle and pulled it toward him so I was spread across the bed. He secured the cuff as he explained, "Dominance is all about being able to read what your partner likes and doesn't like. To listen to their breathing, to know what makes their back arch off the bloody bed and scream my name. If you're not enjoying yourself, all it will take is for you to say no and it's all over. Just like that. So you see, the power is all yours."

"Shouldn't we have a safe word?" I was certain I remembered hearing that before.

"What do you want it to be?"

I thought for a moment. "Red?"

"Red?"

"Like stop," I clarified.

"Red it is." Booker moved up the bed and fastened my right wrist. "Now, are you ready, gorgeous?"

Chapter 6

PEYTON

My heartbeat rang in my ears.
Ba-dum ...

Dum.

Ba-dum ...

Dum.

Ba-dum ...

Dum.

I was spread across the king size bed—open—waiting—*exposed.* No words could come to my mouth as I watched him move to the end of the bed and look directly *up* at me. I wasn't scared. I wasn't nervous. I was ... *ready.* So ready that it felt as though I'd been waiting for this moment my entire life.

Waiting for this night.

Waiting for *this* man.

I nodded my answer.

He smiled. "I never thought you'd be speechless."

I smirked. "And I never thought I'd be laid bare with you looking at me like you want to devour me."

His grin widened. "I want to do more than devour you. I want to make you moan—make you scream—make you *mine.*"

"Yours ..." I whispered the words as though I was testing them against my lips.

Booker slid his boxers down his legs, and I raised my head off the bed to get a good look at him. My stomach clenched, and a drop of desire slid down my pussy. Fuck, he was perfect. So perfect that I ached for him. In the back of my mind I knew this was only for tonight, and once we left the doors of Sensation what we did would never be spoken of again, but I didn't care.

He started to crawl up my body, his gaze roaming across my hot skin. If he didn't touch me soon, I was certain I'd lose my mind.

"Touch me," I whispered.

"I will, gorgeous. I will."

My back arched off the bed, trying to make our bodies touch. I needed to feel his hard chest pressed against me—feel his hand cup my breast and tease me. To feel what his strong hands could do to my body. He was definitely the one steering the direction we were headed in.

Our gazes locked, and his stormy blue eyes held so much desire that I wanted to reach up and run my hands through his short, blond hair. I longed to feel his beard against my face again—to have his lips against mine and taste me.

"So long," he muttered.

"What?" I asked, not breaking our eye contact.

He didn't respond. Instead, his lips crashed against mine, and I got what I wanted. It started off slow, but it wasn't like the kisses we'd shared before. This kiss spoke volumes. This kiss told me that he was serious and this wasn't a game. Our mouths were at war, fighting to consume—to overtake—to conquer.

Booker's hand cupped me, and I gasped in his mouth at the sudden addition to the mix. "Yes!" I wanted to cry out. I needed the release, needed to know what he was capable of. Instead, I moaned into his mouth.

A finger slid in, and he pulled his lips from mine. "You want me, beautiful?"

"Yes," I breathed.

I tugged at my arm restraints as he added another finger and started to push in and out. My body was on fire, needing to come. I expected him to kiss me again. Instead, he lowered his head. His mouth clamped around my nipple, and my back arched again. His tongue slid from my nipple down my torso to my belly.

I was close, so close. I'd been worked up for most of the night, and now that my body was finally getting the attention that it wanted, it wanted to explode, to come apart over and over. Booker added a thumb to my clit, and I bucked, my back returning to the bed so my hips could start to move with his hand. I was so close, and ready to tip over the edge into a world I never wanted to leave. My eyes rolled back into my head, I pulled on the restraints again ...

And then I fell.

I fell so far that I screamed my release. I screamed so loud that the neighbors probably thought we were in a competition.

My breathing was starting to return to normal when Booker rose and began to take the cuffs off my ankles. *That was it? That wasn't so bad.* He removed the cuffs on my wrists, and I started to sit up.

"No," he snapped.

"No?" I asked.

"Roll on your stomach."

Oh!

I did without hesitation. We weren't done. I could hear the rustle of what I assumed was a condom packet, and after a few seconds, I felt each shoe being removed from my feet. They thumped onto the hardwood floor, and then he was over me again. He grabbed one wrist at a time and hooked them back into the cuffs. Nudging my legs apart with his knees, his hand slid between my hips and the bed, and he pulled me up slightly. It was enough for him to slide in, and I moaned as he entered. It wasn't a slow and steady ease in. It was an I'm-tired-of-fucking-around thrust.

My hips pressed into the bed as he slammed into me. He grabbed the chignon at the back of my nape and pulled. My head tilted back, and he continued to pull until my hair fell loose and draped around my shoulders. Bobby pins dropped around me, but I didn't care that he'd just messed up my hair. It felt like pure bliss as he tugged harder.

Hips pumping.

Hair pulling.

The sounds of arousal filling the air.

"I can't wait to smack your arse," he groaned, thrusting into me over and over.

I moaned in response. I wasn't sure I wanted him to smack my ass, but if it was anything like what we were currently in the middle of, I might be open to it. Then it occurred to me ...

I *did* trust him.

After all those years of thinking he was a cocky attorney who wanted to make my cases hell, I realized that I would never look at Booker Jameson the same way. After tonight everything would change. Even if he continued to request a God awful amount of discovery, I knew I would comply in a heartbeat.

I was done for.

Completely and utterly submitted to this man and all it took was for his lips to touch mine.

He groaned, I moaned, and the harder he thrust, the closer I came to falling over the edge again.

"You feel so good," he groaned.

"Yes!" I moaned. "Yes, right there!"

Oh God, I sounded like the women I could hear from my bedroom, but I didn't care. With each drive, Booker hit that spot that made tingles race up my spine. It was about time I was the one on the receiving end of a good fucking. I'd heard too many nights of women getting what I didn't have—what I fantasized about.

Booker yanked harder on my head, and my arms tightened against the restraints. I had nowhere to go as he pumped into me over and over.

"That's it, gorgeous. Milk my dick."

That was my second undoing. I came around his cock, his name slipping from my lips as I screamed again, and the pleasure raced through me like an electric current. He groaned again, this time following me over the edge into oblivion.

Booker rested on top of me as our breathing came down from its high. I was positive I never wanted to move.

We'd been laying in the bed for a few minutes when I finally asked, "What time is it?" There were no clocks around the room, and I didn't have my cell phone. It felt odd not knowing what time of night it was.

"Not sure," he answered.

I looked over at him beside me, seeing his arms crossed behind his head. "We should probably go so we know what time the party ends."

"Want to leave me so soon?" He smirked.

I chuckled slightly. "I just don't know the rules. Do we need to leave right when the party ends at three?"

"No. They allow thirty minutes to finish what or *who* you're doing before security makes you leave."

"But how will we know we only have thirty minutes left since we're up here?"

"There'll be a knock on the door. Like a warning."

"Oh ..." I trailed off.

"And I'm not done with you yet." He rolled on top of me.

I smiled up at him. "Is that so?"

"You don't think I'd leave here tonight without tasting your pussy, did you?"

My belly dipped at the thought of his face between my legs.

Booker smirked again then eased down my body, trailing his tongue along my skin as he went. He started at each breast, making each nipple hard. My hands were free to touch him as he went, so I gripped his hair, holding on like it was a ride that was about to throw me off course.

When he got to the place he wanted to be, Booker spread my lips, winked up at me, and then his mouth disappeared. A hiss escaped my lips as he took his first taste, and my hands fisted tighter into his blond hair. I withered beneath him, pushing his head into me as I wanted more. So much more.

He didn't stop.

His mouth licked—sucked—*devoured* me. Devoured me to the point of no return. To the point where I didn't want it to end.

"Oh, God," I moaned. Fuck, I was close. I'd never gotten off with just a man's mouth on me before. They'd usually have to add a finger or two, but the way Booker was consuming me was sending me into the depths of what I wanted—*needed*.

"Fuck," I hissed. "Right there. Oh God ..."

Yeah, I was close. So close. So close that at any moment my body was going to spiral out of control and I was going to shatter—break into tiny pieces on the bed. How? I didn't know, but I was positive my body was going to come apart.

A pulse started to beat in my pussy, and before I knew it, the beat turned into an explosion. My back curved up, my legs closed tight around Booker's head, and I came. I came so hard that I saw stars. How was it that this man knew exactly how to make me a puddle of water in seconds flat?

Booker slid up my body, and again used his tongue as he went. I was trying to get my pulse to return to normal, but it was no use because then he kissed me. This one was laced with the taste of myself, and I welcomed it. I knew that I was starting to get used to the feel of his lips against mine. Used to the way his tongue went to war in my mouth. He thought we were both trying to fight for the upper hand when in reality he had it.

I wasn't sure how I was going to face him after tonight. How did you make eye contact with a man who knew every inch of your body? Did you pretend it never happened? Did you wish it could again? Did you fantasize about it nightly? I was confident I would do all three.

Booker sheathed himself with another condom. We didn't speak. Instead, he lowered himself on me and entered me slowly. Our eyes remained locked, and I could feel my heart breaking inside with each thrust of his hips. I didn't want this to be the last time we were together. I wanted more. But I couldn't have more. Tonight would be the last time ...

Unless I became a member.

He kissed my lips again.

Gentle.

Unhurried.

Slow.

So slow that I could barely breathe. It was as though we both knew that the night was about to end and we were savoring it. But my body had other plans. Before I knew it, I felt the wave of ecstasy in my core and my eyes closed on their own. There was no warning. No build up. Just me coming apart with his cock inside me, repeatedly hitting just the right spot.

"I love watching your face when you come."

I opened my eyes to see Booker still watching me as he continued to pump his hips. "Knowing I'm the one who put that look on your face, gorgeous, is enough to bring me to my knees."

Again, I was tongue-tied. No man had ever spoken to me the way Booker did. Before I let myself get too close to the ones who didn't care about my job, I'd broken the relationships off. I didn't let myself win. Either they didn't want me, I didn't want them, or I didn't give them a chance because I dealt with divorces on a daily basis. I guarded my heart. *That* was how my career played into my dating life. I wouldn't take a man for all his money. I'd never let one close enough to experience the possibility. Now, with just one night, Booker was chiseling away at the steel bars that kept my heart safe *because I trusted him.* Was it because we now shared a secret or was it because I was actually starting to realize I felt things for him?

He stopped moving, sat back on his heels and pulled me to sit up with him. We were still connected, and my arms wrapped around his neck, his around my waist, and we held on as he started to pump into me again. We were going slow again, in no rush for the night to end, but before long his hips started to thrust harder and I knew he was close. I was close again too. His mouth met my lips, and this time he stifled my cries of pleasure in our kiss as we both came together.

Then, a knock sounded at the door. Our thirty-minute warning.

We stayed locked together for I don't know how long. We both knew it was over. My head rested on his shoulder, and his hands lightly trailed up my back. Only minutes remained until it was back to reality.

"Get dressed, and I'll drive you home. I just need to use the bathroom before we go."

I nodded, and we pulled apart. Booker climbed off the bed, and I watched his perfect ass saunter to the attached bathroom after he grabbed his clothes.

This was it. It was really over.

A knock sounded on the door again as I was slipping on my heels, but when I opened the door, it wasn't security. A blonde I vaguely remembered seeing throughout the night stood there with a wide grin.

"Is Booker ready?"

"What?" I asked.

"Is he ready to go home?" she asked, sliding passed me and into the room.

"What?" I asked again, wide-eyed. "Who are you?"

She stopped and turned toward me. "I'm his wife."

Chapter 7

BOOKER

"What did you do?"

The moment I stepped out of the loo, I knew Peyton wasn't in the room. Carrie was leaning against the wall, and when our eyes met, she smiled. Usually we'd meet downstairs, but tonight of all nights she decided to come get me.

"What? Her?" she asked, hooking her thumb toward the door.

"Yes, *love*. Peyton. Where is she?"

"Calling me love? You only use that term of *endearment* when you're being an ass."

I glared down at her. "Where's Peyton?"

Carrie shrugged. "I don't know. She left."

"What did you say to her?"

"Why do you think I said something? They all leave satisfied, don't they?"

I started to see red. "Answer my fucking question, or you're walking home, *love*." I growled the last word at her.

Carrie moved to leave the room, and I followed her. It was for the best since security was bound to find us at any minute. "I was next door, so I came over to see if you were ready to leave or if you had already gone downstairs."

"That doesn't explain why she left," I clipped.

"She started to question who I was, so I told her."

I stopped walking and grabbed her arm. "You told her what?"

"The truth." She smiled.

My grip tightened on her arm without me realizing it. "Fucking tell me what you told her!" I ordered.

"You know I like it rough."

I pushed her against the wall, my arm going just below her throat. I was pissed, but Carrie loved hardcore shit, and my dominance wasn't scaring her. Granted, I'd never laid a hand on her before right now.

"Jesus fucking Christ!" I yelled, spit flying on her face.

She raised her hand and wiped at the saliva. "All right. I told her we were married."

I no longer saw red. Black clouded my vision, and my head was about to explode. I took a deep breath and then ran down the stairs to try to find Peyton and explain. Yes, Carrie and I were married, but we weren't married in the traditional sense. It was a friendship—*I'll scratch your back and you'll scratch mine* situation.

I couldn't find Peyton in the sea of people as I made my way to the front. It was like a concert had ended and everyone was going for the door. However, it was only one hundred and fifty people or so and not thousands. The bad part was that they were all trying to get to their limos and shit. I just wanted to get to my girl.

My ... girl.

I stopped walking. What the hell made me think that? Tonight was just that—*tonight*. I only wanted to explain to Peyton that Carrie was a bitch and wanted to scare her off. I was going to kill my *wife*.

I started to move around people again, and my eyes found Trent. "Hey," he said, his arm around a redhead. Right ... his divorce.

"Sorry, mate. I don't have time. I need to find—" *Well, I need to find your wife's attorney because I've been fucking her for the past few hours.* "Have you seen your wife?" Peyton was Ava's guest, and therefore, they probably had come together.

"No, I haven't seen that cunt."

The redhead slapped his shoulder. "Don't say that word."

"What?" he asked. "She is one."

I knew Trent and Ava well. Ava wasn't a cunt, and Trent was just pissed that she wanted a divorce, but it was bound to happen eventually. No one in Hollywood stayed married, and that was why I made the big bucks.

"Mate, can you call her please?"

"I'm not calling her. What the fuck is this about?"

"I ..." *Fuck!* "I need to talk to the woman who ... you know." He didn't know the actual truth, but I hoped he'd think it was about his divorce.

He clapped me on the shoulder. "Book, that can wait until Monday. Candace and I are going to go back to her place and continue the party. You're welcome to join us."

"You know I'm not into that." I didn't like sharing. It wasn't my thing. I wanted my woman to come apart because of me and only me.

"All right, but you're missing out."

"Thanks, but no thanks."

The crowd had moved, and we were just coming to the front doors. "There's the cunt now." Trent pointed, and I followed to where he had indicated.

"Stop calling her that," I said, and rushed to where Ava was. "Where's Peyton?" I asked her.

Ava was with Michael Zapino. It was clear she and Trent were moving on. "I don't know. I haven't seen her. Her purse wasn't with our stuff when I grabbed mine. Pretty sure she left. Why?"

I rubbed the back of my neck. "I need to speak with her about ... stuff."

Ava stepped closer to me as though she was trying not to let anyone around us hear her. "I'm sure she didn't come here to work all night. Just call her on Monday."

Monday seemed so far away when really it was less than twenty-four hours away. "Give me her number," I said as Ava's limo pulled up.

She rolled her eyes. "Peyton was right." Ava's driver opened the door for her and Michael to slip in. "I'm not giving you her personal number, Book. Leave the poor woman alone, and call her on Monday."

My alarm blared, waking me. I slept like shit. Pure, fucking shit. I tended to get shitty sleep after a night at Sensation. My body was out of sorts staying up until five in the bloody morning. It was like I was a twenty-something who went bar hopping. But I wasn't. I was thirty-four, and while I might think I'm a spring chicken, my body told me otherwise, even with the hours I put in at the gym.

At least it was only once a month and worth it. *Totally worth it.*

When I left Sensation Sunday morning, I'd messaged Peyton on Facebook. We weren't friends, so my messages were probably going to her other folder or some shit. By the time I got home, I was internet stalking her something fierce, but nothing gave me her private mobile number or her home address. Then I couldn't fall asleep because I was replaying the night over and over in my head. Sleep did come eventually, but it wasn't for long. My alarm woke me at ten so that I could go to the gym.

Peyton still hadn't seen my messages.

That night, I tried to go to sleep early because I had to get up at five to head to the gym before work. Of course, all I could think about was what I imagined her face looking like when Carrie told her we were married. I pictured a look of betrayal on her face before instantly running from the room.

Carrie was right. Usually I wouldn't care if she told a bird I'd hooked up with at Sensation that we were married. But she never had before, and most members didn't know we were married. So of all the people she had to open her big fucking mouth to, it was the one person I actually cared about. Like I'd told Peyton, I'd fancied her for years. She was beautiful, feisty, smart and her body—well, now that I knew what it looked like naked, I was fucked. Royally fucked.

I'd never approached her before now because we were on opposite sides. Peyton was right, we could get in trouble if things were to progress and we didn't tell anyone. I always thought that if I had that one taste, it would be all about sex. But as the day went on, and I couldn't get her out of my head, I realized I actually bloody cared for her. If nothing else, I just wanted a chance to tell Peyton the actual truth about Carrie. It might have only been a one night thing, but how was I going to face her in court knowing what she tasted like? *I couldn't.* That was the answer.

Rolling out of bed, I threw on a pair of black basketball shorts and a white *Under Armour* tank. My gaze drifted to the top of my dresser. I'd left Peyton's knickers there to stare me in the face whenever I was in the room. I couldn't have that, so I stuck them in the top drawer. I had no intention of returning them.

After putting on socks and shoes, I grabbed my wallet, keys, phone and headed to the kitchen. My blood started to boil when I saw Carrie making her coffee.

"Are you still mad at me?" she asked as I reached to grab my protein powder in the cupboard so I could make my pre-workout shake.

"What do you think, *love?*"

"How long will it last?"

I turned to her. "I don't know. Might want a divorce."

She laughed. "No, you don't."

She was right, but it was still brilliant to think it in the heat of the moment. We could get a divorce, but that might turn into a nightmare for me, so it was better to stay married. We'd been married long enough that I could become a citizen, but there just wasn't a need for it right now. Plus, I didn't have time to go to all the appointments and study for the tests I needed to take to become one.

"You're my best mate, but seriously, you have a big fucking mouth. We agreed no one was to *ever* know." Okay, that wasn't true. Only the people who *needed* to know knew we were married.

"Who cares? It was a chick from Sensation. You know nothing gets talked about that happens there. It's in the rules."

I crossed my arms over my chest. "That's where you're wrong. Peyton's a colleague."

"She works at your firm?"

I shook my head. "No. We have cases against each other, though."

Carrie shrugged. "So what? She knows you're married. Big deal."

"We know we're married," I said, motioning my hand between us. "Now Peyton knows, and if she tells someone, then shit could come back on us."

"Why would she tell someone? Being married isn't a crime."

"I don't know, *love*. You bints love to run your fucking mouths off." I was mad. Yes, Carrie could be a bitch, but I'd never called her that before.

Carrie rolled her eyes. "But she knows the rules, doesn't she?"

I sighed. "Yes, I assume she does. I'm just saying that you shouldn't have even opened your mouth no matter where we were."

"All right, fine. It's our dirty little secret." She smirked.

I groaned. "I'll catch you later." I grabbed my protein shake sans water and left.

After the gym, I grabbed a giant cup of coffee before heading into the office. I'd showered and changed after my workout, and then put on my backup suit that I'd left in the locker at the gym. In my rush, I'd forgotten to grab a suit from home.

I'd been working for Lee & Thompson, LLP since I graduated from law school. I'd come to the States to attend the University of California Los Angeles. While attending UCLA, I worked for a law firm as a file clerk to make money so I could survive. That was when I knew what I wanted to be when I grew up.

I obtained my law degree from the UCLA School of Law. My initial plan was to return to Leeds after I graduated from UCLA.

However, since I decided I wanted to become a lawyer, I wanted to stay in the States. If I returned to England after I obtained my law degree, it would have been pointless because the law is completely different. But how could I stay in the States after my student VISA expired? I hadn't found a job to sponsor me, and I needed something within thirty days or I'd be sent back to Leeds, so to make a long story short, my best mate and I came up with a plan so that I could stay in the States after graduation.

"I can't believe we're finally graduating in a week," Carrie said, sitting on our sofa in the apartment we shared off campus.

"It's going to be brill."

"I'm not looking forward to the bar exam, though."

I looked away from the TV. "We'll get through it. We always do." That was, of course, if I was still in the States.

She was silent for a bit. "I'm going to miss you."

"You'll come visit me." It wasn't a question. I knew she would.

"Yeah, but I wish there was something we could do so you could stay."

"I'm looking for a job that will sponsor me for a work VISA."

"I know, but if you don't find one, then you'll leave me."

"We'll visit each other, sweetheart."

"What if ..." she started then stopped.

"What if what?" I asked, raising an eyebrow at her.

"Nothing. It's stupid."

"Tell me."

"What if we got married and you applied for a Green Card? That way you can become a permanent resident, and you'll only have to renew every ten years—or whatever it is."

I started to laugh. "You want to get married?"

She rolled her gunmetal colored eyes. "You know I'm never getting married."

"Just because you like pussy doesn't mean you won't ever get married. California might change their laws or another state."

She started to laugh as if she didn't believe me. "Right."

"Fine. I'll make you a deal."

"What's that?"

"Look for a job for a civil rights law firm. I want you to specialize in LGBT rights, and once the changes happen and you can marry a fit bird, we'll get divorced."

"Let me get this straight. You want to tell me what to do with my career before you'll marry me? I think I'm getting the short end of the stick here, Book."

I grinned. "No, sweetheart. There's nothing short or small about me."

"You're so cocky." She slapped my arm.

"What? You want my cock now?"

She rolled her eyes. "No, thanks."

I lunged for her and wrapped her in my arms. "Getting married might work for real. And I know one day I'll walk you down the aisle."

Carrie lost her father in a motorcycle accident when she was a little girl. I'd heard stories about how, when she was growing up, he would dance with her as if they were at her wedding.

When she got older, she realized she liked women and not men. I knew the time would come when she could marry whatever woman she fancied, and I also knew that I would be the one to walk her down the aisle and give her away.

So, the day before we graduated from UCLA Law, we got married at the courthouse. It wasn't anything to write home about. In fact, I didn't. My parents didn't know I'd married my best mate so that I could stay in the States. They just thought I'd found a job and was on a work VISA. The only people who knew were our friends Amelia and Randy because we'd needed them to witness our nuptials. There was no reason for anyone other than HR to know.

Yes, two attorneys were breaking the law. And now Carrie had opened her mouth and told someone outside of the "need to know" circle.

I parked my black Mercedes in my assigned spot of the garage at L&T, and then took the elevator up to the eleventh floor. I had an agenda for the day, and it needed to happen before I lost my fucking mind.

I wasn't sure why I felt the need to make things right with Peyton. Before Saturday night, the only thing we'd ever mostly talked about were cases. What I did know was that she was beautiful, and that had made me cockier around her. I was like a little boy with a crush on a girl who had to be mean to her for attention.

Now I couldn't get her out of my head.

I'd never had that problem before. I'd been with many women. *Many*. That was what I liked about Sensation. I could go have safe, no strings attached sex, and I didn't have to worry about someone wanting me for my money or anything of that nature. And I had money. L&T paid me well because I had the most billable hours and hooked the wealthiest clients. In fact, I was on my way to making partner.

"Hey, Booker." The receptionist smiled and waved at me as I stepped off the lift. I knew she wanted to fuck me. All the women in my office eye-fucked me on a daily basis.

But I had a rule: don't eat where you shit.

I'd actually learned it the hard way. My old assistant and I were having an affair until her husband found out. That was a bloody mess I'd had to deal with, and it almost got me fired. Luckily, L&T couldn't afford to lose me, so they paid her a handsome amount of money to quit.

"Morning, Sandra. Hope your weekend was a good one."

"It was, thank you."

I continued toward my office, passing the conference room/library. That was where my old assistant and I used to shag. Good times.

My new assistant, Monica, was at her desk as I walked up. "Morning, Monica," I greeted. "Can you get me Peyton Winters' office number, please?"

"Sure thing." She smiled, and I entered my corner office.

I shrugged off my grey suit jacket, hung it on the door, and walked over to my glass desk. I had a shit ton of work to do, but my mind was on one thing and one thing only—or one person for that matter.

Monica walked in carrying a sticky note. "Here you go."

"Brilliant, thank you. Can you also get me a cup of tea?"

"No, problem." She smiled and turned to leave.

Without hesitation, I picked up the phone and dialed the number Monica gave me. It rang twice before it was answered.

"Chandler and Patterson, how can I direct your call?"

"Peyton Winters," I clipped.

"One moment."

My pulse started to race as the call connected.

"Ms. Winter's office," a lady—not Peyton, answered.

"Peyton, please."

"May I ... May I ask who's calling?"

"Booker Jameson."

"One ... one moment, please." I was placed on hold.

Why the fuck was she stuttering? I turned, looking out the floor to ceiling window as I waited. Peyton's office wasn't far from mine, and I had a half a mind to just go there.

"I'm sorry, Mr. Jameson. Peyton's not available." That was code for she didn't want to speak with me. "Can I take a message?"

I groaned. "Have her call me." I gave her my mobile number as well as the office number before disconnecting.

I went to the court's website to see if she had any cases today. She didn't. I decided to give her until the afternoon to call me, or I was going to show up at her office. I *knew* Peyton wouldn't call me back, but I was going to give her until after lunch. In the meantime, I had Response papers to prepare for Trent.

Chapter 8

BOOKER

A nd I was right.

Peyton didn't return my call.

A few minutes before midday, I strolled into the courthouse and filed Trent's papers. He'd swung by the office around ten and signed them. I knew most of the info, and I had emailed him some documents he needed to fill out when I was internet stalking Peyton Sunday. Usually, I would only file the Response because discovery came later. However, Peyton filed Ava's financial pleadings when she filed the Petition, so I felt that I should too. We also had thirty days to respond to the Petition, but it was an excuse to explain myself in person to Peyton. I couldn't wait thirty days. I needed to speak with her now. Yes, I could have had my paralegal or the court runner file the Response, but I needed it done right away, and since I was out, I could swing by Chandler and Patterson and serve Peyton in person like she'd done to me.

I walked through the double glass doors of C&P, back straight and on a fucking mission. Peyton might think she could ignore me, but I don't fuck around. Not only did I want to tell her—

I stopped walking.

I was going to explain what? I was married to my best mate, but it didn't mean anything because we were cheating the government so I could stay in the country? Yeah, that would go over well. I was being as stupid as Carrie opening her mouth. I needed to think about what I should say to Peyton instead of listening to my dick.

I turned around to leave and came face to face with the one I'd been thinking about all weekend. The envelope with Trent's filed papers was in my hand, but I couldn't move. Peyton was more beautiful than I'd remembered. Her dark brunette hair was down around her shoulders like the last time I'd seen her in bed at Sensation. She was wearing a grey trouser suit with a magenta blouse. I'd seen her dressed the same way on many occasions in court, but knowing what was under all her clothes made my dick jump to attention.

"What are you doing here?" Peyton asked.

"I'm going to go check our messages," the woman she was with said. I hadn't realized she was with someone until she spoke. I just stared at Peyton.

"Well?" she asked, crossing her arms over her chest. My eyes went to her tits. Tits that I knew the feel of—the taste of.

"Booker!" Peyton hissed, and my eyes snapped to hers.

Then I remembered how she'd screamed my name in bed, and my eyes moved to her lips then back up to her eyes. She rolled them, and my dick twitched again.

"Do that again," I finally said, not caring where we were.

"Do what?"

I stepped closer and said in a low voice, "Roll your eyes."

"We can't do this here," she stated.

"Then let's go to your office."

"Booker ..." she said low.

I stepped even closer and whispered into her ear, "I'm serving you, gorgeous."

"Give it to me." She stuck out her hand.

"I want to give *it* to you," I admitted, but I wasn't referring to the papers. She wiggled her hand, silently asking for the envelope. I shook my head. "I need to speak with you first." I wasn't sure what I was going to tell her, but I didn't want to leave.

"I have nothing to say to you."

"I have something to say to you," I returned.

She sighed. "Booker, please."

We could go back and forth all afternoon. Neither one of us had time for that, so I turned and walked to her office. I knew where it was because I'd been here a handful of times for other cases and had seen her sitting at her desk. I didn't stop as she called my name, following me. When I got to her office, I unbuttoned my suit jacket and sat in a chair in front of her desk. I wasn't leaving until we sorted our shite out.

She closed the door as she entered and walked around to her desk. I placed the envelope in front of her.

"You have some nerve."

I smirked. "Don't be like that."

"Don't be like that?" She raised her voice. "You used me."

"I didn't use you," I corrected. "We were at a sex club. What did you think would happen?"

She blinked her beautiful chocolate brown eyes. "You're right. I don't know what I was thinking."

We were silent, both thinking. I was trying to think of how to tell her I wanted to do it again—literally.

"Can you just go? Go back to your wife."

"Gorgeous—"

"Don't call me that," she groaned.

I ran my hand over my mouth and sighed. "Why are you so mad?"

I knew why she was mad. I was pissed myself. However, I wanted her to say the words. I wanted her to tell me that what we shared on Saturday was more than sex. I hated her being mad at me. Granted, she seemed to always be annoyed with me when we saw each other, but that was before I'd had my mouth on every inch of her silky body.

She stared at me, not speaking.

"Well?" I prompted.

"I didn't know you were married," she answered with a sigh.

I grinned and leaned forward. "So what if I am? We were at a sex club. People switch all the time."

"It's just not my thing. I don't like sleeping with married men."

"My wife doesn't care."

"Great. Good for her. I just felt blindsided with her showing up at the door. You could have told me—"

"When? When I had my mouth on your tits? When I was between your legs? When I was buried so far inside you that you screamed my name?"

She rolled her eyes again, and I was so close to locking her office door and bringing her across my knee.

So close.

"We just need to forget Saturday happened. You said it yourself, what goes on behind Sensation's doors stays there."

"No," I clipped.

"No?"

"I'm not going to forget it, and we're *going* to do it again."

She laughed. "No, we aren't."

"Don't you fucking dare throw that ethics crap at me. I want you to come to the next party. Talk to Ava and come as her guest again. Come as my guest."

"You've lost your mind."

"Why do you say that?"

"Booker, you're a member of a sex club. You can screw any of those women. Hell, you can bang your wife there. You don't need to fuck me."

"That's where you're wrong."

"I'm not wrong. You see me as a challenge or some shit, and I'm not going to be used again."

I stood and buttoned my jacket. "There are things you don't know. Come to Sensation next month, and I'll tell you."

"Why do I need to wait until then?" she asked, raising an eyebrow.

"Because it's confidential, and you're in the mindset that only secret stuff can happen at the club. So I'm going to play your game. The ball's in your court, gorgeous."

"I hear you're mad at Carrie?"

I looked up to see my friend Randy strolling through my office door. He worked for Lee and Thompson with me. He had red, slick-backed hair, a red beard and green eyes. We worked out together at the gym, so it was safe to say he was fit. He was also a member of Sensation.

"Piss off, mate. This is between my *wife* and me," I clipped.

He closed the door and walked to the chair at my desk. "Tell me what happened."

I rolled my eyes and instantly thought of Peyton. "Carrie didn't tell you?"

"She only told me that you were mad at her and that I should talk to you today."

I shook my head, annoyed. "So you could smooth things over?"

Randy shrugged. "I guess. Just tell me what happened, or I'll get Amelia to hound you."

Of course Carrie would sic people on me who knew our situation. "She told someone at Sensation that we're married," I answered.

He arched an eyebrow. "Really? Who?"

I sighed. "Some bird I fucked."

I hated calling Peyton "some bird." She was more than that to me —or had been. Since the ball was in her court, anything was bound to happen. If I didn't see her at Sensation again, then I'd know it wasn't more than sex to her.

"Big deal."

I shook my head. "It is a big deal. It's ..." I hesitated because he knew Peyton. He had cases against her too.

"It's?"

"Peyton Winters."

His green eyes widened. "Peyton Winters from Chandler and Patterson?"

I nodded. "That's the one."

He grinned. "You mean to tell me that you banged one of the hottest attorneys in Beverly Hills?"

My eyebrows arched. "Why is that so hard to believe?" I mean, I was Booker Jameson. People referred to me as a womanizer, and I was okay with that because I wasn't looking to settle down. Well, not that I could. I was *married* after all.

"Well, for one, she was at Sensation Saturday? I didn't see her."

"She's representing Ava Ashley. She's getting divorced from Trent, and Peyton came with Ava so she could serve Trent at the club."

"Well, fuck me. I missed a lot Saturday." He chuckled. I watched as he crossed his leg over his opposite knee and got comfortable. "How was she?"

"Good enough so I want to fuck her again," I admitted. I wasn't going to give him more info than that.

"You? Booker Jameson want to go back for seconds?"

And thirds. And fourths. And then top it off with an all-night buffet again.

I smirked, not answering.

"Damn, Book." His forehead crinkled. "Wait. What about your clients? What about Trent? Does he know?"

I shook my head. "He doesn't know, and he won't find out. No one will."

"Does that mean she won't go back to Sensation again?"

I shrugged. "I don't know. I told her I wanted her to, but she's pissed off that I'm married and I can't fucking tell her the truth." Unless she came to Sensation. That would be the only place for me to tell her.

He nodded slowly. "Sounds like you're up shit creek without a paddle."

"I have a solution. Get her to come to Sensation next month so I can taste her again."

"You're willing to risk your law license for a chick? Willing to risk hers?"

"No." And I wasn't. "You know as well as I do that what happens at Sensation, stays at Sensation."

"Until Trent or Ava sees you."

"If Peyton even comes."

"Right," he agreed.

If Peyton came as my guest, we'd have to figure out the details regarding Trent and Ava's case. If she came as Ava's guest, then it would be possible she already talked to Ava and was okay with us being romantic together—or whatever we'd be. I had a month to convince Peyton to return to Sensation, though. The ball was in her court, but that didn't mean I couldn't cheat. And it was obvious I didn't play by the rules.

"Well, it's time for our weekly meeting," Randy stated as he looked at his watch. The meetings were a way for the partners to keep track of their staff and make sure we had a revolving door of clients. The meetings were usually in the morning but Mitch, the head partner, had been in court today.

I sighed. "Great."

We both stood and headed for the conference room/library. Randy and I sat next to each other. When Clint walked through the door, I rolled my eyes. I hated that wanker. We were both running for partner, and everyone knew we were competitive. The current partners ate it up because it drove in more money.

"All right, let's begin," Mitch said. He sat at the head of the large rectangular table that sat at least ten people. Others, including paralegals and assistants, were standing around the room, and everyone had legal notepads to scribble on. He briefly went through everyone's cases, and then turned his attention to me.

"Booker, Clint, you're both up for partner, as you know." People clapped and cheered at the announcement. My eyes flicked to Clint's and his to mine. *Fucker.* "While we would like both of you to make partner, we're only able to promote one of you, so we're not taking into account who has been here longer. We are solely basing it on who's bringing in the most money, and right now, you two are neck and neck."

I sighed.

"We have three more months left of this year. Whoever pulls in the most money by then will be made partner January second."

And now it looked as though I had two games to play. One with Clint that I knew I'd succeed in, and the other with Peyton that I wasn't sure I'd ever win.

Chapter 9

BOOKER

After a long day at the office, I walked into the house I shared with Carrie and stopped in the threshold. Carrie was on her back on the sofa, naked and with another woman between her legs, that woman's arse in the air. I'd walked in on this scenario before. Being married to a lesbian had its benefits, and this was one of them. Live, in the flesh, porn.

I closed the door quietly, and watched. Carrie moaned as she reached up and grabbed her own tits. My dick hardened and all thoughts of a long day flew out the window. I moved to the armchair across from the sofa and started to enjoy the show. Carrie's eyes met mine, and she smiled.

"*Wife*," I greeted tersely with a whisper. I was still mad at her, but this show was wearing me down.

She smirked and reached down to the woman's head and ran her fingers through her hair. It was then that I noticed the woman was a brunette, and my mind went to Peyton. I didn't like to share the woman I was interested in but imagining that it was Peyton in front of me only made me harder.

I slouched down in the chair, spread my legs and began to unbutton my trousers. The brunette reached up and grabbed Carrie's tit, and it caused her to moan again and throw her head back. My hand pulled my dick out, and I licked my lips as I started to stroke myself.

Images of Peyton's mouth wrapped around my cock entered my mind, and I groaned. My motion increased, and my grip tightened thinking about Peyton and her tight body. Peyton and her long legs.

Peyton and her long brown hair I'd fisted in my grip as I fucked her. Peyton bound with cuffs as I thrust into her. I continued to work my shaft as I watched Carrie come and then the brunette crawled up her body until her pussy was on Carrie's face. I could smell the arousal in the air, and that made me even harder.

I jerked and jerked, watching the two women enjoying each other. The brunette's back was to me, and I couldn't see her face, so I kept pretending it was Peyton. Peyton and the look in her mocha eyes as she came around my dick. Peyton and how she screamed my name with me buried deep inside of her. My grip tightened as I pleasured myself. I was close.

Carrie used her hands, opening the brunette more, and the brunette threw her head back, her brown hair cascading over her shoulders. My pace quickened, and just as the brunette moaned her release, I came. Ropes of cum squirted my belly as I continued to milk my dick and watch the two girls in front of me.

The brunette rose off Carrie and turned to meet my gaze as I cleaned my stomach with the tissue that was next to me. She looked nothing like Peyton, but it was still fun to imagine it was her.

"Oh ..." she said when she noticed I was sitting across from them.

"Don't mind me," I joked as I tucked my cock back into my trousers.

"I didn't realize your roommate was home," the brunette said to Carrie.

Carrie tugged her down to sit next to her on the sofa. My eyes immediately went between their legs. "You don't mind an audience, do you?" Carrie asked and kissed the brunette.

When they broke apart, the brunette turned back to me. "No, but I'd like it better if he joined us."

I smiled. "You see Carrie doesn't like dick, and I don't like to share. I'm happy with just watching." The brunette nodded.

"Are you still mad at me?" Carrie asked me.

I tilted my head a little to the side as I thought about her question. "This was planned, wasn't it, *love*. For me to walk in on you and her?"

Carrie smirked. "Maybe."

I stood. "Well played, but if Peyton doesn't come to Sensation again, you'll need to do a lot more than put on a show for me."

Today I was going to do something I'd never done before.

I was going to try to settle a case outside of court. It had been two weeks since I filed Trent's response papers, and usually, I would slow play things, making sure we filed every document and asked for every financial statement from the time of marriage to separation. The more hours I put into a case, the more we were paid. I wasn't cheating my clients, per se, I was only being thorough.

Right.

Thorough.

Trent and Ava didn't have anything to really to fight over. They had a few houses they bought while married, but they had different bank accounts and a prenup that stated they'd waive their rights to the division of separate property, whether currently held before marriage or after. Meaning whatever they purchased with their own money belonged to that person. Usually an appraisal would need to be done on each house and then they'd divide the properties, or one would buy the other out. They both stated in their financial disclosures that they purchased three homes together, so it was just a matter of who kept what, and apparently, Trent wanted to keep them all.

I wanted any excuse to see Peyton, even if it meant I'd have to work overtime on more cases, so I was going to convince Trent to agree to a settlement so that I could show up at her office again. Normally I would email it to her, but not now. Not since every bloody hour I was thinking of her. Would things be different if I had driven her home after Sensation that night? If she didn't know I was married? Would we be having secret rendezvous because the night we shared was something we both had never experienced before? I'd never know thanks to my *wife*.

Monica buzzed my office phone. "Booker, Trent Inglewood is here."

"Send him in," I replied.

I grabbed Trent's file from the corner of my desk and flipped it open in front of me. As he walked in, I stood and greeted him with a handshake.

"Trent, how's your day going?"

"All right," he replied.

"Want a cup of coffee? Tea?"

"No, I'm good. Thanks."

I gestured for him to take a seat in front of my desk. A Case Management Conference, where the judge helps decide a good process to try to settle a case, was scheduled in a little over a month. If an agreement couldn't be reached, the judge would schedule a trial, but I didn't want to wait a month to see Peyton again. I needed to convince her to come to Sensation in less than two weeks.

"So, Ava's all moved out?" I asked as we both sat.

He sighed. "Yeah, she moved all of her stuff this past weekend."

"Did you two discuss who's keeping which houses?"

He shook his head. "No. As far as I'm concerned, I get to keep them all, remember?"

I laughed. "That's not really how it works."

"So I fight her for them."

Usually I would be all for fighting, but not now. I wanted Trent to agree to settle everything because of Peyton, but also because I was friends with Ava. "Even if you fight for it, the judge won't give you a house unless you paid for it with only your money. Did you?" I knew the answer but asked anyway to prove my point.

"No. We bought the Montauk property, the villa in Lake Como and the Beverly Hills home together. Ava already left the house here. She gave up her stake on that one."

I chuckled and shook my head. "Again, not how it works."

"I don't care how it works, Booker. I hired you to get me what I want. Ava has embarrassed me by doing all of this, and I'm not backing down easily."

Ah, so there it was. The real reason he was pissed off. It wasn't because the love of his life left him. It was because she bruised his ego.

I leaned forward and rested my elbows on my desk. "Listen, mate. Any judge will make things fair for both parties. If you want to keep the houses, you need to buy Ava out. No one needs to know. You can tell people you bloody took her for all she's worth. No one will know the truth unless they go to the courthouse and pull your records."

"My luck they would. Some jackass paparazzi trying to make money off of my divorce will do it in a heartbeat," he groaned.

"Then you need to just let it go. We can fight this all you want and set a trial that will cost you more money. More time. Time I know you don't have because you're filming. Then you still might not like what the judge orders."

"I can't go down without a fight."

"I understand, mate. But is it worth it?"

"She's worth it." I stared at him, and he continued. "I mean ... Fine. What do you suggest?"

I'd been dealing with divorces for a long time. I knew when one still loved the other, and this was one of those times. Trent was still in love with Ava, and he felt that the more he fought, the longer they would stay married. Even though they weren't together, it was a reason for them to stay in contact. Even if it was through their attorneys.

"Well, I suggest you keep the Hamptons, she gets the villa in Lake Como, and you buy her out of the Beverly Hills home." I leaned back in my chair. "Or you fight for her."

He laughed. "Fight for her?"

"I've known you two for a long time. You were great together.

Maybe it's time you realize the same and fight for her. Prove she's the one you want, and not those birds you screw when you're away shooting."

"It's too late for that."

I shook my head. "It's never too late. Tell me what you want to do, and I'll talk to her attorney."

I strolled through the double doors of Chandler and Patterson unannounced.

Again.

I hadn't heard from Peyton, and I knew she wouldn't take my call or schedule a meeting with me. If I were at her office, she'd have to see me, even if she made me wait all day. I wouldn't leave.

Yes, I was that desperate.

It wasn't only because I wanted to see her again. I wanted to prove to her that she couldn't ignore me. That she couldn't ignore what could potentially happen between us.

"I'm here to see Ms. Winters." I smiled my smile that always worked on a woman.

"Do you have an appointment, Mr. Jameson?" She smiled back.

She knew who I was. Perfect. "I don't, *love*," I clipped. I just wanted to see Peyton.

"Let me call her assistant."

I was pretending to look at the abstract art on the wall as I listened to the receptionist ring Peyton's assistant, Lorelei. If things didn't go as planned with Peyton, I was going to have to win over Lorelei. She'd help me get in.

"Mr. Jameson."

I turned and walked back to the receptionist's desk.

"I'm sorry, but Ms. Winters isn't available."

"Is she with a client?"

"I ... I'm sorry, I can't give you that information."

Actually, she could. She only had to keep the client's name confidential. But judging by her reaction, I didn't think Peyton was with a client, so I took a chance.

"Thanks," I called as I walked around her desk toward Peyton's office.

"Mr. Jameson," she hollered. I didn't stop. "Mr. Jameson!"

I smiled as I made my way down the hall. As I approached Lorelei, she looked up from her desk and smiled. It instantly gave me the impression that she knew what had happened between Peyton and me.

"Don't mind me," I said and kept walking.

Lorelei chuckled, not saying a word. *She definitely knew.*

I entered the open door of Peyton's office. She looked up from her laptop and opened her mouth to say something, but then stopped when she noticed it was me. "Hello, gorgeous. Miss me?" I closed the door.

Peyton rolled her eyes. "You need to stop doing that."

"Doing what?" I asked then sat across from her at her desk.

"You can't just walk in here whenever you want."

"But I did."

She rolled her eyes again. "Book—"

"You're going to regret that."

"Regret what?"

"Rolling your eyes at me."

"I'm getting tired of this game we're playing." She leaned back in her chair and crossed her arms. The slit of her blouse stretched, and my eyes moved to her tits. This shit was driving me insane.

"I brought you something." I looked back up to her chocolate colored eyes.

"What's that?"

I pulled two separate small stacks of paper from my briefcase and stood. She watched me curiously as I walked around her desk. "I met with Trent yesterday."

Her tone changed. "Okay, I'm listening."

"He's making two settlement offers."

"Two?" She furrowed her brow.

"Two for Ava to choose from."

"Okay, let me see them." She stuck out her hand.

I shook my head and leaned against her desk, holding the papers back. "But I have a stipulation."

"What?" She chuckled. "*You* have a stipulation?"

"I do."

"And what's that?"

I leaned down and whispered into her ear, "You give me a chance."

"Booker—"

Still an inch from her ear, I said low, "Listen to me, gorgeous. If you only want to be with me once a month at Sensation, then come in two weeks."

"I'm not interested in joining in on your—swinging."

I closed my eyes and took a deep breath. I needed to use my words wisely. I stood and buttoned my jacket. "To partake in swinging, you would need to have been intimate with your partner to, therefore, have swapped."

"What does that mean?"

I set the papers on her desk, knowing the conversation wasn't going to go the way I'd wanted. "I told you that I would tell you at Sensation. You have two weeks to decide if you want to come. You know how to become a guest. Do it under my name. Do it under Ava's. I don't care as long as you do it. Show up, and I'll tell you what I mean. Don't show up, and I'll go back to being opposing counsel only."

"What about your settlement offers?"

I made my way toward the closed door. "Review the settlement agreements and have Ava decide what she wants to do. If she doesn't agree, then we go to court. You know I like to fight. But in this case, I hope Ava chooses to stay with Trent."

"Stay with Trent?"

With my hand on the doorknob, I said, "Like me, gorgeous. When he wants a woman, he's persistent."

Chapter 10

BOOKER

In the last two weeks, I still hadn't heard from Peyton. It was starting to feel like it was a losing battle and I should cut my losses. I hadn't heard from Trent either, so I assumed that meant Ava hadn't made her decision.

Trent was proposing what I'd suggested about dividing the houses and buying Ava out of the one he was living in Beverly Hills. He was also asking for Ava to give him another chance. One offer was an actual pleading, and the other was a letter to Ava. If she were to choose the latter, Peyton would need to prepare a Request for Dismissal for me to sign and then file with the court.

If Ava and Trent were together tonight, I had that answer. If Peyton showed up tonight, I had that answer, too.

"Are we going together tonight?"

I looked to the door of my bedroom to see Carrie in the threshold. She was wearing a black trench coat. I knew from over the years that she was only wearing lingerie under the coat. I straightened the cuffs of my tux as I turned.

"Don't we always?"

"What will happen if that woman comes tonight?"

"What do you mean?"

"You like her."

"I've liked plenty of women before," I clarified.

She shook her head. "Not like this. Usually they do the chasing, not the other way around."

"Who said I'm chasing her? We haven't even talked about it."

"Because you've shut me out since the last party," she whined.

"Exactly, so how do you figure I'm chasing her?"

"I talked to Amelia."

I started for the door. "*I* haven't even talked to Amelia."

"But *you* talked to Randy," Carrie said as she followed me down the hall.

I should have guessed. Carrie and I were close like Randy and Amelia were. However, they weren't married or even dating. Amelia was married to someone else and had children. Carrie probably vented to Amelia, who then called Randy to get the gossip since Randy and I worked together and he could find shit out for them.

"Look, if Peyton comes tonight, get a ride. I'm not chasing her, but if she shows, then that means something."

"I could help, you know."

I stopped walking and turned to face her. "I think you've already helped enough, *love*."

She rolled her eyes, but my dick did nothing in my trousers. It only craved Peyton's mocha ones.

"For *us*, I hope she gives you a chance."

"We'll get over it, but first she needs to show up."

I pulled my Mercedes into the circular drive of Sensation. We'd been in the queue to enter for twenty minutes, and I was more nervous than the first time we attended the club. That night I'd had no idea what to expect. I was invited by a classmate of mine who had used inheritance money for his membership. It's not every day you get asked to attend a sex party, and somehow my classmate knew I'd be into it. I mean, who wouldn't be into walking around a mansion in Beverly Hills with people fucking everywhere?

That night, I'd only observed. I was in my mid-twenties and knew exactly what it meant when people said, "Like a kid in a candy store."

That was me. I came home and jerked off until the sun rose. I couldn't get the images out of my head: women together, men together, threesomes, bondage ... If you can imagine it, I probably saw it, or have since.

Now I was a regular and, of course, I had Carrie get a membership, too. She was still set on the fact that she would never get married (even though laws had changed), so I brought her along to eat all the pussy she desired. We each started with the Ruby level. Back then it was five-hundred dollars a month to join. Now I had no idea how much it was, but over the years I'd upgraded, and now I could afford to be a Diamond member. Granted, when I became a Diamond member, it was cheaper than it was now.

"If she doesn't show, at least have a good night, Booker," Carrie said from the passenger seat as we pulled up to the valet.

"I will, sweetheart. Don't worry about me."

"I do worry about you."

I cupped her head and pulled her toward me so I could lay a kiss on her forehead. "Go eat some pussy."

She laughed and pushed me away just as the valets opened each door. Once we were out of the car, I winked at Carrie, and she hooked her arm in mine. We walked up the red carpeted stairs together. After Luke had made sure we were on the list—we were always on the list—we entered, and Carrie checked her coat.

"How will I know if I need to get a ride?" she asked.

That was a good question. We usually met here as we left and got in the car. I rubbed the back of my neck. "How about you just get a ride and I'll meet you at home?"

She reached up on her toes and kissed my cheek. "Okay. Again, I hope she shows."

I sure the fuck hoped so, too.

I usually had a plan. I would get a drink, find a fit bird and do my thing. Sometimes we would watch others so she would get turned on, or she'd give me a blowjob in front of people because that seemed to turn some women on. I never really cared. Other times I would go up to my room to get away and stare at the view of LA in the distance, almost like I needed to regroup.

Tonight was different.

I had a plan, but that didn't involve me finding just anyone to be with. Tonight I was walking around, searching for Peyton. I stopped and chatted with people I knew, grabbed a drink, but every second I was looking at the women in the area to see if one was her.

Carrie was right. I'd never acted this way about a woman before. Peyton was the forbidden fruit, and once I'd tasted her, I was on the verge of being kicked out of the garden. I knew it was wrong, Peyton knew it was wrong, but when you are forbidden to do something, you only want it more.

The night was in full swing, and the longer I walked around, the more I started to think Peyton wasn't going to show. I didn't blame her. Being married was a kink in starting any relationship, but I had my reasons, and I wanted to share them with her. If she still didn't want anything to do with me then I would leave her alone. I got plenty of pussy. The difference was Peyton was more than sex for me and I wanted to explore things with her.

My gaze fell to a sofa, and I watched as a man lay naked, his dick inside one woman as another woman straddled his face. Sharing wasn't my thing, but this scene was turning me on. It had been a month since I'd fucked, and that wasn't like me. Sure I came to Sensation for sex, but that wasn't the only place I was getting it. The women I slept with outside of Sensation weren't necessarily into the same things as me, and with Sensation, I could find someone to tie up for the night or whatever I fancied.

"I'm surprised you're not in your room."

I turned my head to see Randy leaning against the same wall table as me. "No one to bring up there," I answered.

He smiled. "Book, there are plenty of women around to bring up there."

"Not the one I want."

He laughed. "Aw, man, you've got it bad."

I did. "Whatever. I'm just waiting to see if she shows, okay?"

"You mean her?"

I looked to where he pointed near the window that led to the pool. We were about fifteen meters from each other and people were all around. The moment my gaze fell on her, my dick twitched. She was laughing with Ava. They were alone.

They were alone ...

Did Ava decide to continue the divorce proceeding? Did Peyton come for me or as Ava's guest so she could meet someone else? I thought once I saw Peyton, I'd know what the fuck was going on. Now I still didn't have a bloody clue.

Without saying a word, I took two steps toward them and stopped. Jason Motherfucking Black walked up and handed Peyton a drink. I watched as her face brightened and she smiled up at him. It caused my chest to ache—literally. I grabbed it and started to massage my pec as if to soothe the hurt.

"You better get over there fast. I've heard that Jason puts shit in women's drinks," Randy said next to me.

"What?" I asked, turning my head to look at him. That was against everything Sensation was about, and he could get kicked out for doing it.

"He told Cole that was how he got them to loosen up so he could DP them."

"What?"

"Double penetrate—"

"I know what it means, but why the fuck would he do that?"

"Some men are sick."

I watched as Peyton looked down at the glass and then raised it to toast Jason. I broke out into a sprint, and just as the glass touched her lips, I pulled it away. The crowd around us fell silent, and I glared at Jason.

"What the fuck, dude?" he asked.

I took the glass of red liquid and shoved it in his face. "How about you take a sip?"

He tsked. "I got the drink for Peyton."

"What are you doing, Booker?" Peyton asked at my side. "Give me my drink back."

"No," I clipped. "I want Jason here to take a sip first."

"Dude." He furrowed his eyebrows. "Give the lady back her drink."

I got within an inch of his face. "Not until you take a sip."

Peyton tugged at my arm. "Booker. Please."

"Gorgeous," I hissed. I didn't have more to say as I stared Jason in the eyes.

He stepped back and turned his gaze to her. "I'll get you another one."

"The hell you will." I grabbed his white tuxedo shirt with my free hand.

"Why are you acting like this?" Peyton asked.

"You should ask this wanker."

He stared me down, not talking. I glared more, silently urging him to tell the truth. "You gonna fight me one handed?" Jason dared.

I chuckled. "You want me to?"

"No one is fighting. Booker, let him go. You're causing a scene." Peyton tugged at the arm that still held the glass.

"It's better I cause a scene than you not remember this night."

Her tug stilled. "What?"

I stepped closer to Jason, my chest connecting with his and hissed, "That's right, motherfucker. I know what you do, and you're not doing it to my girl."

He laughed and wiggled out of my grasp. "Your girl? We were just getting acquainted. Looks like she didn't choose you."

My fist clenched hard around his shirt. "You think I'm going to let her anywhere near you from now on? I know, mate. I know!" I shoved the glass in front of his face.

"I don't have to deal with this shit. She's all yours."

Yeah, she is.

He tried to break free from my grasp, and I let him go. I walked to the door, tossed the liquid out, and then set the empty glass on a black tray. All eyes were on me, including Randy's who had walked up at some point.

"He was going to drug me?" Peyton whispered when I was near her again.

I sighed. "Yeah, gorgeous. That's his MO."

She sat in the empty chair, and I knelt down in front of her. "It's okay."

"It's not okay," she stated. "I never thought that could happen at a private club."

"Neither did I, but apparently he's into kinky shit and he slips something in drinks so the women do what he wants."

Ava walked over and patted my shoulder. "Thanks, Book. I'm going to go find Trent."

My head snapped up to her. "You are?"

She smiled. "Yeah. I told him once you found Peyton that I would find him so we could talk."

That meant they were probably going to get back together, and to them it wouldn't matter if I was with Peyton. "I like the sound of that." I smiled.

She smiled back before she walked away. My gaze fell on Randy, and he nodded and left too.

"So you weren't looking very hard for me," I said, looking into Peyton's chocolate colored eyes.

"We found you five minutes ago, but you were engrossed in the— show." She waved her hand in the direction of the sofa where the threesome was still going strong.

When I looked back, I reached up and ran my thumb along her bottom lip. "I was thinking about you."

She smiled. "Do you want to talk now?"

I laughed. "Well, I'd rather do other stuff."

She rolled her eyes. *How many times was that? Her arse was mine.* "I only came because Ava said she didn't know you were married. If she didn't know, then that meant there might be a good reason."

Great, now Ava knew I was married.

"You told her about us?"

She shook her head slightly. "I didn't go into detail, and I waited until she made her decision about what to do with Trent. Looks like we won't be representing them, so I asked her if she knew your wife. She didn't. So I took a chance and asked her if I could come as her guest again because I needed to talk to you."

Well, Ava did know my wife, but I wasn't going to correct Peyton. "Okay, let's go up to my room and talk." I stood and reached out my hand.

She furrowed her brows. "Your room?"

"The one we were in last time," I clarified.

She stood. "What do you mean by your room, though?"

"All Diamond members have a room."

She blinked. "You spend twenty-thousand a month on a sex club?"

I grabbed her hand, needing to feel her soft skin on mine. "No, gorgeous. When I became a Diamond member, it was half that."

"Ten thousand," she whispered. "For one night a month."

I leaned in and whispered in her ear, "I actually make money by coming here. A lot of my clients are members."

"And your ... um, wife?"

I shrugged. "She has money." When Carrie's father passed, she was left with a handsome Life Insurance policy because her parents were divorced and she was the sole beneficiary.

"But—"

"Let's go upstairs where it's quiet so I can explain."

I saw her throat work as she swallowed then whispered, "Okay."

Chapter 11

BOOKER

We walked up the familiar stairs that lead to my room at Sensation. I'd used them many times, but this time was different. We were going to *talk*. Who talked at a sex club? I didn't care. Peyton needed to know the truth, and I was going to tell her whatever she wanted to know. I trusted her.

As we walked up the stairs, and I stared at her arse, I finally noticed what she was wearing. Before I hadn't noticed anything except the glass of alcohol that was threatening to fuck up my girl. But now, as I watched her arse in her tight turquoise dress, my dick stirred. And it didn't stir only because of her arse. No. The back of the dress was open and dropped down just before it showed the top of her perfect globes. *Fuck, she was going to kill me.*

Just as we passed a few doors, Peyton stopped. "Why did you check all the doors to see if they were open the other night if you have your own room?"

I looked up at the cream ceiling and ran my free hand down my face. "I never expected there to be more than one night between us. I didn't want you to know, so I just pretended I didn't know where to take you."

A month ago when I was leading her up to my room, I thought it would just be sex. I didn't care if she knew I liked to tie women up. What went on behind the doors of Sensation, stayed here. Of course, the more I thought about it, if things didn't progress tonight, it might be a little awkward in court. I'd cross that bridge when I got to it.

"Seems there's a lot you don't want to tell me."

I yanked on her hand and brought her flush with my body. "Was, gorgeous. *Was* a lot I didn't want to tell you."

She looked into my eyes. "You're going to tell me everything?"

"I'll tell you anything you want to know," I responded, staring at her pink lips.

Lips I wanted to taste again.

Lips I dreamt about.

Lips that I wanted around my dick.

I resisted and turned to walk to my room, her hand in mine still. I let Peyton enter before me.

"Did you decorate this room?" she asked, looking around as though she'd never been in it.

I chuckled. "No. It's more that I just rent it for the night."

"This is one expensive pay by the hour room." She laughed.

"It's worth every penny so I can ..."

"So you can what?" she prompted.

I rubbed a hand across my neck. "Nothing."

"Booker. Tell me."

"So I can be with you again."

She didn't say anything as she slowly blinked.

"See? Stupid," I conceded.

"I just don't understand."

"Come sit on the bed, and I'll tell you whatever you want to know." I walked the couple of feet to the foot of the King size bed, then sat and waited for her to follow. She bit her lip as she hesitated and then moved to sit next to me. She turned in to face me and our knees pressed together.

"Where do you want to start?" I asked.

"I guess we should start with the big question."

"Which is?" I knew what she was referring to, but before I opened my mouth, I wanted to make sure.

"How do you justify having a wife and thinking I'd be okay with it?"

"Well, I don't think you'd be okay with it, per se."

"I'm not." She shook her head.

"Do you promise to keep whatever I tell you between us?" I reached out and linked her hand in mine.

"Who would I tell? I'm not planning on ruining my career."

"That's not entirely what I mean."

"What do you mean then?"

I was just going to lay it all out there. A take it or leave it situation. "Carrie and I are married, but it's not your traditional marriage."

She tilted her head slightly as if to process what I was saying. "Meaning you're swingers, and therefore it's okay for you to have sex here?"

I laughed. "Kinda."

"Kinda?"

I took a deep breath. "I came to the States on a school VISA." She scrunched her eyebrows. "After college, I was to return to Leeds, but I didn't want to go back, and Carrie didn't want me to go back, so we came up with a plan."

"To get married?" Peyton asked.

I nodded. "Yeah, we got married a week later at the Courthouse, and I eventually got a Green Card."

She went silent, staring at me with her beautiful mocha eyes. "So you're only married so you can stay in the U.S.?"

I nodded.

"Okay. I get why you would do that, but why would Carrie?"

I grinned. "Because she's my best mate and we both like pussy."

Peyton's eyes widened. "She's a lesbian?"

I nodded again.

"But women can get married to each other," she countered.

"Now they can, but not nine years ago."

"You've been married for nine years?" she exclaimed.

"Fuck, I guess so." I chuckled.

"But four or so years ago same-sex marriages became legal in California."

"Yeah ..."

"And you're still married."

"You want me to be deported?" I joked. That wouldn't be the case. I would apply to become a citizen before I'd let that happen.

Peyton laughed. "No, but you're telling me that Carrie hasn't found someone else to be with?"

I shrugged. "She's had relationships, but most don't live the same lifestyle."

"You mean wanting to go to a sex club?"

I nodded. "Yeah, or they can't afford to become members like her."

"Right ..."

"I mean, she's brought women here before, but she usually just likes to have fun."

"Or she doesn't want to start a serious relationship because of you."

"What?" I asked and blinked. Was that true? I'd always assumed Carrie was happy playing the field.

Peyton shrugged. "I'm not sure what I would do in her position, but I have to imagine it's hard to get serious with someone if you don't have an endgame because you aren't able to pursue one. Especially since your marriage is a secret."

Had I been cheating Carrie out of happiness? Was I a selfish douchebag?

"She's never said anything to make me think otherwise."

"Maybe because she can't?"

"I'll talk to her. Worst case, I try to become a citizen. I've had my Green Card long enough."

"Okay, so your marriage is a sham. What else?"

What else?

I wanted to kiss her—*badly*—that was what else. So I did. I leaned forward, my lips falling upon hers. She didn't pull away, so I slipped my tongue out, seeking approval. She opened, and I finally got my taste of her. It was a mixture of mint and champagne, and it tasted divine. I cupped her cheek and threaded my hand in her loose curls. My hand brushed against the tie of her halter-top dress.

Fuck, I ached for her.

"That's what else. Every fucking time I've seen you since last month, I wanted to feel your lips against mine again, gorgeous," I said when I needed to breathe.

"I've wanted you to," she replied as she slowly opened her eyes.

"You always gave me a hard time," I reminded her.

"I had to." She chuckled. "I was hurt."

I palmed each cheek and looked directly into her soul. "I would never do it on purpose. I'm truly sorry for Carrie opening her mouth."

Peyton looked down at our laps, not saying anything.

"Can we forget that part of the night happened and see where this will go?"

She looked back up, my hands still cupping her cheeks. "Where this will go?"

I smiled. "Now that you know my secret, we can have one together." I kissed her lips softly and then dropped my hands only to grab hers again.

"Booker. It's bad enough we have a thing here. Are you talking about outside of the confidential walls of Sensation?"

"No one has to know. If I can be married and no one knows, I'm sure I can keep our relationship a secret."

"I don't know ..." Peyton trailed off.

"I want you, Peyton. I want you badly. Our jobs shouldn't prevent us from pursuing this."

"We both went through a lot of schooling and a vigorous bar exam to become attorneys. Are you sure you want to risk it?"

"For you? Yeah, I do."

"If you really want a relationship with me, why not withdraw from the cases we have against each other and do things the right way?"

I took a deep breath. "I would. I would do it in a heartbeat, but

I'm on track to make partner, and I need those cases. Do you want to withdraw?"

She thought for a moment. "I need those cases too."

"Let's just see where this goes for a few months until I make partner. Then I'll withdraw."

"Okay," she agreed. "But what do we do if one of us is retained by a client and the other person is opposing counsel already?"

"We don't take the case. It's a conflict of interest."

"And you'd do that even if it meant not making partner?"

That was a valid question. What if Peyton and I didn't work out? Would I risk making partner to be with her? "Can we just cross that bridge when we get to it then? I have three months to make partner."

"Yeah. That's awesome you might make partner."

I gave my cocky smile. "I will make partner."

She laughed. "Same old Booker."

"Admit it. You'll miss going against me in court."

Peyton snorted. "I'll miss kicking your ass."

"Now you can do other things to it."

We stared at each other for a few beats and then both of us were laughing. Finally, I asked, "Is there anything else you want to discuss?"

"There's one more thing I can think of." I watched as she slid off the bed and knelt at my feet. Her dress rose up her thighs, and I took a deep breath. All laughter had died, and I was instantly hard at the sight of her on her knees. "I've never had a man protect me like you did downstairs."

I looked down into her brown eyes as she looked up at me, her hand on the button of my trousers. "I want to kill that wanker," I confessed.

"I can't let you do that." She smirked. "Then I wouldn't get to thank you."

"Thank me how?"

Without a word, Peyton unbuttoned my black tuxedo trousers and then slowly unzipped them. I leaned back on my hands and watched her wicked grin go wider as she reached in and grabbed my dick. The moment her warm hand engulfed my length, I groaned. I'd been missing this woman for a month, and finally, her hand was working my cock.

"I like your thinking," I said.

"Oh yeah?" she asked before her head descended onto my shaft. Her warm mouth wrapped around my dick, and the heat caused shivers to race up my spine. I'd had plenty of blowjobs in my day, but Peyton doing the sucking only made it that much more enjoyable. I couldn't take my eyes off her as she continued to lick, suck and twist her hand around my dick in sync with her mouth.

"Gorgeous," I warned. "I'm going to come, and I'd rather do it with your pussy wrapped around my dick."

She lifted her head, and her eyes met mine. A popping sound filled the space when her mouth came off my cock. "We have all night, right?"

"We have more than tonight," I clarified.

"Then let me do this. I've been thinking about it for a long time."

I smirked. "You have?"

"Yeah, but only because I know you'll return the favor." She grinned.

"I'm going to do more than eat your pussy, baby."

"Good." Peyton returned her mouth to my cock.

Twisting her lips over the head, she sucked, then ran her tongue down the underside of my sensitive, yet overly throbbing shaft. My hands curled into the bedspread, and I bit my lip to try to stifle my groan. She returned to stroking and sucking me.

"Peyton, slow down. I'm not going to last much longer."

But my woman ignored me. Instead, she sucked harder, consuming my cock from tip to base. I jerked with another groan, cum shooting down her slender throat.

"Oh my God, Peyton."

After I had released every seed, another pop of her mouth caused my cock to bob. It was still hard. "Now, it's my turn." I grinned.

I hoisted her up from the floor, lay her on top of me, and ran my hands up her bare thighs. When I got to her round arse, my hands slid across smooth skin.

"No knickers tonight?"

Peyton giggled against the crook of my neck. "Not when you have a habit of stealing them."

I smiled. "It was one time. How is that a habit?"

"Just a hunch. Plus, I heard panties aren't required."

"No, gorgeous, they aren't. They just get in the way." She came to Sensation without any knickers on. Did that mean she knew what was going to happen between us? Even if my marriage wasn't a sham?

"I have one more question for you."

"Only one?" I smirked.

"For now."

"What's that?" I asked as my hands continued to rub circles on her arse.

She rose a little so that our eyes met. "If you're the only one who uses this room, why do you have a giant bowl of condoms on the table by the fireplace?"

I jerked my head back in shock at her question. Not because I didn't want to answer it. It was because I wasn't expecting *that* to be her question. I chuckled as I answered, "Because we're in a sex club."

"Yes, but if you're the only one who uses this room, then why do you have more than a few? It's not like you have days to use them."

"I don't only use them in this room. Plus, I think they thought it would look better than having a box of condoms on the table when they decorated the room." I shrugged.

That caused her to laugh. "Condoms as decorations? That's funny."

I smiled back. "I really don't have another answer for you."

"But you don't use all of them do you?"

"I think my dick would fall off from over-usage if I did."

"Oh." She chuckled.

"Speaking of, it's time to use one."

"Mr. Romantic," Peyton teased.

I quickly rose and rolled her to her back. She squealed, but once I was on top of her, I silenced her with my mouth again. Her leg hooked around my hip, and I ground into her as I ran my hand up her smooth leg. We fit together perfectly.

Peyton moaned into my mouth as my hand continued up her thigh, seeking for that one spot that I knew was throbbing for her. I rolled to the side, only covering half her body with mine, and continued my journey to find her soft, wet, swollen pussy. My cock was still hard as a fucking rock, and I ached to be buried deep inside of her again. My fingers found my treasure, and I smiled against her mouth.

Running two fingers up her slit, her arousal coated them, and her chest heaved as she took my mouth more aggressively. She seemed to be as hungry for me as I was for her, and I returned her kisses and slipped my fingers into her pussy at the same time. She moaned again in my mouth as my fingers worked inside of her. Her fingertips ran up and down my back causing a shiver to shoot straight to my dick, making it throb with need. It didn't matter that only ten minutes ago I'd shot a load in her mouth. I was ready again.

I slipped my fingers out of her and Peyton broke our kiss. Before she could utter a word, my hand continued down, gliding across her perineum, and she sucked in a breath.

"Shh," I whispered and then attached my mouth to her neck, licking her skin to taste her, needing my entire body on her. Her arms tightened around me as I sought out the specific spot that puckered.

"Ah fuck," she hissed.

My finger rimmed the hole, and I whispered against her neck, "You like that?"

I wet my finger again with her arousal and slid my hand back the short distance, adding pressure as she moaned, "I ... I don't know."

Everything stilled, and I rose my head to look into her eyes. "You've never done this before?"

She shook her head. "No."

I smiled. "I've wanted to take your arse since I first saw it."

She stared into my blues, and I wet my finger again before rimming the sweet puckered flesh. My finger slipped in the tiniest bit, seeking approval. She sucked in a breath and then whispered, "Okay."

I felt the small opening relax, allowing my finger to slip in just a little more. Her hands left me and fisted the bedsheets as she leaned her head back exposing her throat. I latched on, sucking again as my finger pushed in, retreated and then pushed in some more.

"Oh, god," she groaned.

"Does it feel good?"

"Yes," she breathed. "Don't stop."

She was so tight as I worked my finger in more. "Hold on," I stated and rose.

"Wait," Peyton protested.

"One sec." I opened the top drawer of the nightstand and grabbed the bottle of lube.

"Oh," she said, looking over at me.

I didn't say anything as I lay beside her again and coated my finger with the lube. She spread her legs, tilted her hips up, and I returned my hand to her puckered rim.

"Give me your mouth again, beautiful," I said and kissed her again. I wanted her to focus on my tongue as I slipped my finger in inch by inch. She moaned into my mouth as my finger worked its way to stretch her. Once it was fully in, I added another one slowly.

"Does it feel good?" I asked, breaking our lips apart.

She hesitated before answering, "Yes. I want more."

I grinned down at her. "You don't need to ask me twice."

I rose and quickly discarded my clothes while Peyton tossed her dress onto the floor. After I grabbed a condom and made sure the lube was within reach, I sat on the end of the bed, my knees bent and my legs on the floor. I sheathed myself, put a load of lube on my dick and then I motioned for her to straddle my hips.

She blinked.

"You'll be in control," I clarified. Since it was her first time, I wanted Peyton to go as slow or as fast as she wanted to.

A small smile graced her lips, and she did as I wanted. We were face to face, only an inch apart. As she lowered onto my cock, our eyes stayed locked on each other. I spread her arse as wide as it would go while she held my shaft steady. Peyton's breathing became labored as she got lower, so to build her arousal, I reached between us and circled her clit with my thumb. She moaned and slipped down another inch. *Fuck, she was tight.* As my dick penetrated her, I groaned because it felt phenomenal. The thought of going where no man had gone before was causing my balls to tighten, and I was on the verge of coming before she was seated.

"Are you okay?" I asked, needing to focus on her words instead of the way she was making me feel.

"It's tight, and not really the best feeling."

"Keep going," I urged. "Once I'm in all the way, you'll understand."

She nodded and rose slightly and then lowered again. Our eyes stayed locked on each other, and never before had I felt so consumed by a woman than with Peyton at this moment. She rose again, and this time I added more lube before she lowered. It made it so she fully engulfed me.

"Are you okay?" I asked again.

"Yes," she breathed, and started to glide up and down.

I returned my thumb to her clit, circling it as her moans filled the room. "That's it, baby."

"It feels—good," she panted.

I groaned in response, and as she rode my cock with her tight, wet, hole, our breathing built. We both got closer and closer to falling over the edge, and before I knew it, my hips were thrusting up, meeting her movements. My hand left her clit, and I reached around, grabbed her arse in each hand and spread her once more. Fuck she was beautiful. Her skin was flush, and her face wore a look of pure ecstasy. She looked absolutely beautiful, especially while on my cock.

Peyton threw her head back as I used my arms to slide her up and down. My mouth connected with her exposed throat and I sucked.

"I'm gonna come," she gasped.

"Yes, baby," I groaned, pumping harder.

And then she did. Her anus tightened around my cock, and I jerked as she milked me. As she moaned her release, she rested her head on my shoulder while I thrust into her. The sound of her coming around my dick was enough for me to follow her and I groaned my release.

She didn't move. I didn't move. After a few minutes, our breathing returned to normal and she rolled off of me.

"So, what did you think?"

"Could you not tell?" She smiled.

I grinned. "I could tell, just making sure."

A blush crept up her neck, and I leaned over and placed my lips on hers. "Come on, let's get cleaned up." I reached for her hand, and we stood from the bed. Then I dragged her into the bathroom and into the shower where we cleaned up in between making out.

"What do your tattoos mean?" she asked, running her finger over my left pec.

I looked down at my wet chest. "The Chinese script is my daughter's name."

"What?" she shrieked.

"Kidding." I grinned. "It's my grandma's name. I was really close to her when I was growing up, and she passed away five years ago."

"Oh, I'm sorry."

"Thanks. I got the roses because they were her favorite flower, and her name is around clouds since she's up in heaven."

"That's really sweet."

"Sweet like you." I kissed her lips, and then did other things with her under the warm water. I didn't want to talk about my grandma when I had the most beautiful girl naked in front of me.

Chapter 12

PEYTON

wo months ago if you had asked me who I thought I'd be dating, I wouldn't have said Booker Jameson. *Not in a million years.* He was cocky, arrogant, self-centered and smug whenever I saw him. In fact, I hated seeing him weekly, or sometimes daily, in court. Even when it wasn't against me, I still would see him because the courthouse was our home away from home.

Even a month ago I didn't think I would be dating Booker. Sure he was pursuing me, but I never thought I would give him another chance or that it would go beyond Sensation. I honestly didn't think he wanted to do anything but fuck me at the club.

Apparently, I was wrong about him. He was more than the cocky attorney who drove me up the wall. He was potentially willing to risk his career for me.

But secrets always come out.

Was I really willing to risk my career for him?

Sure we had a plan, but what if? What if something happened and the wrong person found out about us before he made partner? Most attorneys couldn't care less who was dating whom, but there are assholes in our field, and it would only take one to report us.

"I'll call you tomorrow," Booker had said when he dropped me off the night before. Was tomorrow really today since it was Sunday, or did he mean Monday? I was too infatuated to get a clarification, and now I was like a lovesick teenager waiting by the phone.

A knock came to my door, and my heart fluttered. *Lawd. Spend a night with a hot guy and I act like a crazy person.* I walked to the door, peeked through the peephole, and sighed. Not him.

"Can I help you?" I asked as I opened the door.

Lorelei pushed passed me. "Yeah, I want all the details. Don't leave anything out."

I threw my head back and rolled my eyes. I knew she was coming over. Just like she had the month prior, she was at my door for lunch and an interrogation. Though last time I wasn't in such a great mood.

"Only if you brought me honey walnut shrimp," I answered and closed the door.

"I've been your assistant *forever*. I think I know what you like to eat."

I smiled as I walked toward the couch she was now sitting on, and watched as she pulled out Chinese takeout boxes. "And potstickers?"

"Yes. Now start talking while I dish you up." She stood and moved to my kitchen. I watched as she went straight to the cabinet with my plates. It was safe to say she'd been over a few times in the last five or so years.

"Remember if you say a peep of what I have to tell you, I'll tell Kenny you're in love with him."

She stopped walking and then rolled her eyes. Kenny was a law clerk at our firm, and *he* was in love with her. He wasn't her type at all. She went for the hunky type, and Kenny was ... well, not.

"You wouldn't."

"I would." I grinned.

She started to walk back to the couch again. "Whatever. You know I won't say anything. So is he really married?"

We didn't need to say *his* name. We both knew why I went to Sensation again.

I nodded. "Yeah, he is. For nine years now."

Lorelei stopped scooping out shrimp and looked up at me. "*Nine years?*" she exclaimed.

I nodded again. "Yep."

"Nine years," she said again as though she couldn't believe it. "So they go to Sensation to swing like we suspected?"

I chuckled and took my plate from her. I scooted back on my teal couch and sat cross-legged. "Kinda."

"Kinda? What does that mean?"

"Pinky swear," I said and stuck out my hand with my pinky finger extended. I didn't care that we were grown ass women. Everyone knew a pinky swear was like sealing your lips and you were to *never* tell anyone. In fact, according to Japan where the gesture was created, if the person told the secret then they would have to cut off their pinky. It was *that* important.

She reached out her hand, and we entwined our pinkies. The promise was made.

"He's married to his best friend, who's a lesbian, so he can stay in the U.S. and not have to go back to England."

She balked. "What? Are you serious?"

I nodded. "Dead serious."

"So his marriage is fake?"

"Pretty much."

"That's some crazy shit."

"I know, right?" I agreed.

"Why did he have to wait until the club to tell you? He could have told you any of the times you two were locked in your office."

I chuckled. "First of all, we weren't locked in my office."

"Uh-huh," she muttered.

"We weren't," I confirmed. "And second of all, I told you that Sensation is a confidential place. What goes on there, stays there, so he wanted to tell me there so I wouldn't tell anyone. You don't count, *obviously*." I smiled.

We both stuck bites of food in our mouths before Lore continued to question me. "So, did you two screw again?" She was never one to sugarcoat things. I turned my head to look out my window that led to the street.

"So that's a yes."

I looked back to her. "Of course we did."

A smile spread across her face. "I want details."

I shook my head. "You're not getting details."

"Aw, come on."

"Nope." I shook my head again.

"I'm going to get you drunk one Friday night so you'll tell me everything."

I rolled my eyes and shoved a forkful of fried rice in my mouth.

"So what else happened? Were you the one to approach him or did he seek you out again?"

"I found him. He was watching a threesome, and as I was waiting for him to finally notice me, Jason Black walked up and handed me a drink."

"Seriously? Damn, I need to get invited to this club."

"Not to meet him. He tried to roofie me."

Her eyes widened. "What?"

"Apparently he does that so he can take advantage of women."

"But he's a celebrity. He can have any woman he wants."

"I know. I don't fully understand why, but Booker said that's how he gets women to let him and another dude DP her."

Lorelei's mouth dropped open. "But he's at a sex club. I would think that would be something he could find women to do no problem."

I shrugged. "Maybe he drugs the ones he really wants knowing they wouldn't be okay with it?"

"You're blowing my mind right now. And my hard on for Jason Black."

I laughed. "I know. Try living it."

"So you said he tried to roofie you. He didn't?"

I smiled and shook my head. "Booker apparently knew, and he saw him give me a drink. He ripped it out of my hand and got in Jason's face."

"Your own knight in shining armor."

"Yeah, but not Mr. Romantic." I laughed. "He just flat out told me we were going to have sex this time. There was no trying to work me up or anything."

"Really?"

"Well, it was after I gave him a BJ." I smirked. "And he realized I wasn't wearing panties."

"Ahh," she groaned. "Get me on the list. I want to go so bad."

"I'd have to join for me to invite you."

"Well, join. It's not like you don't want to go back."

"You want me to spend thousands of dollars so you can go to a sex club with me?"

"Yes," she deadpanned.

I laughed. "You know I can go as Booker's guest, right?"

"Wait. What?"

"Yeah, so we're kinda together now."

"What?" She stood, her plate almost spilling onto the floor.

I shrugged. It was all I had because I knew she was mad I didn't lead with that information. It *was* a big fucking deal.

"You're seriously blowing my mind now." Lorelei sat back down next to me and hooked a leg under the other as she faced me.

"I'm scared, though," I admitted.

"About what?"

"It's unethical."

Lorelei sighed. "Yeah, it is. But you two are adults. Just keep it on the down low until you see if it's going to get serious."

"That's pretty much what we said we were going to do."

"Wow," she breathed. "I never thought you'd be dating Booker Jameson."

"I know." I laughed. I knew what she meant. It was crazy.

"Well, you know I won't say anything. I'm happy for you."

We smiled at each other. "Thanks."

"But seriously. Is he a beast in bed or what?"

I laughed—hard. There was no way I was going to tell her about my sexcapades. Therefore, I changed the subject to her love life. She didn't mind sharing details.

Booker didn't call Sunday. I figured by tomorrow he really meant Monday and not a few hours away. It was okay with me, but I had a hard time sleeping. I kept thinking about him and our night at Sensation. I'd been starving before we were together, and now I was dying of thirst without him.

I made it to the office after a quick appearance in court. It was a status conference, and since the case was going smoothly, a settlement conference was set because we felt we could reach an agreement. To my displeasure, I didn't see Booker. I really just wanted to see him again. Have him kiss me like he needed *me* to breathe.

After saying hello to Maria as I entered the doors of Chandler and Patterson, I made my way down the hall to my office. The moment my gaze connected with Lorelei's, she grinned.

"What's that look for?"

She shrugged. "No reason."

"Why don't I believe you?"

She shrugged again, not responding.

"Any messages?" I prompted.

Lorelei handed me a few message slips, still not saying anything.

"Thanks," I responded and started to walk into my office only to stop dead in my tracks when I noticed the bouquet of red roses sitting on my desk. I turned my head to Lorelei, and she grinned. I grabbed the tiny card that was sticking in between a few stems.

Gorgeous,
For every hour I've been missing you.
Mr. Romantic

I laughed slightly at the note. Guess I couldn't refer to him as not being romantic any longer. Lorelei was staring at me as I looked over to her desk. She smiled, and I realized I was too. I set the roses on the credenza behind my desk and thumbed through the messages I'd set down when I read the note. Booker had called.

Once I sat in my chair and took a deep breath, I dialed his number. When a receptionist answered, I realized it was his office number.

"Booker Jameson, please."

"May I ask who's calling?"

"Peyton Winters."

"Which case is this in regards to?"

Ahh. "Um, Ashley versus Inglewood," I lied.

"Please hold."

I took another breath as I leaned back in my chair and waited for Booker to get on the line. I swear I could feel Lorelei's eyes on me, and I knew at lunch I'd be grilled once again. Maybe I *should* find a way for her to come to Sensation. That way she could have her own stories and not want to know mine.

"Miss me?"

A shiver washed over me as I heard his accent through the phone. God, it was sexy and so was he. Especially with his muscular body and tattoos that not everyone got to see. "Yes," I admitted. "Thank you for the roses."

"You're welcome, gorgeous."

"People are going to ask about them." I bit my lip and looked to Lorelei to in fact see her still staring at me. I shooed her away and glared.

"Let them ask. I didn't put my name on them."

I smiled. "I know, Mr. Romantic. But I haven't gotten flowers delivered—well, ever."

"Now you have. And every time you look at them, you'll think of me."

"Don't need the flowers for that."

"When can I see you again?"

My stomach fluttered at the thought. "I ... I don't know." It wasn't like we could go on dates.

"I'll come to your place tonight."

"But what if someone sees you?"

"Who will see me?"

I shrugged. "I don't know. I'm just worried."

"I'll dress in black and climb through your window," he joked.

I chuckled. "That's not creepy at all."

"It will be fine. I want to see you again. I'll even bring dinner."

"I'll cook you dinner," I offered.

"The only woman who has ever cooked for me was my mum."

"Not even Carrie?" I frowned as I brought her up. It was still weird to me even if it was a sham.

Booker laughed. "Carrie burns toast."

"Then I'll fix dinner."

"It's a date, gorgeous."

My grin widened as my heart warmed. "Okay."

"Have you heard from Ava?"

"Oh," I blinked at the sudden change in subject. "She might have emailed me, but I haven't had time to check them. Some guy sent me roses, and I haven't had a chance to turn on my computer." I didn't even have time to check my emails on my phone. I went to court, was the first case to be called, and then I left.

"Do I need to kick this guy's arse?" Booker teased.

"Maybe. He *is* pretty cocky."

He groaned. "Don't make me hard."

My eyes widened, and I smiled, my cheeks turning a shade of pink as well. "Booker," I scolded.

"All right, fine. I'm already hard."

"Oh my God." I laughed. "Let me check my emails. I'll see you tonight."

"I need your apartment number."

"Oh right." I gave it to him.

"And your mobile number."

Well, that explains why he didn't call me on Sunday. I gave it to him.

"See you at seven, gorgeous."

Chapter 13

BOOKER

Monday morning my alarm blared, waking me from my dream of Peyton. Every morning I woke up to go to the gym, and every morning I was happy to do so, but this morning, I wanted to slip back into dreamland. Instead, I crawled out of bed, got dressed, and made my way to the kitchen.

As I made my protein shake, I couldn't stop thinking about Peyton. After five plus years of watching her arse in court and having cases against her, I was finally, *finally* going to get to spend time with her outside of the courthouse to get to know her. And it wasn't only going to be at Sensation.

From day one I had been smitten with her. There was just something about a strong woman that turned me on. It also helped that she was fit as fuck. I knew I wanted to continue to pursue things, and I'd pretty much begged on my knees for her to give me another chance.

Now I just needed to make sure I didn't fuck it up.

"When do I get to meet her?"

I jumped at the sound of Carrie's voice from behind me, the protein scoop falling from my hand. "Jesus, woman. Don't do that to me."

"Did you forget I live here too?" she asked as she reached for a coffee mug.

"No, but fuck. You're like a ninja and shit."

She laughed. "I think your mind is just elsewhere, or should I say on *someone* else?"

"Should I say someone else?" I mocked. "Yes, *love*."

She stopped pouring her coffee and glared at me. "Okay, someone is in a bad mood this morning."

I shook my head. "It's not that. I'm just worried about the whole secret relationship thing."

"Relationship?" Her eyes narrowed. "You're dating her?"

"Yes."

"Why are you worried?" She took a sip of her coffee, and I started to shake the brown powder with water in my tumbler.

"I'm not worried about dating her. I want to take her out, go to the beach, stuff like that, but we both agreed that it needs to be a secret so no one finds out until after I make partner."

"I'm sure you'll figure it out."

"Yeah," I agreed though I wasn't entirely certain I would. Los Angeles was a big city, but at the same time, it was small as hell.

Carrie reached up on her toes and kissed my cheek before leaving the kitchen. "But I do want to formally meet her."

"You will, sweetheart."

"Soon?"

"Soon," I agreed.

After my workout, I still had Peyton on my mind. I wanted to see her again, and soon. As I sat in my car before going up to my office, I called a local flower shop to deliver three dozen red roses to her.

Not romantic? We'll see about that!

Randy knocked and then stuck his head in my office door. "Ready?"

"Yeah."

It was time for our monthly staff meeting, and I'd just gotten off the phone with Peyton. She'd got my flowers and was going to cook me dinner. I hadn't had a woman cook for me since I was a young lad jerking it in the shower every night—sometimes twice a day.

Just like every meeting I'd attended, I sat next to Randy at the giant conference table. People piled in and then it commenced. It was boring but necessary.

"Before we conclude the meeting, I just wanted to update everyone on the race to partner," Mitch stated at the end of the meeting.

My eyes shot up to him.

"Sure," Clint responded, and I nodded in agreement.

"As you know, we only have two more months until the decision is made, and you two are still neck and neck."

Clint grinned at me, and I rolled my eyes.

Fucker.

"Keep up the good work, fellas."

"Thanks," I replied, and everyone stood.

I needed to step up my game.

You'd think I wouldn't be nervous going over to my *girlfriend's* apartment, but I was nervous as fuck. I hadn't had a serious girlfriend in—well, ever. I was playing the field and focused on school and then my career before I wanted to settle down. I wasn't scared because I was going to see Peyton. I was looking forward to it. She was like the color of my world. What was bothering me was the fact that I was starting a relationship when I needed to spend every waking hour at work. I wanted to see her every night. Fuck, I wanted to. But I also wanted to make partner, and that fucker Clint was still on my arse.

I rode up the lift to Peyton's floor. Tonight I wouldn't think about work. I truly missed Peyton, and it had only been a day. Tomorrow I would figure out a plan, but tonight I needed my fix.

After I'd stepped off the car, I walked down the hall toward her apartment number. Just as I was lifting my hand to knock on her door, the one next to hers opened. The sound caused my hand to still mid-air, and out of instinct, I looked and saw some wanker stepped out. When he turned to lock his door, he saw me. It was a few seconds, but we made eye contact. This was Peyton's neighbor, and I needed to be polite, so being the gentleman that I was, I gave him a head lift.

"You're ... You're going to Peyton's?"

I furrowed my eyebrows, my hand still raised to knock. "Yeah, mate," I replied. So much for hiding our relationship.

He puffed up his chest causing me to do the same as my hand came down. *What the fuck?*

"Just a word of advice, bro. The walls are super thin." He gave a chin lift and left.

Did that mean he's heard Peyton fucking before? I finally knocked, and the door swung open. "Hey, gorgeous." I stepped forward and wrapped her in my arms.

Peyton's arms went around my waist, and she murmured against my chest, "Hey."

I sniffed the air. "Something smells good."

We broke apart. "I didn't know—"

She didn't finish her sentence as my lips came crashing down on hers. An hour was too long to go without kissing her, and it had been about forty of them. Her mouth opened for me, and I got a taste of wine as my tongue met hers. She tasted fucking good.

"And you taste good," I said when we pulled apart.

She blushed then closed and locked the door behind us.

"Don't want me to escape?" I teased.

Peyton laughed. "No, it's just a habit."

"A good one to have."

"I hope you like chicken piccata." She smiled.

"Yeah, gorgeous. I like most everything."

"Good. Would you like a glass of wine?"

"Sure," I replied, following her to her kitchen. I would tell you that I took a look at her apartment, but I wasn't looking anywhere but her arse as it swished in her tight jeans. I'd never seen her in jeans before. It made me want to grab a fist full of her arse and squeeze.

"Do you need any help?" I offered.

"Nope," she replied as she poured a glass of white wine. "Just sit here, and it will be ready in about ten minutes." Peyton motioned for me to sit at her breakfast bar. She slid the glass in front of me and turned to a skillet on the stove. "Oh, I heard from Ava before I left the office."

I smiled. "Are we going to only talk about work?"

She chuckled. "No, but you asked if I had when we spoke earlier, so I'm telling you what she said so I can save time and not have to call you tomorrow."

"I *want* you to call me."

"People will get suspicious, don't you think?"

"Why?" I asked, and took a quick sip of the tart wine. "You're calling about an active case."

"Right, just like I did today."

"We kinda talked about the case." I kept my eyes on her arse. Since taking her arse at Sensation, that was all I thought about honestly.

"Anyway, Ava said that she talked with Trent, and they are going to try and work it out. I'll prepare the dismissal in the morning."

This was what I wanted. For me to see Peyton again, and for my friends to get back together. However, I needed more hours to bill. Hollywood was always breaking up, and I just hoped they called me.

"Brilliant. I'm happy they're going to work it out."

"You know them better than I do. Trent will be good to her?"

I nodded. "Yeah. He knows he fucked up, and Ava was the best thing to ever happen to him. If they don't work out, then they know who to call."

Peyton looked over her shoulder and smiled. "True."

"Now that that is out of the way, let's talk about why you're cooking with clothes on."

"What?" She turned around, a pair of kitchen tongs in her hand.

I grinned. "I thought you were cooking me dinner naked?"

She laughed, and my dick stirred. "I never said anything about getting naked."

I slid off the chair and walked the few feet to her, a smirk spread across my face. "How long did you say dinner would be?" I slid my arms around her waist.

"Not long enough for *that*," she protested and poked a finger into my chest.

"Are you saying I can't make you come in under three minutes?"

"That's exactly what I'm saying," she challenged.

I took the metal tongs from her hand, set them on the counter then spun her so she was facing the cabinets, and stepped forward, my front was flush with her back. "I've never met a challenge I couldn't beat," I whispered in her ear.

I felt her shiver against me. "Then try."

I began working her jeans. I popped the button and then slid the zipper down. Peyton's head tilted forward. I wanted to see my hand disappear inside her, but from this angle all I could do was taste her skin on her neck.

My fingers slid along the hem of her knickers and then descended inside. She took a deep breath, preparing her body for the pleasure I was about to bestow upon her. Her head tilted to the side, and I sought her taste as my tongue ran up the slope toward her ear. My hand continued down into her knickers, and once I found the heat I was seeking, my finger went right for its target. She bucked against me as I rubbed the bundle of nerves.

"You're already wet," I groaned against her skin.

She pressed harder against me. My throbbing dick was rubbing against the fabric of my trousers as the friction between us built. There was a chance I would come in three minutes if she kept rubbing her delicious arse against my cock.

"I've been craving you since I heard your voice this morning." I inserted a finger, and she rode my hand. My thumb was still circling her clit, and she moaned. My teeth sank into the slope of her neck causing her to hiss.

"Oh God ..."

"If you're not careful, I might just eat you for dinner."

"Yes," she whispered. "Please."

Removing my fingers, I used two of them to rub against her clit. The timer on the stove was counting down, like a ticking time bomb. Her breaths became pants, her knees starting to buckle beneath me. I held her up with my leg, still rubbing the spot that was on the verge of exploding. And then she did. Her hands clutched the counter, and she cried out as a rush of cum coated my fingers. I slowed my motion, our bodies still pressed together and my hand in her knickers.

"That was a good appetizer," she finally said.

"Now it's time for the main course." I withdrew my hand and spun her in my arms and kissed the shit out of her.

My cock was throbbing against the zipper of my trousers, wanting to break free and seek warm, pussy shelter.

And then the timer on the stove buzzed.

Peyton tried to break free from me, but I didn't let her. Instead, I kept her pinned to the counter, reached over and found the button to turn off the blood buzzing, and then I turned off the stove.

"Anything else needs to be turned off?"

She shook her head.

"Nothing's in the oven or anything?"

"No," she frowned. "Just the chicken on the stove, and I have salad in the fridge."

"Good," I stated and picked her up.

"What are you doing?" she shrieked, her legs going around my waist.

"Eating my dinner."

She laughed. "What about the piccata?"

"Trust me, beautiful. I'm going to eat your home cooked meal. But first I'm going to eat you."

"It's going to be cold."

I stopped walking and pulled my head back so I could look her in the eyes. "Are you telling me you don't want this?"

She stared at me for a beat then shook her head. "No, I do. I just don't want you to think I'm a horrible cook because we'll have to reheat it."

"I would never ... say that to your face." Peyton threw her head back and laughed as I smiled. "Just point me in the direction of your bedroom or dinner will really be cold."

She turned a little in my arms and pointed at a door to the left of the hallway. Once we were in her room, I placed her on the bed and started removing her jeans completely. I tossed my shirt on the floor with her trousers and moved back to her. She spread her thighs, and I got a view of her pussy. Pre-cum coated the tip of my shaft. *God, she was beautiful.* Even with her T-shirt halfway up her stomach. I didn't need to see all of her to know she was perfect.

I spread her, and my mouth followed, licking the arousal seeping from between her legs. Her back arched, and a moan slipping from her mouth as I felt her grip the sheets beneath us. Then I heard another moan that didn't come from my girl. My head lifted, and I waited a moment to see if I would hear it again.

"What's wrong?" Peyton asked.

"Yes! Yes, right there!"

I turned my head to the wall behind Peyton's headboard. The wall I assumed was her neighbor's wall too.

"Ahh," Peyton groaned, and I turned back to her. "He would be getting busy right now!"

"Who?" I asked, though I already knew.

"My neighbor, Sam. Usually he waits until Friday and/or Saturday night. I'm not sure if I've ever heard him on a Monday."

"This is a normal thing?"

She took a deep breath. "Yes, and the one time I banged on the wall for him to stop, he came over and asked me to join him."

My body stilled. *Was this the same wanker who told me the walls were paper thin?* "He wants to fuck you?"

"He wants to fuck any woman, I'm sure."

"I think I saw him."

Peyton rose up on her elbows. "What? When?"

"Right before I knocked. He was leaving, and when he saw me, he asked if I was coming to see you. Then he gave me *advice* that the walls were paper thin." Apparently Sam didn't go far before coming back home or he'd changed his mind and called a bird to come over right away.

We were both silent as the woman next door kept shouting to God. "Are you good friends with this wanker?" I asked.

Her forehead furrowed at my question. "No. I've literally only talked to him about his propositions."

Propositions—plural. My blood was starting to heat.

"You want to show them how it's done?" I smirked.

"What?"

"We both know that he's doing it to try and make you jealous. Or to try and prove he's the better man or some shit. So, I say I fuck you hard, headboard banging against the wall and all that. Let him hear *you* for a change."

"I don't know. That will probably make him do it more."

"If he keeps it up, I'll talk to him."

"You will?" Her eyes widened.

"He's gonna know who I am eventually. I'm not going anywhere."

She smiled warmly at me. "Yeah?"

"Yeah," I confirmed. "Now, lose all your clothes, get on all fours, and be prepared to rock that headboard." I nudged my head in the direction.

"I can't believe we're doing this."

"Baby, it won't be the only time I rock your world in this bed." I shucked off my shoes, socks and then my trousers. Peyton tossed her top on the floor with her bra.

"I'm not going to be able to make eye contact with Sam ever again."

"Do you have a reason to?"

"Well ... no."

I discarded my boxers. "Exactly. And if he says anything, tell me."

"Always coming to my rescue." She smiled and turned to get on her hands and knees.

"Always," I confirmed. There was no chance in hell some other wanker was ever getting close to her again. She was mine. All fucking mine. And even if I had to crawl in her bed late at night after working eighteen hours, I would.

I gave my dick a few tugs, making sure it was hard as steel. Of course it was. We were both arrogant, and now had a show to put on. I sheathed myself with the condom I'd pulled from my trousers, and made my way behind Peyton in the center of the bed.

"Ready, beautiful?" I asked, and ran a finger through her slit. Yeah, she was ready.

"Yes," she responded.

"When I'm in all the way, grab the headboard and hold on."

"Okay," she breathed.

I took my cock, ran the latex tip in her arousal a few times and then slid in slowly. Her pussy immediately sucked my dick like a winter glove. *Yeah, this was better than any home cooked meal.* I wanted to survive solely on Peyton's pussy until the day I died.

I rocked my hips to slide fully in. Once I was to the hilt, I spoke, "Hang on."

She reached up and grabbed the headboard. Her body tilted, causing my shaft to hit the spot that I knew would drive her insane. I picked up my speed, Peyton's tits bouncing with each drive, and I grunted. She felt fucking amazing.

"Oh, God," she moaned.

So she spoke to him too ...

"Your pussy's so fucking tight," I bellowed. "God, Peyton, you feel so good."

Well, shit, I was talking to him too.

She moaned, the headboard banging against the wall. "Don't stop."

Stop? Fuck no. I wasn't stopping until she screamed my name so that Sam knew who the fuck I was. I groaned. She moaned. The bed squeaked, and the headboard started to mark the grey paint.

Peyton came once.

I continued my thrusts, willing my explosion to hold off. Sweat slicked my entire body as I pumped, the head of my cock hitting the end of her slick heaven.

"Fuck," she hissed as her body moved in sync with mine.

She came again.

My balls started to pull up, and I knew I was close. I also knew that the spot I was thrusting against was more aroused after an orgasm—or two—and if I kept up my pace, Peyton would come one last time before I blew my load.

And then she came again.

"Booker!" she screamed, cum gushing out of her.

"Ah fuck," I hissed, and drove a few more times and then came.

She leaned back against my chest, my arms holding her up as the milky fluid soaked her bedspread. I lazily played with her tits as our breathing slowed.

"What was that?" she asked.

"That, beautiful, was you squirting." Yes, I totally said it loud enough for that Sam dude to hear.

Beat that, motherfucker.

Chapter 14

BOOKER

Carrie: *Are you ever coming home?*

I stared at the text message and sighed. I hadn't slept in my own bed for almost a month, and when I did go over to grab my clothes, she wasn't home. Therefore, I hadn't seen much of my *wife*. Everything was weighing heavy on my shoulders. I thought about how I needed to work my arse off each day, how I needed to make sure Peyton was happy, and now how Carrie was basically telling me that I'd been neglecting her.

Carrie: *Miss me?*

A few seconds later she texted back.

Carrie: *I have something to tell you.*

That sparked my interest.

Me: *What is it?*

Carrie: *I want to tell you in person.*

Me: *Is everything okay?*

Carrie: *Of course.*

Me: *Okay, I'll talk to Peyton and I'll come tonight.*

Carrie: *Bring her.*

I blinked at the words on the screen.

Me: *Bring her?*

I knew she wanted to meet Peyton officially and probably apologize for being a bitch toward her that night at Sensation, but if she had something to tell me, I didn't think she'd want to do it in front of my girlfriend.

Carrie: *Yes, let's order Chinese.*

I swear these women knew nothing about my diet. While I burned an excessive amount of calories at the gym each day, I needed to go back to chicken, ground turkey and sweet potatoes. I'd put a lot of hours into sculpting my body, and I was trying to not let the women in my life make me fat. Granted I loved Peyton's cooking. It felt like home.

Me: *All right. See you tonight at seven.*

Apparently, I was getting off work *early* too.

I started to type out a text to Peyton, but instead, I decided to call her office. After going through the receptionist, Lorelei picked up the phone.

"Peyton Winters' office."

"Lorelei, Booker."

"Hey, Mr. Jameson, let me put—"

"Actually, I want to talk to you."

"Oh."

"Peyton told me that you wanted to come Saturday?"

"Yes."

I nodded, even though she couldn't see me. "I talked to my mate Randy, who you met at Rick's."

"Okay ..."

"He said you can come as his guest."

"Really?" she shrieked. I had to pull the receiver away from my ear.

"Yes, but remember—"

"I know, confidential."

"Right."

"Thank you so much. I'll put Peyton on now."

"Thank you. I'll see you on Saturday."

A few seconds later Peyton picked up. "Hey."

"Hey." I smiled as soon as I'd heard her voice.

"What's up?"

"Dinner at my place tonight?"

There was a brief pause. "Yeah, sure."

"It's not that I don't want to go to yours, but Carrie wants us to have dinner with her tonight."

"Oh," she breathed.

"You're okay with that?"

"Well, I mean—it will be weird at first I'm sure."

"Don't worry. She'll probably apologize for starting shit between us, and then she'll give you wine and you'll be best friends."

Peyton laughed, and my dick jerked. "I do like wine."

"I'll pick you up at six-thirty."

"Okay."

"Oh, and one more thing. Bring clothes for tomorrow."

"How will I get to work?"

"After I hit the gym I'll pick you up and bring you back to your place so you can get your car."

"Should I just meet you at your place?"

"And if you get there before me, will you feel comfortable with Carrie alone?"

"Good point."

I chuckled. "Don't be nervous. Carrie's harmless, and I promise you'll love her."

Peyton was coming home with me where I shared a house with my *wife, but* I knew they'd hit it off after they got over the awkwardness of their first meeting.

I wasn't the last one to leave the office for once. More and more Clint tried to stay later than I, but I never let him. He had a wife and a kid he had to get home to, and there was no way I was going to let that wanker take my raise and promotion from me. If I had to go stand outside of nightclubs, waiting for couples to exit who were at each other's throats, I would. Anything to get more clients. In fact, I was going to hit up a few people at Sensation on Saturday who I knew were on the verge of calling it quits.

As I exited the lift onto Peyton's floor, my *good mate* Sam was walking toward it.

"Hey, wallbanger." He chuckled as he slid past me.

I turned to face him. "Jealous?"

He threw his head back, laughing. "Why would I be jealous of you? You're probably only fucking one chick, and I have an entire list on speed dial."

First of all, everyone was technically on speed dial these days. Second of all, I'd had plenty of arse in my day, and I was happy with the one I was with.

"Keep thinking that, mate." I turned to walk down the hall toward Peyton's door. I knocked and waited for her to answer. I *really needed my own key or something.*

The door swung open, and my gaze roamed from her booted feet all the way to her loose brown curls. She was in jeans and a cream colored sweater that hung off one shoulder. Instead of greeting her with a kiss like I normally did, I stepped forward and placed my lips on her bare skin.

"We'll be late if you keep that up," she teased.

I grinned against her skin. "Carrie would understand."

"Just contain yourself for a few hours." She laughed and stepped passed me into the hall.

I closed the door and reached for her keys so I could lock it. "I'm trying, gorgeous, but I haven't seen you all day."

"I think you'll live."

"Maybe. Maybe not. Are you willing to risk it?" I joked.

"It depends. What are we eating for dinner?"

As we walked toward the lift, I grabbed Peyton's overnight bag and handed her back her keys so she could put them in her purse. I reached for her hand, needing to feel her skin on mine.

"Chinese."

She sucked in a light breath. "My favorite."

I grinned. "Yeah?"

"Yeah. This night just might turn out great."

I laughed. "Trust me, will you? Carrie's a sweetheart."

"You keep telling me this, except the first words out of her mouth were rude."

"She assumed you were just some random bird, and she was ready to go home. She was probably hungry, too."

A slow grin spread across her face. "Women are bitches when they're hungry."

"Exactly my point. Tonight I have no doubt she wants to redeem herself."

"Have you seen her in the last month?"

I nodded. "But only for a few minutes at the beginning of the month when I went home to get my clothes for the gym and work."

"Maybe if things work out, I can come over after work or something to hang with her while you're working late. We can switch off days or something. I go to your place one day. You to mine."

"Don't want to spend a night without me, baby?" I teased.

"Please. You're the one who told me to pack a bag for tonight."

"You're right. I don't want to go a night without you," I admitted.

She smiled but said no words in response. I didn't need them. Even though she joked about it, I knew she didn't want to go a night without me either.

Twenty minutes later, we pulled onto my street. After parking in the garage, I grabbed Peyton's bag, and opened her door.

"Ready?" I asked, taking her hand in mine.

"Do I have a choice?"

I finally pressed my lips to hers. The moment they met, I realized I hadn't kissed them since early that morning. "I'm going to say it one more time. I've got you. Carrie won't be a bitch, and if she is, I'll threaten her with a divorce." I grinned.

Peyton slapped my chest. "Shut up."

We walked into my house through the door of the garage that led to the kitchen. Carrie sat at the dining room table with another woman who I didn't know.

"Peyton!" Carrie exclaimed and rushed to her. My hand fell away from Peyton's as Carrie engulfed her in a hug. "It's so nice to finally meet you. I mean, we met before, but that was—"

"She knows what it was, sweetheart. Peyton was there." I cut Carrie off because I didn't know who the other woman was, and I wasn't sure if Peyton would be comfortable with a stranger knowing we go to a sex club.

"Right," Carrie said, not moving her hands from Peyton's shoulders. "I'm sorry about what I said and how I said it."

Peyton gave a small smile. "Thank you. It's fine now."

Her eyes moved to me, and I smiled back. "All in the past," I agreed.

"Good," Carrie said.

"I'm Booker." I stuck out my hand to the stranger at my dining room table.

"Taylor." The blonde returned the gesture.

"Booker. Taylor's my ..." Carrie hesitated as she smiled at Taylor, and then turned back to me. "My girlfriend."

"Oh." I smiled down at Carrie. "This what you wanted to tell me?"

She bit her bottom lip. "Not entirely, but that can wait until after dinner. I think we should order the food and get some drinks going first."

My head tilted slightly. "Now I'm really intrigued."

"Don't worry. I'm just hungry, and I'd rather tell you after the food is ordered."

I sighed. "Okay. Grab the menu, and I'll show Peyton to my room so we can put her stuff in there."

Peyton followed me down the hall to the room that I'd never let a woman in except for Carrie and Amelia, and neither one of them ever sexually. I rarely spent time in my room except to sleep, so it was bare for the most part except my dresser, a nightstand with a lamp and clock on the top, and my bed. I had a picture of Big Ben on one wall to remind me of home, and that was it. Carrie was the one to decorate our house. It was, in fact, *her* house. She bought it not long after we graduated and married.

"You doing okay?" I asked as I closed the door behind me.

Peyton nodded. "Yep. Wasn't expecting a hug or to meet your *wife's* girlfriend."

I chuckled. "I wasn't expecting to meet my wife's girlfriend either."

Peyton sat on my bed. "From our conversation last month at Sensation, I'm sure this is new for her too."

I rubbed the back of my neck. "Probably. I'm not sure what she wants to talk about, though."

She shrugged. "Maybe just to understand this next part of your lives. You both haven't had serious relationships since getting married. Maybe she wants ground rules or something. Like if the house is a rockin' don't come a knockin' type a thing."

I sat next to her. She leaned her head on my shoulder as I wrapped my arm around her. "The house has rocked a lot of times since we've been married. That hasn't stopped her."

"Then I guess we just wait until she's ready."

She lifted her head to look at me, and before I spoke again, my lips brushed hers. "Let's go order your favorites."

A huge grin spread across her face. "After my heart, Mr. Jameson?"

I stared at her, not sure how to answer the question. I felt something completely different for Peyton than any other girl to cross my path. I never wanted to go a day or night without seeing her, and I knew for sure that the last month was one of the best times of my life. Was this love? I'd been too busy with everything to stop and think about how love should feel. So I answered jokingly, "I thought I already had it?"

It was her turn to stare at me. Before she could answer, there was a knock on my door.

"Stop making out and come look at the menu!"

Fucking wife.

"Come on, gorgeous. Let's get you fed." I held out my hand and helped Peyton off the bed.

An hour later, we were all sitting around the dining room table, scooping various dishes onto our plates. While we'd waited for our food, Carrie told us how she and Taylor had met. A week before the last party, they met at a coffee shop down the street when they were both customers, and they started seeing each other the day after the party. Apparently, Taylor had approached Carrie and one thing led to another. Taylor didn't go to Sensation. I knew that because Carrie and I went together, and I didn't recall seeing Carrie with anyone. Granted I had other things on my mind. While Peyton and I were doing our thing, so was Carrie and Taylor. The mornings I would come home and didn't see Carrie were the mornings she was with Taylor.

Our lives were definitely changing.

"So now that we all have food," Carrie started, "I was wondering how serious you two were?"

I dropped my fork onto my plate causing a clinking noise to radiate the open floor plan dining room. "What?"

"Well, I mean, you two have been together every night. Is it serious?"

"Why do you care?" I spat. Carrie was with Taylor and didn't need to butt into my life.

"I'm getting to that."

"Well, bloody hurry the fuck up."

"Don't get your panties in a bunch, Booker."

I narrowed my eyes at her.

"So one night Taylor and I got drunk—"

"And?" I wasn't mad at her per se, but I was irritated that she was asking me about my business.

"I may or may not have told her we were married." She gave a tight, worried smile.

"Are you serious?" I stood, the chair falling back as it slid backward.

"I'm sorry."

"What is wrong with you?" We went years without anyone knowing, and now she was telling people like it should be public knowledge.

She stood and put her hands out in front of her. "Hear me out."

"There very bloody well be a good explanation, *love*."

"There's not a good reason I told her—"

"Maybe I should go wait in your room?" Peyton muttered as she started to stand.

"I'll go with you," Taylor said.

"No!" I hissed. "Everyone in this fucking room knows what's going on, and since my *wife* has a big fucking mouth, she might as well tell us why she is curious about our relationship." I looked to Peyton, and she sat back down. Taylor did as well.

"Continue, *wife*."

"I want to know how serious you are because I want a divorce."

My head felt as though all oxygen left my brain. "What?" I whispered. Sure we'd discussed it before as a possibility, but nothing was ever certain or written in stone, and now it f[[;;;;;;;;pback to me. "I researched how you can become an American citizen."

I knew how to become one, but I wanted her to continue. "Go on." I leaned toward her while placing my hands on the table.

I saw her throat move up and down as she swallowed. "You meet all the requirements. For examplūe; being a permanent resident for over five years (or three since we're married), you have a good moral character, and you speak, read and write English. I don't see why you'd be denied if you were to submit the Application for Naturalization, and then, when it's time, you learn U.S. history and whatever else before taking the oath of allegiance. Of course, there's more to it, but I think you'll be okay. I just think that you should do it soon because it could take six months to a year to happen. Or more."

I righted my chair and sat back down, processing what she'd said. Carrie had a good point. I had no desire to return to the UK. My life was here, my work was here, and now my woman. But if things didn't work out with Peyton, I still wanted to be in this country.

"You should have started off this conversation saying you researched how I could become a citizen, not asking if Peyton and I were serious. That's no concern to you."

"But it is," Carrie returned. "Taylor and I are serious too, and one day this secret could bite us in the ass."

"Not if you kept your mouth shut," I growled.

"I'm sorry, but—"

"It's fine," I clipped. "Let's just eat."

"Are you mad at me?"

My gaze flicked to hers. "I'm angry that you did this in front of our girlfriends. You should have talked to me privately."

"You're right. I'm sorry."

We all started eating in silence, the clock on the wall ticking every second that passed. "You know," Peyton spoke, her gaze on Carrie, "I've been sitting here for the past hour trying to remember where I knew you from. It isn't from when you walked into the room and told me you were waiting for your husband. You were the first person I saw at Sensation."

"Really?"

"As I walked through the black velvet drapes, I saw two women kissing by a fireplace. You were one of those women."

My gaze turned to Taylor. Did she know about Sensation? Was she going on Saturday?

"Bitches love making out in front of fireplaces." Carrie laughed. "It was probably me."

"Are you coming on Saturday?" Peyton asked Carrie.

"Of course."

"And ...?" Peyton looked to Taylor.

"Carrie has been talking about Sensation for a few weeks. I'll be there too."

"Perfect. We should get a limo or something. My friend Lorelei is going with Randy."

"What?" Carrie asked, her gunmetal eyes going big and round.

"Not like that." Peyton chuckled. "Lorelei just needed a way to get invited, and Randy said it was okay."

Carrie's eyes cut to me, and we both started to laugh.

"What?" Peyton asked.

"Randy's going to do more than just get Lorelei in if you know what I mean," I answered.

"Really? He said he was interested in her?"

"Randy doesn't invite anyone to Sensation unless he's interested in fucking them."

"I thought he was doing you a favor?" Peyton asked me.

"It was more that I planted the seed. Apparently, they had a good time at Rick's."

"Nothing happened at Rick's," Peyton retorted.

"Not physically, but Randy thinks she's hot."

"Well, I'm not going to tell Lorelei. She'll get all worked up if she thinks it's a date. Randy needs to make his move."

"He will." I winked at her.

Chapter 15

PEYTON

I woke to a blaring alarm that caused me to shoot straight up only to see darkness. There were fumbling sounds, and then the alarm stopped. An arm hooked around my waist.

"Sorry, that's my alarm," Booker said against my naked side.

"Alarm? It's pitch dark."

"Have to go to the gym."

I blinked down at him. Gym? Who the fuck went to the gym at this hour?

"But first, I need to stop and get my suit and shit for work. Wasn't expecting to stay the night, and I've been forgetting to replace the backup one I used to have in there."

After we'd discarded my soaked sheets the night before, I'd placed them in the washer before heating our dinner in the microwave. The piccata was still delicious despite being reheated. Then we lounged on my couch until the sheets were dried (because the best feeling was putting fresh sheets out of the dryer on your bed and then crawling into it), took a shower together, and did *it* all over again minus the headboard banging. Sometime after, we both fell asleep.

I lay back down and moved so my leg wrapped around his waist, almost spooning him. "Everything was going so well until you woke the dead."

He chuckled. "If it isn't loud, I don't wake up. I'm a hard sleeper, especially after multiple rounds of sex."

"Want me to make you breakfast?"

I could feel his head move against the pillow, but it was still dark, only a sliver of light slipping through my blinds. "If you do that, I'll never make it to the gym or work, and neither will you."

I smiled. "I like the sound of that."

"I do too, gorgeous, but I need to get as many billable hours as I can these next two months."

"Oh right. Partner."

Booker rolled, his arm still under my head, but now he was on his back. "Yeah. Clint thinks he's hot shit."

"Like you?" I teased. I didn't want to get Booker worked up and remind him that Clint had asked me to drinks once.

He chuckled. "Yeah, exactly like me."

"I understand." A thought occurred to me. "But Ava and Trent's case getting dismissed means fewer hours on that case."

He sighed. "Yeah. But they're my friends, so it's okay."

"And if we have a conflict of interest with potential clients, that's less for you too."

"I've already thought about all this. It will be fine."

I was silent for a few moments. "Okay."

"I gotta go, though. Go back to sleep, and I'll call you later." Booker leaned over, kissed my lips softly, and then my forehead. I melted. I could get used to waking up with him every morning. However, we'd need to figure out a solution for his alarm situation.

He got out of bed, and I heard him as he put on his clothes. Before he left, he came to my side of the bed, kissed me again, and then he was gone. I stared up at the dark ceiling and sighed.

Then I fell back to sleep.

My entire body ached. No matter how much I stretched, every

muscle was yelling at me. Maybe I needed to go to the gym too. I thought it would get better since it wasn't the first time Booker and I had tangled in the sheets for hours, *but damn*, my body needed to get used to my new exercise regimen.

I didn't need to be in court this morning, so I went straight to the office. As I approached Lorelei's desk, she looked up and met my gaze. A smile spread across her face and mine followed.

"Details. I want all the details."

"You know damn well I'm not giving you details," I stated as I stopped at her desk.

She huffed. "I'm living vicariously through you."

"You've never had a problem getting action."

"I don't have a problem, but I'm also not sleeping with—"

"Shh," I scolded.

"I wasn't going to say his name."

"Still. No one can know my business."

"You know everyone wants to know where the roses came from yesterday."

I shrugged. "Too bad."

"I won't say anything, you know that." She leaned forward and whispered, "But he did come over last night, right?"

I nodded. "I'll tell you one thing. But later."

A look of excitement lit up her face. "I'm intrigued."

I laughed. "Just give me my phone messages." She did, and before I left to go to my desk, I said, "Oh, and if anyone calls and it's a conflict on my end, can you refer them to ... *him*?" I'd whispered the last word.

Her brows drew together. "Okay. I thought you'd want *him* to spend more time with you, not have a ton of cases."

"I do," I agreed. "But he's trying to make partner."

It wasn't an everyday occurrence or anything for me to have a conflict, but it did happen. I never thought I'd ever help Booker out. Now I wanted him to make partner because I was happy for him.

"You got it, boss." Lorelei smiled.

I laughed and went into my office. My red roses were starting to open, and the smell hit my nose as I got closer to my desk.

Definitely could get used to this.

An hour later, I emailed the Request for Dismissal to Booker. We had two other cases together that weren't on the verge of settling or being dismissed, but those cases weren't set for hearings for a few more months—after the first of the year.

Ten minutes later, my email dinged with a new message. It was from Booker.

Ms. Winters,

Attached please find the executed Request for Dismissal. Once filed, please provide my office with a copy.

Yours,

Booker Jameson

I stared at the message. I wasn't expecting a lovey dovey email from him, but ...

Whatever.

Lorelei stuck her head in my office. "Ready for lunch?"

I glanced at the clock on my computer, realizing it was noon. "Yeah, where do you want to go?"

"*Chipotle?*" She smiled.

I nodded. "Sounds good."

We each ordered a burrito bowl, and before I could take a bite, the questioning started.

"So, what do you have to tell me about last night?"

"I swear to god, you're like a dog with a bone."

"You're teasing me," she whined.

I took a bite and then looked around. I didn't see anyone that I knew, so I felt it was safe to tell her one little bit of the night. "So last night we heard Sam."

Lore blinked. "Heard Sam?"

I nodded. "Yeah, as in *heard* him."

"Ohhh." Her face lit up. "And?"

"Well, I guess when ..." I looked around the restaurant again. "When *he* went to knock on my door, Sam was leaving his condo or something. Sam proceeded to tell *him* that the walls were thin." I took another bite of food.

Lorelei's brown eyes widened. "Shut up!"

"So I don't know if Sam called up one of his girls, but not long after, he was, you know." I lifted a shoulder.

"What did ..." She groaned in frustration. "You know what, we need a nickname for *him*. How about BJ?"

"What?" I chuckled. "We're not calling him BJ."

"Those are his initials," she clarified.

"I know that, but I'm not calling him *that*."

"Well, what do you want to call him? And not him or he or he's or whatever else refers to *him* in a non-specific way."

I thought for a moment as we both ate a few bites. "How about Cuffs?"

"Cuffs?" She drew her head back a little, confused.

I smiled remembering Booker and my first night together. "Yeah."

"Why Cuffs?" she inquired.

"Let's just say he likes to use them."

I swore her eyes were going to fall right out of her head. "Shut up!"

"Shhh," I whispered.

"I swear to all things holy that I'm getting your ass drunk Friday at Rick's and then making you tell me *everything*."

I laughed. "Whatever. So anyway, Cuffs heard Sam and whatever flavor of the week, and he got all superior or some shit because we both knew that Sam was only doing it so we would hear. I mean, it was Monday. He's never had a thing on a Monday that I can remember."

Lore nodded and took more bites of her chicken bowl.

"Anyhow, Cuffs turns to me and asks if I want to ... you know, so Sam would hear." Her mouth dropped open. "At first I was against it because it was like we were stooping to his level or being immature. Then Boo—Cuffs said that he wanted Sam to know who he was and that he wasn't going anywhere."

"So you did it—loud?"

I smiled. "Loud. Headboard banging, me screaming his name, *loud*."

Lorelei dropped her black, plastic fork in her bowl. "I need a Cuffs. I want to get a concussion from hitting my head on the headboard."

I laughed. "It wasn't like that."

"Sounds like it was."

I shook my head. "It wasn't my head. I was—facing and holding onto the headboard."

"Ohhh." She smiled. "Gotcha, but please, please, *please*, take me with you to the next party. I'll love you forever."

"You'll love me forever no matter what," I corrected.

"Yes, but I will love you more if you get me in."

I grinned. "I'll see what I can do."

Later that afternoon, Lorelei buzzed my office phone's intercom. "Cuffs is on line two."

I turned my head and looked at her through the window that separated my office and her desk. "Don't call him that if it's about a case. Just say his real name so it's not suspicious."

"So many rules," she murmured and hung up her handset.

I rolled my eyes, grabbed my handset and pushed lined two as I motioned for her to close my door. She was still staring at me through the glass.

"Hey," I greeted.

"Hey," he said back. "Have a moment to chat?"

"Sure." I smiled.

"I'm going to be at my office until late. I'm not sure until when."

"Oh," I sighed.

"I'm sorry."

"It's okay. We didn't have plans or anything."

"I know, but I want to see you."

"I want to see you too, but I know you want to make partner. I told Lorelei to refer any conflicts I have to you."

"You did?"

I grinned. "Yeah. I heard some hot shit is trying to take it from you."

He laughed. "Yeah, he is. I called Trent to tell him you're filing the dismissal, and to also have him spread the word that I'm hot shit."

I giggled. "Yeah, you are."

"I do want to see you tonight. I just don't know how late it will be, and you'll probably be asleep."

"Just call me, and I'll let you in."

"Okay, gorgeous. I'll see you later."

My heart fluttered at the thought. "See you later."

"Oh, and Peyton?"

"Yeah?"

"Be naked."

I laughed. "Maybe."

"Bye, beautiful."

"Bye."

Chapter 16

BOOKER

My eyes were starting to cross. I'd been preparing discovery requests all afternoon, and those things are a pain in the arse. At this point, I didn't care if my clients already knew all the info we were requesting. I wanted it all: bank records, mortgage statements, pensions, airline miles—basically everything financial. I also prepared special interrogatory requests asking for the opposing party to produce details of monthly living expenses, all monthly income, employment information, real estate, etcetera. Even though we had basic forms already prepared that needed to be tweaked to fit the cases we were working on, I still made sure I asked for *everything*.

I was also the last person to leave the office.

The office had cleared out six or so hours earlier. I'd worked sixteen hours. All I wanted to do was see Peyton. I didn't know how much energy I'd have when I got to her place, but I didn't want to sleep alone. I needed the comfort of her body pressed against mine. I needed to smell her skin. I needed to taste her skin. *I needed her.*

I sent her a text before I exited the garage:

Me: *I'm on my way.*

A few seconds later, she replied:

Peyton: *I'm awake.*

I smiled. I figured she'd be fast asleep, but since she was awake, it led me to believe she was waiting up for me.

Twenty minutes later, I pulled into the garage of her building, found a guest parking spot and then rode the lift up to her floor. As I passed Sam's door, I glared, wondering if he'd said anything to her.

What would he say? "*I heard you last night getting your brains fucked out.*" Or "*Next time, love, call me and I'll rock your world.*"

No—just no.

I knocked softly on the door, trying not to wake Peyton's neighbors. A few seconds later, the door swung open, but there was no Peyton.

"Hello?" I said to the empty doorway.

"Just come in," she whispered.

I stepped in, and the door closed behind me. I turned, seeing Peyton standing there in nothing. Absolutely nothing. I'd work twenty-four hours straight if it meant this.

"Gorgeous." I smiled.

She grinned back. "You said to be naked."

Shit, it felt like days ago that I'd spoken with her on the phone. "I did," I remembered.

"And you're just staring at me."

"I am."

"Are you going to strip or what?"

I wanted to take all my clothes off, lift Peyton and fuck her against her front door. "Not tonight."

She blinked. "What?"

I cupped her cheek with my hand. "I didn't come over to fuck you."

She blinked again. "You didn't?"

I shook my head. "No, I came to be with you. I'm beyond tired."

"Why did you want me naked then?"

"I always want to see you naked. I'm a man. But honestly, I said that before I realized I was going to work past midnight."

"Oh. Well, are you hungry?"

At her question, I realized I hadn't eaten since one that afternoon. "I'm fucking starving."

She smiled, reached up on her toes and pressed her lips to mine. Then she pulled away. "I made spaghetti. Do you eat spaghetti?"

"I told you I'd eat anything."

"I know, but you wake up at the butt-crack of dawn to go to the gym. I have no idea if you can eat pasta."

I grinned. "I do have a strict diet, but right now, I'd eat an entire loaf of bread."

She grabbed my hand and laced our fingers. "That can be arranged."

"What?" My gaze was on her naked arse, and I had no idea what she'd said.

"If you want all the carbs, I have all the carbs." She looked over her shoulder as she walked toward her kitchen, me in tow.

My eyes moved up to hers. "The spaghetti is fine."

"Okay. Sit, and I'll make you a plate."

My gaze roamed over her body. "You're going to make me dinner naked?"

"No." She laughed. "I'm going to put the leftovers in the microwave, and while it's heating, I'm going to put my clothes back on."

"No—"

"No?"

"Go get in bed, and I'll be there in a bit. I think I can figure out how to serve myself."

She stared at me for a beat. "Okay. Make yourself at home. Everything's in the fridge."

I nodded, and then watched her arse again as she walked toward her bedroom. *Definitely could get used to this.*

Twelve minutes later, I was walking into her bedroom, dragging my arse. I'd eaten an entire plate of spaghetti, but it didn't give me any energy. Instead, it made me even more tired. How the hell was I going to get through the next two months working myself to the bone and keeping a relationship with Peyton?

I'd never had a steady girlfriend. I never had time. I fucked around with chicks, had fun at Sensation, but nothing lasted longer than a few weeks. I was in school for seven years, and then I was busy trying to prove myself with L&T so I could get raise after raise. I still went to the parties at Sensation, and still met women on the weekends. I was a man with needs after all. But I'd never really had something that was every night. And I wanted every night with Peyton.

I wanted to go to sleep with her arse pressed against my cock.

I wanted to wake up to her hair a mess, sleep in her eyes, and be the first thing she saw each every morning.

Peyton's dark hair was fanned across her pillow, and I thought about how things had gone from nothing to this. How in the world did she give into temptation and ever let me cuff her the first night we were together? And how the hell she'd ever let me be the first to claim her arse was beyond me. But she had, and the thought made my chest tighten.

I discard my clothes before crawling in next to her. When I pulled the duvet back a little to slide in, I noticed that she was still naked. I smiled and moved in closer, bringing my arm around her waist.

"Did you get enough to eat?"

I opened my eyes to see her staring at me. "Yeah, beautiful, I did."

"Good."

"I thought you were sleeping?"

She smiled. "Nope, just waiting for you."

I grinned and leaned down to press my lips to hers. "Thank you for making me dinner."

"You're welcome."

I rolled over, reached for the lamp and turned off the light. It was going on one in the morning, and four-thirty was going to come fast. *Fuck!*

Peyton's arm moved around my waist, and she moved closer to me. "You're so warm."

"If you had clothes on, you wouldn't be cold," I teased.

"I'm not sure of all the rules."

I blinked. "What rules?"

"Us."

"What do you mean?"

She sighed. "I like you a lot, but I don't know if this is only sex between us."

I brushed my lips against her forehead. "Gorgeous, I told you I wanted to see where this would go between us. I want you. All of you, and not only for sex. Sure, I'd love nothing more than to be buried deep inside you right now, but it's late, and we both have to work in a few hours. If I only wanted you for sex, I wouldn't have come over tonight, because honestly, I'm positive I'll be asleep in two minutes."

"Okay," she breathed.

"Okay?" I asked, seeking clarification that she understood.

"Yep, okay."

"Good." I leaned the few inches to bring my lips back to hers.

Peyton's mouth mirrored mine as I opened, seeking her tongue and a goodnight kiss. It started off slow. I'd intended for it to be short and sweet, one that would leave us both happy. Instead, it turned to fire. My dick hardened and pressed against her belly.

"Are you sure you're tired?" she panted.

"Yeah," I affirmed.

"Then let me do all the work."

I opened my eyes. "What?"

Peyton's hand reached between us, and she fisted my shaft. I sucked in a breath at the contact. "You don't have to do that."

"Shh," she whispered.

I shut the fuck up. No matter how tired I was, I wasn't about to turn down a hand job. My hands ran up and down her back lightly, still facing one another as her hand pumped my cock. Our mouths returned to tasting each other, and before I knew it, my hand was between her legs. Her velvet pussy was sleek, wet, and even though she said she'd do all the work, she was as turned on as I was.

"Shit," I murmured against her lips. "I really—"

"Shh," she said again, and her hand moved faster.

Two of my fingers pumped into her, matching her speed. She moaned in my mouth, her pussy clenching my fingers. Pre-cum seeped from the tip of my dick, her hand catching it and gliding the secretion around my cock as her hand began to move quicker. I removed my hand from her center, coated my thumb with her juices and moved to her clit. The faster she worked my shaft, the harder I rubbed her clit. I groaned, on the verge of coming in her hand.

"Roll over," I instructed.

Her hand paused for a beat, but then she continued to bring me closer and closer by pumping me.

"Peyton," I warned, my hand still working her pussy like we were both in a race. "On your back. *Now*," I growled.

Her hand left my dick as she rolled on her back as I'd ordered. I removed my hand from her body, too, threw off the sheets that were covering us and got on my knees. My hand returned to her pussy, and I continued working the bundle of nerves that caused her to moan over and over. My other hand worked my cock, pumping up and down, twisting on the head, my thumb giving the underside more pressure.

She reached up, grabbed her delicious tits in each hand and twisted her nipples.

Then I came.

Ropes of cum landed on her belly, her chest, her tits.

"Fuck," I groaned.

Her body jerked, and she followed my groan with a moan that sounded so deep in her throat that I was sure it started in her pussy and worked its way up.

I rolled to my back, about to pass the fuck out. "I really didn't come here for any of this." I wasn't sure why I kept telling her that my motives were pure, but they were.

"I'm not complaining."

I rolled onto my side, took her mouth between my fingers and kissed her. "I'd help you clean up, but I don't think my feet will work right now."

I heard her chuckle in the dark. "I'll be right back. Go to sleep." She kissed me and then rolled out of bed.

I listened to water run as sleep starting to overtake me. Just as I was beginning to drift off, the bed dipped, and her naked arse moved back so it was against my cock.

Right where it belonged.

I'd sworn I'd just fallen asleep when my alarm blared. Peyton shot up next to me, and I fumbled for my phone to shut it off.

"Okay. We seriously need to fix that. One of these mornings, I'm going to have a heart attack."

I laughed. "Go back to sleep, beautiful."

"You're really leaving?"

I kissed her shoulder. "Yeah. Once again I didn't bring my suit for work, and I need to hit the gym."

She sighed. "Maybe this weekend you can bring clothes over so you can stay in bed longer and keep me warm."

I smiled. "I'll put extra clothes in my car when I go home."

"Okay," she replied sleepily.

"I'll call you later."

"Hmm ..."

I kissed her bare shoulder again and rolled out of bed. It was still dark, but if I didn't keep my workouts up, I wouldn't have the stamina I needed to get me through the next few months. It was crazy to think that less sleep would give me more energy, but it was true. Sure I would need to get more sleep tonight, but having the blood pump through my veins as I ran and lifted weights gave me a shit ton of energy.

Plus, I needed to work off that plate of spaghetti.

"How about we go to dinner tonight?" I suggested after Peyton woke me Friday morning. We'd come to the decision that her alarm would go off and then she'd wake me. I hated waking her in the first place, but it was either her jolting up in bed, or her kissing me awake. Of course, I chose the latter. And no matter how tired I was, hearing her voice first thing was worth waking up for.

"I can't."

My body stilled. I wasn't expecting that response. "We'll go somewhere no one knows us."

"It's not that. Every Friday after work, Lorelei and I go to Rick's on—"

"I know the place. I'll come back here when I leave work tonight. Tomorrow we'll sleep in and spend the weekend together."

"You don't have to go to the gym tomorrow or Sunday?"

"I do," I corrected. "But I don't need to go early."

"Oh. Okay. I'll meet you back here."

"Go back to sleep, beautiful."

Just like every morning, I left my Sleeping Beauty fast asleep. Tomorrow would be a different story.

"Are you going to Peyton's after work?"

I looked up from my computer screen to see Randy in my doorway. "Don't say her bloody name," I hissed.

He held up his hands and walked forward. "Dude, sorry. Chill."

"You know you can't go walking around here saying her name."

"No one is here," he stated, waving an arm behind him to indicate the office was empty.

I glared. "Someone could be around the corner, and it's not like she has a common name."

"She could be a dude." He laughed.

"Just don't say her name again."

"Well, what do you want me to call her?"

I set my pen down, leaned back in my chair and thought about his question. What could we call Peyton? Randy was one of my best mates, so it was a given that we'd talk about my love life—or my life in general.

"Call her Manning."

"Manning?" he questioned.

"Yeah," I confirmed. "Like Peyton Manning." The only Peyton I knew besides my girl was the famous quarterback.

"All right. Are you going over to Manning's place after work?"

I looked at my watch. It was only seven, but after the week I had, I was ready to call it a night. "Actually, you want to grab a drink at Rick's?"

He smiled. "Is Manning there?"

My mate knew me all too well. I grinned. "Maybe."

"Cool, let's go."

Ten minutes later, Randy and I were walking into the swanky bar. We went straight to get a drink, and I scanned the area until my gaze landed on Peyton. She was with Lorelei.

I wanted to walk over to the high-top table they were sitting at, but a lot of our colleagues frequented Rick's. It was close to the courthouse, and therefore, people spent a lot of time blowing off steam with drinks.

Instead, I pulled out my mobile just as her friend stood and walked toward the loo.

Me: *Having fun?*

I watched as she looked at her mobile on the table, picked it up and typed back.

Peyton: *Yes, though Lorelei's trying to get me drunk so I'll tell her all my secrets.*

I smiled.

Me: *What secrets?*

Peyton: *Our secrets.*

Me: *Like what?*

The bartender stepped in front of me, and I ordered a vodka and water. It's the easiest drink to order without sugar and other crap that would fuck with my body.

Peyton: *Like what we do at Sensation. In bed. On my kitchen counter.*

My smiled widened.

Me: *She knows about me?*

Peyton: *Of course. She's my best friend, but I haven't told her details.*

Me: *I wouldn't mind.*

Peyton: *Seriously?*

Me: *If you trust her, so do I.*

"Are you going to be on your phone all night, or are you going to walk over there?"

I looked up to see Randy glaring at me. "I can't go up to her. Someone might see."

"Dude, you two have cases against each other. No one will think you're fucking each other. They'll just assume you're being cordial."

"Go find a bird and piss off," I said as I read the reply text from Peyton.

Peyton: *She doesn't need to know details. Though she has bought me four drinks in hopes I'll spill.*

Me: *Are you drunk?*

I saw her laugh and text back.

Peyton: *A little buzzed.*

Me: *Are you wearing knickers?*

She laughed again.

Peyton: *Wouldn't you like to know?*

Her friend came back, and I groaned inwardly. Our texting was just getting good. I continued anyway.

Me: *If I ran my hand between your legs, would I feel your wet pussy or cotton?*

Peyton looked at her friend and then back to her mobile.

Peyton: *Cotton, but I'm wearing jeans, so there's that.*

Aw, yes, casual Friday. I couldn't wait to see the denim hug every curve of her arse. The arse that I wanted to grab a fistful of as I plowed into her.

Me: *Would you go in the vodka room with me wearing the fur coat so I could find out for sure?*

I saw her mouth drop open as she read my text. Her friend was trying to see the screen, but Peyton turned, hiding it.

Peyton: *Yes, if you were here.*

I didn't need more of an invitation than that. "I'll be back," I said to Randy and walked over to where Peyton was. Without her seeing me, I got behind her and whispered into her ear, "Then do it, gorgeous."

She startled, her back falling against my chest. I didn't want to move away from the contact. I wanted to lean down and kiss her neck followed by her luscious pink lips. But I held her up with my hand and stepped back.

She turned, met my eyes and said, "What are you doing here?"

I didn't know who was around because I hadn't been paying attention, so to be safe I replied, "Going to *taste* vodka in the tasting room."

And then I walked away.

I walked to the stand in front of the refrigerated glass box, and paid for Peyton and me to have a vodka tray each that contained six different samples. It theoretically equaled three shots. I also told the host that we wouldn't need an instructor and to only bring the trays in and leave because we'd done the experience before and only wanted to try more of their selection. The host agreed.

When I turned to see if Peyton was coming, I saw her grab the coat from the attendant. She hesitated, and the host stepped inside the box to pour our samples. I met Peyton's stare, and she motioned that she was going to the loo. I smiled. I wasn't sure how she was going to pull coming in without any trousers or knickers on. As she left, I distracted the host so he didn't realize that she took the coat with her.

A few minutes later, the door opened, and Peyton walked in, her purse on her shoulder. I had to fight everything in me not to touch her. We weren't the only ones in the tasting room. A handful of people stood around the center counter, sipping their samples. From the restaurant, you could see inside the room, and again, I had no idea if anyone was here that we knew (besides Lorelei and Randy). When I looked out the window, I saw Randy talking to Lorelei at her table. *Good thinking, mate. Distract the friend.*

The host poured our twelve clear samples, and then he turned his attention to the other patrons, asking if they had any questions.

"If we turn our backs and lean against the glass, no one will tell it's us," I said, motioning with my head to the glass windows. Only the center three panels were floor to ceiling, the other four (two on each side) were half walls, and would be perfect for me to find out what was under Peyton's coat.

"Okay," she said and moved. I followed. Once she was in the corner, and I was beside her, I dropped my hand and laced our fingers.

"Show me," I ordered.

Peyton turned her head and looked up at me. "What?"

165

I grabbed a shot glass and handed it to her, then grabbed one for me. "Take my hand and show me what's under your coat while we sample this delicious vodka."

After a few moments, she moved closer to me, our shoulders pressed together, and then she pulled my hand in front of her. She slipped our adjoined hands through the slit of the coat that was being held together by only buttons. My body shielded anyone from seeing, though no one was paying attention to us nor could they see. With our coats camouflaged together as one, she pressed my hand to her heat. She was burning despite the twenty-eight-degree box that caused our breath to come out as smoke.

"Is this what you were looking for?"

I sucked in a breath and groaned. "Yeah." I slipped two fingers inside of her. "And, of course, you're wet."

Peyton spread her legs a little, welcoming me as she casually downed the vodka she was holding. I shot mine back, reached my arm out and set my empty glass back on the tray. I did the same for her, and then got us two more all while my fingers continued to work her velvet pussy.

I took the other shot and whispered, "I want to fuck you against the window so fucking bad."

She groaned and took her shot. "Yeah?"

"Yeah."

My dick throbbed against my trousers, and Peyton's arousal dripped down my hand. I didn't care who the fuck was watching. We quickly downed three more shots, and I couldn't tell you if they tasted any different from each other. What I knew was that it burned as it went down. All my focus was on Peyton's shallow breaths, her pussy clenching my fingers and forcing myself not to unzip my trousers, bend her over, and fuck her right here.

We each had one shot left, but instead of reaching for it, I took my slick fingers and rubbed her clit vigorously.

"Oh God," she moaned.

I leaned down to her ear. "After this, I'm taking you home and fucking you so hard that we'll have to stay in bed tomorrow because you won't be able to walk."

I wasn't sure if that was possible. What I knew was my dick was aching to the point that, if I didn't find release soon, I was going to come like a boy looking at his first tittie magazine before he got his trousers down. At my words, Peyton let go. Her pussy convulsed, and she turned her mouth against my shoulder to stifle her moan of ecstasy.

Maybe I wouldn't go to the gym in the morning. Because now, I had an entirely different workout in mind.

Chapter 17

PEYTON

That weekend we stayed in bed except when I needed to go to my parents' for Sunday dinner. While I was there, Booker went home and got more of his clothes to bring back to my place. I was starting to get used to him sleeping next to me every night, and I didn't want that to change. We didn't even have sex every night like I thought we would. Sometimes we'd just talk and, of course, our morning talks were worth waking up at the butt-crack of dawn for.

Tonight Booker was still at the office, so I'd opened my laptop to research Sensation more while I watched one guy make out with ten girls in a single night on my TV. Another party at Sensation was on Saturday, and while I assumed I was going as Booker's guest, Lorelei was hounding me to get her in. Then there was the fact that I actually enjoyed going to a sex club. Never in my wildest dreams would I have ever thought that my lifestyle would include watching people have sex, but I was turned on by it.

While Booker and I had sex a lot outside of Sensation, there was just something different about being at an elite sex party. As though it was okay to let him do whatever he wanted to do to my body. Of course, I would more than likely let him do it without the club, but he hadn't mentioned anything about cuffing me, spanking me, or anything like that since we were at Sensation. The headboard banging continued, and it wasn't because we could hear Sam. It was because when Booker fucked, he *fucked*.

I typed in the website for Sensation. A homepage opened that had the 3D dodecahedron logo at the top. Under it was a bar that listed all the pages you could visit. Under that was the history of how the club got started as well as how to apply to become a member. The history portion intrigued me at first. I'd heard sex parties had been around since the Greeks had their first orgy sometime before Christ.

Sensation started twenty years ago. It didn't say by whom or why, but the fact that it had been around for twenty years and I never knew about it baffled me. I felt as though I was living under a rock. But that had all changed, and now I wanted to become a member. There was probably some rule that I couldn't be Booker's guest forever. I mean, they charged thousands for memberships. If one could invite someone over and over, they'd never need to join.

I scrolled down. The only way to get a membership was to be invited by a member. You would then need to submit your application with a picture or video and get approval. All members had a member ID, and that number was to be inputted on the application. It made sense to have an application process. After my first night, I knew Sensation was for the rich and famous. I was neither of those, but since I owned my own condo, and had a steady job where I made decent money, I assumed I could at least afford the pearl package—whatever that entailed.

I clicked the apply button.

Applicants are required to receive an invitation by a current member.

Applications missing any requested information will be deemed incomplete and will not be considered. Clear, recent photos, or a video of your face and full length, must be provided. All submitted information and content shall be held in the strictest confidence. If application meets Sensation's approval after review by our founder, an approval email will be sent. The chosen can create a dodecahedron account where payment is to be obtained via our secure site. After purchase is verified, Sensation's address and party dates will be revealed.

Would you like it rough?

Would you like to be caressed and worshipped?

Or would you simply like to observe?

What do you desire?

Let Sensation be the place to let your clandestine fantasies come to life.

After the disclaimer, there was a list of questions: your name, date of birth, email address, employer, occupation, if you'd ever been to the club before, and various questions regarding your fantasies and what turned you on. *Did I really want to become a member?* What if things with Booker didn't work out? I still wanted to go to the club and experience the lifestyle, but could I handle seeing him with other women? Would he do things if he saw me with another man? Booker had already expressed disdain toward Jason and Sam, so I wasn't sure how he'd react.

I needed to talk to Booker to see where his head was regarding the club. We were good, but if we ever broke up, I'd deal with the outcome. And there was still the fact that he was married, and I didn't want to date a married man for the rest of my life. I wanted the husband, the kids, the white picket fence all girls dream about. I had the career, and I hoped I had the man. The other two would hopefully follow after the man became *my* husband.

Wait. What?

I was a lunatic for thinking that after only a few weeks of dating we'd eventually get married. Sure, when you dated, that was the endgame. But not even a month of dating and I was thinking about it? It was probably because we were together every night, and he was the first thing I saw every morning.

My phone buzzed with a text.

Booker: *I'm on my way.*

I looked at the time. It wasn't even after ten.

Me: *You're early.*

Booker: *Got another man at your place, beautiful?*

I rolled my eyes.

Me: *No, but how do you feel about reality TV?*

It took him a few minutes to reply.

Booker: *Depends on the show.*

Me: *The Last Rose?*

The Last Rose was a dating reality show where each week the bachelor or bachelorette sent people home until they were left with one person who they were supposed to get engaged to at the end.

Booker: *Not my cup of tea, but I don't care.*

I smiled.

Me: *You'll love it. There's this chick that's crazy!*

That wasn't something new. Every season had at least one chick who thought love at first sight existed for her and only her. Then she caused tension in the house and *hello drama.*

A few minutes passed and no reply from Booker. Finally, there was a knock on my door. I looked through the peephole and smiled as I saw his blond bearded face in view. He was looking toward Sam's door, but as I opened mine, there was no one in the hall.

"Hey." I smiled.

Booker grinned back. "Hey." He entered and kissed me hello.

Every night was the same, and even though he treated my home as if it was his own, I still loved serving him his dinner. My mother always told me that the way to a man's heart was through his stomach. Thankfully, I could cook.

I pulled the pot roast from the fridge and then put it in the

171

microwave. When I turned around, Booker was staring at where my ass had been before I turned.

I rolled my eyes. "How was work? Why did you get off early?"

His eyes moved up to mine. "You think nine is early?"

"For you? Yes."

"I only had an hour consult this afternoon, and afterward I got ready for court in the morning. Then I decided to come see my girl."

"Yeah?" I grinned.

He stood and walked toward me, wrapping his arms around my waist. "Yeah what? Yeah, that you're my girl?"

"Yeah."

"You know you are." He pressed his lips to mine. The microwave beeped, and we pulled apart. "You think I'm shagging my secretary or what?"

"Are you?"

He grinned. "Not this one."

I balked. "Not this one?"

"A few years back I had a thing with my old assistant. She doesn't work there anymore because her husband found out. Almost lost my job."

"Booker!" I scolded.

"It was years ago. I have too much to lose now to make that mistake. Plus, Monica isn't my type. She irritates me to no end when she rolls her eyes because I'm her boss and that shit doesn't fly with me. Then on Fridays when we can wear jeans, her arse does nothing for me."

I stared at him. *What the hell did all that mean?*

"You, on the other hand," he continued as he cupped my face with one hand, "make my dick hard as stone when you roll your eyes because it's *you* I want to tie up and punish. And don't even get me started with your arse, baby."

I looked up into his electric blue eyes. "You've only tied me up once."

"There's always Saturday when we go back to Sensation,

gorgeous. Or, if you want, I'm sure I can find something around here that will strap you to your bed or the dining room table."

I blinked in shock.

"I could use my tie, your robe tie, or four of your belts to strap your arms and legs bound to the table. I wouldn't mind eating *you* for dinner—again."

The microwave beeped, reminding me that his food was ready. "I actually wanted to talk to you about Saturday." I didn't want to discuss my dining room table. While it intrigued me and turned me on to think about being strapped to the table and spread open with him between my legs, I knew Booker was exhausted because *I* was exhausted and only worked eight to ten hours a day, not his crazy hours.

"What about?"

I grabbed his food, motioning for him to sit. While he began eating, I asked, "So I assume I'm going with you this time?"

He nodded, a mouthful of meat in his mouth.

"How does that work? I can't go as your guest every time can I?"

He shook his head and swallowed. "No, you're only allowed to come twice. They figure one time is to get the feel of things and the second time will seal the deal."

"Two times total, or two times with one member?"

"I think per member."

"Okay. So after the December party, I'd have to get a membership?"

"Yeah. Do you want one?"

I blushed. "Well, I figured that since it's something you're into, I would need to get my own membership so I can keep going with you."

"Okay."

I thought he'd have more of a response. It wasn't as though I was telling him I was going to the grocery store with him. "Okay?"

"Okay." He nodded.

"Well, it's by invitation only. Would it be under you or something?"

He smirked. "Of course."

"How much is it?"

"You'll need to decide what level you want and what you can afford."

"I looked at the website, but it didn't tell me prices or what each level entailed."

"I don't know the going rate, but I do have a general idea of each level. There's no need for you to become a Diamond member since I already have a room. Plus, there's a waiting list. The main perk of being the highest level, though, is you do get the invites to the special parties."

"Special parties?"

"It's more than once a month."

"What?" My eyes widened. "Wait. If there's more than one party, why did you let us wait a month before I returned to the club for you to tell me about Carrie?"

"Because Diamond members can only attend the special parties, not guests."

"Oh. So what are these *special* parties?"

He took a few more bites as I went to get my wine. I needed alcohol to process the ins and outs of Sensation.

"I'm only going to tell you this because I trust you and because you want to become a member. You are *not* to tell Lorelei or anyone else."

I downed the rest of my glass. "Okay, pinky swear." I stuck out my pinky.

He grinned and laughed. "Pinky swear?"

"Yeah, that's like the highest level of a promise."

"I know, but I didn't expect you to do it. You're too cute."

"Just give me your pinky." I wiggled my hand. I was convinced I would pinky swear until the day I died. Some things from your childhood just never go away.

Booker dropped his fork and stuck out his right pinky. They locked, and I swore I would never tell Lorelei. I told her almost everything, but I could do this. "Well?" I prompted.

"They have random masquerade parties for Diamond members. You're required to wear a mask the entire time. It's about embracing unrestricted love and becoming open-minded."

"But people do that at the normal parties. I mean, you've seen what goes on there."

"Yeah, but what if Joe Blow has the power to bring your body to a level of complete bliss where you're almost experiencing an outer body experience? But when you know it's Joe Blow, you don't give him a chance because you're not attracted to him and your eye is on —well, me?"

I grabbed the bottle and poured more wine into my glass. "I have no idea what you just said other than you want me to sleep with another dude."

He smiled. "Baby, we know that's not true and will never happen. I'm only trying to explain the secret party."

I thought about his words, trying to piece them together. "So you're saying that when you don't know who you're sleeping with, you open yourself and get out of your head?"

"Yes." He took his final bite of carrot.

"But I'm comfortable with you, so I do get out of my head."

"You, yes. Others don't. Think about who's a member. What if Lorie Diaz experienced this with her co-star Ty Sage? Do you think they could ever really work together after sharing a night together?"

"I ... I don't know."

"Maybe they could. Maybe they couldn't, but since they work together and have for years, I know for a fact that they will never sleep with each other intentionally. They're like brother and sister."

A sour taste formed in my mouth. "Okay, that's gross."

Booker laughed. "They aren't related. They're just close."

"I know, but thinking about brothers and sisters ..."

"My point is that they could be missing out because they aren't willing to give the other a chance. Being behind a mask allows people to shut off that part of their brain that cares, and allows them just to feel."

"Okay, so what else is included in this Diamond package?"

"You're able to get the high-end liquors at the bar like *Cristal* champagne, *Vieille Bon Secours Ale* that's imported from Belgium, *Glenmorangie Signet—*"

"I only know what *Cristal* is, and really, I'm okay with the cheap stuff."

"What did you drink when you went with Ava?"

"Huh?"

"Did you go to the bar near the pool?"

I nodded.

"Then you had the high-end liquors. Since she's Diamond, you were able to get the good stuff. If you were a regular member, you would have to go to a different bar."

"Okay, but I don't really need the high-end stuff. Two buck Chuck works just as well."

"Two buck Chuck?"

"Yeah, *Charles Shaw* wine from Trader Joe's. Except it's no longer two dollars. Still cheap, though."

"Is that what you make me drink when I'm here?"

I laughed. "No, but this is close. This is *Barefoot*. Award-winning, in fact."

"They probably don't serve that at Sensation." He grinned.

"Probably not." I laughed. "What else does twenty-K a month get me?"

"That's really all the exclusive stuff. The other levels allow you to do more than the one below it. So Diamond you can do it all."

Booker stood and walked behind me to the sink.

"Do you go to these masquerade parties?"

"I have, yes."

"Recently?"

He rinsed his plate and stuck it in the dishwasher as he spoke. "I haven't been in two months."

"Oh." I bit my bottom lip.

He kissed my forehead. "I honestly have no desire to go back because I only want to be with you."

I smiled up at him. "Yeah?"

"Yeah."

"There's one more thing I need to tell you."

"What's that?"

"Lorelei wants to come on Saturday."

"Hmmm," he thought, bobbing his head a little. "I'll talk to Randy and see if he'll invite her."

Lorelei and Randy officially met a few weeks back when Booker and I were in the vodka tasting room. Lorelei knew who Randy was just like she knew who Booker was. She mainly talked to assistants at work and not the attorneys themselves. Now that might be a different story with those two.

"Can you ask him tomorrow so she'll stop bugging me?" I half-joked.

He laced his fingers with mine, grabbed the remote from my coffee table and shut off the TV. "Yeah, I'll ask him after court."

"Thank you."

Booker led me to my bedroom, and once we were in there, I expected him to throw me on the bed and do those naughty things to me. Instead, he spun me to face him and began to slowly take off my clothes. My shirt went first, then my pajama bottoms and panties. Then he began to strip himself of his suit. I watched as he discarded his tie and then every stitch of clothing.

"Time for bed," he said.

"Oh," I murmured and moved to my side of the bed. "Will you tell me about the rest of the levels?" I asked as we slipped under the dark grey sheets.

Booker pulled me to him so my back was pressed against his front. "Yeah, but briefly. I'm knackered."

"Me too," I admitted.

"You could come with me to the gym tomorrow?"

I laughed—hard. "If I were to go to the gym, it wouldn't be when I needed my beauty sleep."

"Fair enough." I waited as he collected his thoughts. "So, Pearl just grants you access. You can get in, engage in the common areas and drink at the open bar. With Ruby you can do all that, plus there's a room downstairs that has ten or so mattresses around."

"Downstairs?"

"The basement. Not the main level."

"California doesn't have basements," I stated.

"We're talking Beverly Hills. I'm sure all the homes are custom, and Winn knew what he wanted when he built the mansion."

"Winn is the founder?"

"And also Savior."

"What?" I sat up to face him.

He chuckled. "You think they'd let just anyone sit on a throne with women licking their feet?"

"Well ... yeah."

"No, gorgeous. That chair is his."

"Wow." I slid back down. "Is that why he gives demonstrations?"

"A lot of people are into BDSM at Sensation, but yes. You have to be sapphire or higher to learn his art."

"And emerald?"

"There's a room on the main floor where people perform."

"Perform?"

"Actors."

"Why would they need actors to put on a show when the mansion is basically an interactive porno?"

"Art or some shit." I felt Booker smile against my shoulder.

"And people pay more for that?"

"To each their own."

"I guess." I shrugged. "So let me get this straight. Pearl, you get entry into Sensation and can drink at the open bar as well as hook up with people in the common areas."

"Yes."

"Ruby, you get all that and access to the basement where you have a little more privacy, but not by much because there are multiple mattresses around the room?"

"Yes."

"And Emerald, you get live *art*?"

"Yeah."

"Sapphire, you get private lessons from Savior?"

"Correct."

"And then with Diamond, you get the whole shebang plus your own room, top shelf booze, and an exclusive party each month?"

"Yep."

"Hmm." I thought for a moment. "So yeah ... I would only need Pearl because I can come to your room and I have no desire to have any of the other perks. Except maybe I'd want to check out the art to see what the fuss is all about."

Booker smiled again against my shoulder. "We'll get you set up after Saturday's party."

As we lay in bed, my head played over the fact that I was going to become a member of a sex club. I smiled as I thought about questions on applications for various things where they asked if you were members of any clubs. A sex club probably wasn't what they were thinking about when they formed that question.

Chapter 18

PEYTON

"We need ground rules," I stated as both Lorelei and I put finishing touches of our make-up on in my bathroom. I had decided to wear my super short, sequined, grey dress with spaghetti straps that went around my neck and crisscrossed in the back before being tied in a long bow. Lorelei was wearing a skin tight, red, halter style dress with a neckline that draped all the way down to her bellybutton. It was perfect for a night at Sensation, and also a dress I could never pull off. Lorelei had the boobs for it, and I did not.

"Like what?"

I shrugged. "I don't know. Maybe we should pretend we don't know each other once we're in there. I really don't need to see you having sex."

Lorelei laughed. "Ditto."

"Plus," I smirked, "I'm sure Randy will keep you company tonight."

"I don't think he'll want a girl like me when he can sleep with a celebrity."

I set my mascara down and turned to her. "Do you forget how Booker and I hooked up? He didn't want a celebrity."

"True. Guess we'll see." Lorelei put the finishing touches on her lips. "He's hot for a ginger."

I giggled. "You're gonna see a lot tonight."

"I can't wait." All week Lorelei had been talking about tonight. What do I wear? Who will I see? Will we eat before we go? Can I bring my phone? Of course I wouldn't answer most of them. She needed to experience it for herself and get the full excitement of what and who she'd see.

A knock sounded on my door. "The wait is over."

I walked toward my door, grabbing my clutch and jacket as I went. With a smile on my face, I opened the door and immediately saw Booker in his black and white tux. That man in anything always made me hot. He was confident in his suits, but a tux made him seem more dapper and elegant like he was picking me up for a ball of some sorts. Though, with my barely-there dress, we were kind of opposites.

I watched as his gaze roamed my body like he always did when he saw me. "Gorgeous," he greeted and stepped forward, cupping my face and silencing any return greeting.

"Are you two going to be like this all the way there?" I heard Lorelei ask from behind me.

Booker and I pulled apart, and Booker spoke with a smile, "I can arrange for you and Randy here to do the same." He motioned behind him to where Randy was dressed in a tux, too.

"Don't listen to him," Randy said. "I'll be the perfect gentleman."

"Who said I wanted a gentleman?" Lorelei winked at Randy, and then moved passed all of us and into the hall.

Randy's eyes cut to me, and I smiled. "Feisty that one. I like it." And then he followed her.

Booker reached out his hand, silently asking for my house key. I handed it to him. "Those two are either going to be really good or really bad together."

"I agree, but it will be good for him. He needs a woman to keep him on his toes."

We rode down the elevator, but instead of going to the garage, we walked out the front doors of my building to a black limo. The driver opened the door, and we piled in. Greetings were exchanged between Lorelei, Carrie and Taylor. Even though Carrie wasn't introduced as Booker's wife, Lorelei knew who she was. It was also clear that Carrie and Taylor were a couple. They stole kisses, touches and were sitting practically on top of each other as we rode to Sensation.

"Am I the only virgin here?"

My eyes widened at Lorelei's question, and then slid over to Randy to see his reaction. Of course she wasn't a virgin, and knowing my best friend, she meant virgin in the sense of being the only one who hadn't been to Sensation before. Randy choked on his champagne, and Lorelei's eyes met mine as the silence became deafening in the car. Then Lore and I started laughing—hard.

"You're a virgin?" Randy asked, clearing his throat.

"I mean, am I the only one who hasn't been to Sensation before?"

"Oh," Randy breathed.

"I haven't been before," Taylor spoke.

My gaze turned to the pretty blonde. I couldn't tell what she was wearing because she had on a long coat, but her piercing blue eyes sparkled from the contrast of her copper-colored eyeshadow. Carrie was dressed similarly.

"Oh good, I won't be the only wide-eyed chick walking in with this group." Lorelei laughed and then took a sip of the champagne Booker had poured each of us.

Wanting to make more of a connection with Carrie, I asked, "What shade is on your eyes?"

"Honeylust." She beamed.

I smiled knowing the color. "I'm a *MAC* whore. I have that color."

Carrie turned her body to face me. "I'm a *MAC* whore too!"

"Oh Jesus," Booker griped next to me.

I turned my head and glared at him. He shook his head, not saying anything further and then I turned back to Carrie. "I think I have almost every color. You never know when you're going to need Bang on Blue, Electric Eel or Bio-Green."

"I don't think I have those. You should bring yours over, and we can compare."

I smiled. "I'd like that."

Booker squeezed my knee, and my heart squeezed in response.

He'd finally realized what I was doing. Carrie and I might have started off rocky, but I was making an effort. An effort for him.

The limo finally pulled into the circular stone drive of the Beverly Hills mansion. They had added heat lamps along the stairs because even though it was early December and we lived in So Cal, there was still a chill in the air, especially when you were dressed in next to nothing.

We all exited the car, and Booker grabbed my hand. I had no idea what the plan was for tonight, but I wanted to check out everything and experience what Sensation was all about.

I watched as Taylor followed Carrie up the red carpeted stairs. Carrie showed the security man her card, and then she and Taylor went inside.

"Ready?" I asked Lorelei.

"Hell yeah." She grinned.

"Then let's go, sexy." Randy hooked his arm for Lorelei to slip hers in, and then they ascended the stairs.

"Want to get a drink first?"

I looked up to Booker. "Yeah." I thought for a moment. "Can we check out that room where there's performers?"

"We can do anything you want." He kissed my forehead and then flashed his card to the doorman. "Luke."

"You have a group tonight," Luke stated.

"We do, mate," Booker agreed.

Luke looked down at the clipboard and then to me. "Peyton Winters. That name's familiar."

"I've been here a few times," I clarified.

"Right. With ..." He took a few seconds to think. "Ava Ashley."

"Yep." I smiled.

"Trying to keep everything straight. Ava came with Trent tonight even though the last two months she hasn't. And I've never seen Booker bring anyone except Carrie."

Well, that was good on both counts for me. Ava and Trent were working it out, and Booker never brought anyone to the club.

"I'm your first guest?" I asked Booker.

Booker nodded. "Never had anyone I wanted to bring."

I smiled. "So I'm special?" I teased.

"Very."

And there went my heart again. The butterflies were swarming around it, making it come to life.

After we had left our belongings at the coat check, we stepped through the velvet drapes. I didn't know where the others had gone, and I was okay with that. Like I'd mentioned to Lorelei as we were getting ready, I wasn't ready to see my best friend, who was also my assistant, get down and dirty, and I didn't want her to see anything on my end either.

Booker led me by the hand to the bar that overlooked the pool. It was the only one I'd been to. "What do you want to drink, baby?"

I blinked, trying to remember what fancy brands they had. I couldn't remember what Booker had told me, so I just said, "Vodka cranberry."

"With the good vodka?" He smiled.

I shrugged. "Might as well. Whatever that is."

"They have *Beluga*."

I shrugged again. "Whatever."

Booker ordered my vodka cranberry, and a *Beluga* and water for himself. I took a sip and tasted nothing except the cranberry juice like I had the other times I'd been to Sensation. When we did the vodka tasting at Rick's, that shit burned. My cocktail tonight was tart, a little sour, and if I hadn't seen the bartender pour the vodka into the glass, I'd think I was drinking only the juice. Maybe that was why this was the *good* stuff.

"Ready?"

I nodded, and Booker grabbed my hand again. As we walked through the house, people were already starting to get into the action. Before becoming a guest of Booker's, I had to provide proof I was clean from any STDs. I had to do the same the time before when I was a guest of Ava's. I wasn't sure how it worked for members, but I assumed it was similar to what I was asked before becoming a guest each time. Each time, I had to provide proof that I was clean if I had partners other than with members. Of course there was a chance people would lie and say they hadn't had sex with anyone else, but if word got out that Haley Snow from one of the hottest cop shows on TV had contracted a disease from a sex club, that would turn ugly. Members paid good money, and therefore, wouldn't want to jeopardize anything.

We stopped at a set of double doors accented with molding in the middle, making it look elegant to fit the vibe of the house. Booker showed a man in a suit with an earpiece his card, and then we were given a nod.

"Ready?"

"I ... I guess," I stammered. At this point, I wasn't sure anything would surprise me.

We entered a room the size of my living room and kitchen combined. Instead of red lights, yellow ones were scattered throughout that shot up the walls from the floor. The room felt warm and somehow inviting. People sat in chairs around a stage that was raised to eye level. Behind them, people flanked the walls, and couples stood talking and sipping drinks. For some reason, I expected to walk into a room where people were already fucking.

I looked up at Booker. "What's happening?"

"Hasn't started yet." He looked at his watch. "Starts in ten minutes."

"Ah." Booker led me to a spot on the wall, and I stood next to him, his hand still holding mine. I took a sip of my drink before asking, "Is every time the same?"

"No." He shook his head. "Each one is different, and we don't know what it's going to be."

"Interesting." I nodded.

Before I could ask more, a brunette with stunning green eyes walked up to us. "Hey, Book, how are you?"

His eyes cut to me before he responded. "Brilliant, Tammy, you?"

"I'm well." She looked down at our clasped hands. "Maybe when you're done with her, we could use your room?"

My body went tight at her words. *What the fuck?*

Booker dropped my hand and wrapped his arm around my shoulders, bringing me closer to him. I fit perfectly under his arm, my shoulder the right height to slide into him. "While I'm flattered, Tammy, this is my girlfriend."

Her emerald eyes moved back to me and gave me a once over. "Girlfriend? Since when?"

"That's none of your concern, *love.*"

I took a long sip of my drink.

She chuckled. "Well, my offer will still stand once you get tired of your *girlfriend.*"

I watched this Tammy women sashay away from us.

"Sorry about that," Booker apologized.

"One of your many conquests?"

"Something like that." He took a long sip of his drink. *Yeah, we were both feeling the awkward interaction.*

Then it hit me. Booker had been coming to Sensation since he was in college—for at least *ten* years. If he'd had a different woman each time, then that meant he'd been with over one-hundred and twenty women or more depending on how many masquerade parties he went to. That was—crazy.

"Have you ..." I stammered because the question was on the tip of my tongue yet I was nervous as hell to ask it.

"Have I what?" He kissed my forehead as he leaned down to meet my eyes.

I decided to change the way I was going to ask him. "Do you ever have sex with the women again, or is it a one-time thing?"

His forehead creased. "What?"

I knew the rule: you never asked your partner how many people they'd been with. No one ever liked the number. But this was different, right? We weren't talking about five, ten or even fifteen people. We were talking about one-hundred and twenty *plus* women. I didn't even know that many women *or* men.

So I asked the question in a different way again. "I mean, will we keep getting women coming up to us asking for you to fuck them again?"

Booker dropped his arm from around my shoulders and then turned me so I was facing him head on. "There's nothing you need to worry about."

"I know," I agreed. The last month had been perfect, and I never wanted it to end, but he was used to sleeping with different women and not the same one every night. "I just ..." Crap, I couldn't get the words out. The thought of all those women was turning my stomach.

"Gorgeous, just spit it out."

I downed the rest of my drink, took a deep breath and just went for it. "I'm good at math, and having that Tammy chick come up to us made me realize that you've been coming here a long time. A decade or more, Booker. That's a long time, and even if you only went to the one night a month party and not the exclusive one, that's still a lot. I—"

"Baby, calm down."

"How can I calm down? We're talking a hundred plus. *Plus!*"

His sky blue eyes held mine. "The answer is no. I *never* go back for seconds."

Heart, it was nice knowing you. I felt it crush inside my chest as I processed his words. He never went back, so that meant a new girl each time.

"But," he continued, "I don't come every month, and sometimes when I come, I don't find anyone to be with."

"What?" I whispered. How was that possible? The clientele at this joint was beautiful. *I'd* sleep with a few of the women I've seen around—*if I were bi.*

"I might come off as a womanizer, but don't forget I told you that I have a lot of clients here. And the ones that aren't my clients, I try to get them to be. Work comes before my needs."

I stared up at him, not knowing what to say.

"I don't know how many women I've been with, but it's not hundreds. And like I said, I've never gone back for seconds —until you."

Until me. Me!

"Don't let your self-doubt get in the way, baby. You're special to me. Remember that."

I went to tell him that I was sorry, but before I could, the lights went out, and we were left in total darkness. I felt Booker wrap his arm around me again. He leaned down and whispered, "It's starting."

A few moments later, the yellow lights came back on. This time, a man and a woman were standing on a stage in the middle of the room with some sort of hoop hanging above them. Before I let my attention become fully on the couple, I wrapped my arms around Booker's waist and hugged him. I hugged him because I wanted to tell him that we were okay. I trusted him fully, and I wasn't going to think about his past any longer.

The actors were both dressed in silk robes. The man started to walk around the woman as though he was admiring every angle of her body. Once he was at the woman's front again, he started to untie her robe. It fell to the floor, leaving her naked with everything on display. The man reached into the pocket of his silk robe and pulled out a rope.

Booker leaned his head down again and whispered into my ear, "Do you like Shibari?"

I looked up and admitted in a whisper, "I don't know what that is."

"It's Japanese rope bondage."

My eyes grew wide, and I looked back at the stage. The man had draped the rope across the woman's neck, and it hung down to the floor against her stomach. I continued to watch as the man started to knot the rope in the section against the woman's belly. Once he was done, there were three knots with at least three inches between each one. He took the end of the ropes and brought it between her legs. Walking around to her backside, he pulled the rope up and through the loop that was wrapped around her nape. The woman moaned as he tugged the rope tight, and my pussy clenched at the thought of the rope going between her folds and then up her crack.

Booker took my empty glass, set both his and mine down and then pulled me to stand in front of him. He leaned down and whispered, "The rope is more than likely on her clit."

I didn't respond as I continued to watch. I was fully engaged and as I leaned back against Booker's front. I could tell he was as well because I could feel his hardening cock pressed into me.

One side at a time, the man took the ends of the rope, pulled them under her armpits and through the gap between the first knot and second knot on her chest. The rope curved around the top of each of her breast. He took the ends and crisscrossed them around the two ropes that were side by side on her back. He repeated the same pattern, but this time the ropes went under her breasts. After he had crisscrossed them on her back, he wrapped the ends around her waist and tied them together below the bottom knot.

He'd wrapped her like a present. I'd never seen something so ... beautiful.

"The knots are positioned on pressure points to increase endorphins," Booker said into my ear.

I'd always associated being tied up with something bad. Like being tied up when you're kidnapped or something. But this was different. The woman was clearly in some sort of trance as the rope pressed into various places on her body.

189

I wasn't in a trance. I was turned on at the thought of Booker doing the same to me, and as I looked around the room, it was clear that others were turned on too. Women rubbed their asses against men's fronts, men played with their woman's breasts, and some were using their hands to bring pleasure to each other.

As I pressed into Booker, I began to grind my ass slowly against him. His hand went inside the top of my flimsy dress, and the moment his finger glided over my puckered nipple, I sucked in a breath.

"This turning you on?" he whispered.

I nodded.

The man on stage brought the woman's hands behind her back and began to crisscross a new rope around her arms. Once he was at the bottom, he took the rope and wrapped it tightly around her wrists and then back up, crisscrossing again until he was at the top. He tied it, and then took the hoop that was hanging from the ceiling and fastened it to the rope near her shoulder blades.

I watched, my eyes as big as saucers and my pussy throbbed. Booker's hand left my breast, moved down between my legs and inside me. I wasn't wearing panties again.

"Yeah, baby. This is definitely turning you on."

Again, I had no words. I only nodded in agreement and moved my hips to gain more friction to ease my ache.

Once the ring was bound to the rope, the man nodded to someone off stage and then the woman was lifted into the air. I watched as the man discarded his robe, ran his hand between her legs and then angled his body so he could enter her. She moaned, her back arched as he slid inside her. When the man began to thrust, Booker's fingers pumped faster into me, matching the man's pace. It was as though I was the one bound to the ceiling unable to move.

"I think I just found out what we're doing next," Booker said, low.

I turned my head slightly to him, my ass still grinding on his cock. "You know how to do this?"

"I do."

His lips started to kiss along the slope of my neck. And that did it. I came in the dimly lit room as I thought about Booker tying me up, this time with rope and his mouth on my skin. I didn't even care if people heard me.

Booker removed his hand from between my legs. "Ready?"

I nodded, and he took my hand, leading me out of the room.

Chapter 19

BOOKER

I couldn't pull Peyton fast enough. All plans I had to mingle and find new clients went out the window the moment I realized she was getting turned on by the bondage scene, and I envisioned my own rope wrapping around her body. Tying a woman up so she was bound and I could deliver any sort of pleasure I wanted, made my dick rock hard. I'd fancied many scenes in my day with a woman tied up and spread wide so she couldn't touch me. But the first time I cuffed Peyton to my bed at Sensation, I realized I never wanted to do that with another woman. She was breathtaking. And now my mind raced as I thought about how I was going to use her body as my canvas, and how I was going to *paint* her with the rope.

We ran up the stairs and to my room, my dick aching so bad that it was hard to move. Once we were behind closed doors, Peyton began to remove her dress as she stood next to the bed.

"We need to talk," I stated.

She stopped, her dress halfway off her body. "Talk?"

I began to loosen my bow tie. "I know I cuffed you before, but that was before I knew we'd be doing more bondage. I want to know what you like, what you don't like, your fantasies."

"I want to do that rope thing."

She tore her dress off and onto the floor, leaving her in only her black heels. She'd come a long way since her first time when she wore knickers. My cock was screaming at me to shut up and fuck her already, but that wasn't how true bondage relationships worked.

"We aren't doing exactly what they did, baby. There's a lot we can do with the rope, and I think your first time shouldn't be with you in the air."

"Oh," she breathed. "Well, I don't know what I like and don't like. This is all new to me."

I tossed my tie and tux jacket onto a chair. I rolled up the sleeves of my dress shirt as I walked closer to her. "I know you liked the cuffs. I heard it in the way you moaned, how wet you were. But your first time experiencing Shibari should be more for pressure points than being bound."

"I trust you to do whatever you want."

"Good," I replied. "We'll learn what you like together."

Peyton bit her lip. "Okay. Where do we start?"

"We start with the rope," I answered, walking over to the dresser that was on the adjacent wall from the bed. The dresser had various toys for my use. I pulled two meters of brand new rope out of the middle drawer. My gaze roamed over Peyton's naked form as though I was using water on a blank canvas to get it ready for paint. When I got to her sexy shoes, I had my answer of what I was going to paint.

"Before we begin, if there's anything that hurts you or you don't like, just tell me. Do you remember your safe word?"

She nodded. "Red, like stop."

"Right. So if you want to stop, say red. There are scissors in the dresser, and I can get you untied fast. Okay?"

She gave a warm smile and nodded.

I stood in front of her, grabbed the ends of the rope, and then pulled it until it came to a loop at the other end. Once I had the loop, I took it and placed it around the back of Peyton's neck, letting the loop drape down to the small of her naked back. Without saying a word, I grabbed her hands, placing each of them on top of the rope along each collarbone.

I took the rope that hung down her belly and made an overhand knot just above her breasts, pulling the entire rope through and pulling the knot tight. I repeated the knot four more times down her torso: between her tits, about a fist length lower, above her bellybutton and then above her pussy. After the knots were secured, she removed her hands, and I ran the rope between her legs, making sure it touched her clit and then drew it up her back, threading it through the loop and pulling it through. I took the midsection of the rope, split them, and brought each length around under her armpits.

My dick was starting to harden again at the sight of the rope biting into her skin. It wasn't tight, but enough to make her soft skin bow below it. Taking the rope underneath and between the first knot I made, I pulled it through, then tugged the ends of the ropes snug—not tight—making small loops that joined the rope above her breasts with the rope under her armpits on each side. I could smell her arousal as I brought the ends of the ropes around her back again, and then to her front and in between the middle rope, above the second knot, and singed it in place. Peyton let out a moan, and my eyes flicked to hers, causing a smile to spread on my face. With all the pulling and tugging of the rope, I had no doubt she could feel it between her legs where it was rubbing against her clit.

I worked my way down her body, bringing the rope around her back and then through the rope above each knot. After all the diamond shapes had been made, I tied the end of the rope together across her arse. When I stepped back, taking in my work, Peyton was standing with a corset made out of the rope. She was fucking beautiful.

"Want to see?" I asked, admiring her sexy body.

"Yes." She grinned.

I took her hand and led her to a floor length mirror that hung on the wall. When she stepped in front of it, taking in my handy work, she gasped.

"Oh my God ..."

"What do you think?" I asked standing behind her but looking at her reflection in the mirror with her.

"I love it." She smiled again, this time through the reflection of the mirror.

"You look sexy as fuck, baby." She continued to stare at herself. "You know what's good about this design?"

"What?" she asked, not looking away from the rope.

"You can wear it under your clothes."

Her gaze finally met mine again. "What?"

"Just imagine you in court with this rope rubbing on your clit. Only you and I would know, and I would be hard as steel as I watched you squirm seeking release."

"Sounds like torture." She giggled.

"I'd take you to the nearest stairwell and give you what you wanted. The rope would rub against your clit, my mouth on your pussy, and at any moment someone could catch us." Peyton's chest started to move up and down.

"Does it turn you on to think of us getting caught?"

"Yes," she admitted. "But we can never—"

"Shh," I said, stepping closer to her back and whispered, "Just pretend. Pretend you're arguing a case against me, and only you and I know what's under your trousers. Imagine my dick getting hard as you bend over to pick up a pen you dropped because I know the bite of the rope is rubbing your clit and your trousers are soaked because you're not wearing any knickers. Picture me *accidentally* rubbing against your arse as I walked by you, apologizing for getting in your way, though my body just caused the rope to rub harder."

She didn't say anything as our stares stayed locked on each other in the mirror. Her chest moved in a silent pant, and the smell of her arousal made my dick ache.

"If we couldn't find a stairwell, I'd take you to my car, pull you into the backseat and pound into you. Still, at any moment someone could walk up beside my rocking car and catch us. Maybe they'd stare at us, getting hard themselves as the rope corset bit into your skin, and your moans filled my car. They'd watched as you came with my dick so far in you that you aren't sure where you end and I—"

Peyton spun, knocking me into the wall as she jumped into my arms, her legs hooking around my hips. Her pussy ground into the

195

fabric covering my cock. I held her up as she tore open my shirt, a few buttons coming loose and falling to the wood floor. Even though no one was watching, the thought of it turned her on. It was the same reaction when we'd used her headboard as a door knocker.

With our mouths still moving together I brought her to the bed and lay her down as she looked up at me with heat in her chocolate eyes—eyes that reminded me of hot, melting fudge.

"Fuck me, baby," she whimpered.

Frantically, I discarded my clothes, grabbed a condom from the bowl, and sheathed myself. Peyton was laying on her back, her knees bent and spread. My canvas was complete.

"You're so fucking beautiful," I said crawling on the bed toward her.

She smiled, and before she could respond, my lips descended on hers. She was sweet, tart and delicious, and I was one hundred and ten percent into this woman, my heart full.

"Please?" she begged.

I knew what she wanted, and I delivered. With one thrust I was inside her, her back arching off the bed and the rope rubbing *both* of us. I brought her leg up, slipping my hand under her thigh. As I pumped into her, my hand cupped her arse and spread her wider. My mouth pressed into her neck and sucked as my hips rocked, meeting the end of her.

Peyton moaned. Her hands ran through my blond hair, down my back and she cupped my arse, grabbing it and pressing us closer together. The moment her pussy tightened around my dick, a current ran through my veins and we both groaned our release. It was fast, wild and rough, and left us breathing hard.

We lay connected, both of us catching our breaths. "So you like the rope?" I teased.

She chuckled. "I guess I do."

My lips brushed over hers, capturing her bottom lip between my teeth. I sucked, wanting to taste her more, but I knew she needed a break. The first time with Shibari could be intense. It didn't matter if she was only in a corset design. After she reflected on what had happened, we could talk about doing more patterns, including hanging in the air like she'd witnessed tonight.

"I'll be right back. I want to show you something." She nodded and I got off the bed. After I'd cleaned up, I returned to her side and reached out my hand. "Come here."

Peyton didn't hesitate as she placed her hand in mine. I helped her to her feet, and then slowly untied the rope. Once it was off, I took her hand again and led her to the balcony. Her steps faltered before we exited the room.

"What's wrong?"

"Can anyone see us?"

I turned, placed my hands on either side of her face and held her eyes. "They can if they look up here. Don't forget people are doing their own thing."

"What if we see Randy and Lorelei? What if they see *us* naked?"

I chuckled. "You know it's bound to happen eventually, right?"

She stared at me, not speaking.

"Even if they are out there, they won't care. If we see them, we'll walk back in. Okay?"

Peyton nodded, and we finally made our way outside onto the balcony that overlooked the pool area. Of course you could see people in the pool, on lounge chairs and some in the grass as they sought pleasure from each other. After ten years, it was normal to me, but I knew Peyton was new to this lifestyle.

"Don't look down. Look in the distance."

My room had a perfect view of Los Angeles. The glittery lights sparkled in the distance, and taking the view in, one tended to forget the hustle and bustle that was happening on the streets. LA never slept.

"It's breathtaking," she whispered.

"Sometimes I would just come up here alone and stare at the lights. It was like my one day to decompress and forget everything at the office, or forget that I didn't have you in my arms."

"What?" she asked, turning her head to look up at me.

"I told you. I've fancied your arse since I first saw you in court."

"Yeah, but you can't seriously be telling me that you used to think about me like that."

"I did, but I figured I could never have you." It was always worse when I saw her in court and knew I couldn't have her.

She turned and wrapped her arms around my neck. "I never thought I'd say this, but I'm glad Ava Ashley wanted a divorce from Trent."

I chuckled. "Me too."

Peyton rested her head against my chest. There was nowhere I'd rather be, and even though I'd been working myself to the bone, my long hours at the office were about to end. I had one more month to prove I'd be the perfect partner and afterward, I was going to come home to my girl's cooking every night at a decent hour.

I never thought I would want a serious relationship, but there was something about Peyton that made me look at the world differently. She was smart, funny, sexy, a damn fine cook, and the more I got to know her, I realized she fancied some of the same fantasies as me. I could definitely spend forever like this.

"Are you scared?" I queried before I realized what I'd asked.

Peyton looked up at me. "Scared of what?"

"Falling."

She looked down toward the ground beyond the wrought iron railing. "No."

"I'm not talking about heights," I clarified. "I'm talking about us."

She blinked, realizing what I was asking. "Are you?"

I shook my head. "I was, but that was before I knew how shattered I'd be without you."

What was I saying? I'd never in my life confessed anything remotely like this to anyone. But it was true. The thought of not crawling in bed with her each night, and the thought of her not being the first person I saw each morning, terrified the shit out of me.

"It's hard to fall when you've already fallen."

I smiled and said the four words I'd never said in a romantic way before now. "I love you, beautiful."

She smiled, her eyes glassy. "I love you too, Mr. Romantic."

No more words were spoken as I pressed my lips to hers, and then carried her back to the bed. There would be another time to reflect on the Shibari scene. Now wasn't that time.

We stayed in bed until there was a knock on the door.

"We've come to that part of the meeting," Mitch stated and looked between Clint and me. "Gentlemen, this is the home stretch. You've both stepped up to the plate and are hitting everything out of the park. We're impressed." The other partners murmured their agreement. "As you know, the office is closed for the week between Christmas and New Year's. You're more than welcome to keep working and billing hours, but we won't be here." Mitch motioned to the other gentlemen. "That said, we're going to give you one more update and then it's in your hands."

All I heard was blah, blah, blah. *Fucking hell, just spit it out already!*

"Booker." My eyes shot up and met Mitch's gaze. "You're in the lead. We won't tell either of you by how much, but we're excited to see who will come out ahead."

I could feel Clint's eyes burning holes into the side of my head. I didn't look at him. I didn't even smile, though I wanted to. The better man would win, and I was certain that would be me.

Chapter 20

PEYTON

W hen you're single, you don't need to worry about what you're going to get the love of your life for Christmas. It's easy and sometimes depressing. This year I wasn't single, though I couldn't go around announcing that fact to anyone except Lorelei. And she wasn't single either. She and Randy had hit it off at Sensation, but their relationship wasn't a secret. She even made it a point to announce it one day in the break room. I, on the other hand, had to pretend that I went home every night and drowned my sorrows in a bottle of wine. That was what I used to do, especially after dealing with clients all day.

I wanted to get away. I wanted to go somewhere with Booker that wasn't in LA and go out, do normal couple stuff. I didn't want to have to worry about someone seeing us. So I started to search for places to book for Christmas in Yosemite.

Yosemite was over seven hours away from Los Angeles. I'd never had a white Christmas. To wake up on Christmas morning, my man next to me, snow falling and a fire blazing in the fireplace, sounded like heaven. Of course, I'd have to tell my parents. Christmas Eve was spent with my cousins and other family members at my parents' house. I'd stay the night, wake up the next morning and exchange gifts. Later in the day, family members would come back for Christmas dinner. We spent Christmas at my folks' because they had the biggest house. But this year I wanted to be with Booker. I couldn't bring him to my parents'. My dad would ask him what he did for a living. I knew my father would never report us to the State Bar, but since he was a retired judge, I didn't want him to know about any wrongdoing.

After I talked to Booker about going out of town for the week while our offices were closed, I'd figure out how to tell my parents.

I heard a key in the door and smiled, knowing Booker was home. Sunday I'd stopped by the hardware store and had a key made. It was time. Not only because we'd each professed our love for one another, but because—*okay, that was totally the reason.* I never thought that I'd ever fall in love with him. He was the opposing counsel I'd loathed. Now he was the sexy attorney who did things to my body that I never knew were possible. Plus, he made me feel special. From the way he held my hand, to the way he always locked my door for me when we left. I didn't need him to bring me flowers or whisk me off to Paris. I was happy with what we were building.

As I heard the door close, I stood and began to walk to the kitchen. I'd made meatloaf for dinner, trying a new recipe that I hoped went with Booker's diet. I knew he enjoyed going to the gym, and I didn't want to ruin all his hard work. *I enjoyed his hard work. Damn...*

"Gorgeous," he greeted, kissing the side of my head when he came to the kitchen.

"Hey, how was work?"

He rubbed the back of his neck and sighed. "I can't wait until this shit is over with."

I turned to the fridge and grabbed him a bottle of water, then reached in my cabinet for the vodka I'd picked up at the store for him. It wasn't *Beluga.* I'd looked for it, but quickly decided I'd rather spend twenty-five bucks on a bottle of vodka instead of ninety.

"Here, I think you need this."

He smiled. "You got me vodka?"

"Yeah, and I made you meatloaf with *Ezekiel* bread."

He took the bottle from my hand and set it on the counter with the water. "You really do love me," he said, pulling me to him. His lips pressed against mine. My arms went around his neck, and I pushed against him, his back hitting the counter. He deepened the kiss, his tongue seeking and finding mine. I had no doubt that I would spend forever in bed with him. I craved him, and all those years that I spent despising him were wasted time.

When we broke apart, I said, "I do."

"Yeah?"

"Yeah." I brushed my lips to his. "Make your drink, and I'll heat your food."

He let me go, and I turned to grab his plate from the fridge. "After I make partner and I come home around six, we'll be able to finally eat dinner together."

I smiled as I looked over my shoulder at him. "I like the sound of that." It wasn't lost on me that he called my place home.

Booker took his seat at my breakfast bar while his food was heating in the microwave. "And I won't get reheated food."

"You're lucky I'm giving you any food," I teased. I really did know how important becoming partner was to him, and if I had to cook breakfast, lunch, and dinner for him to achieve his goal, I would.

"Yeah, beautiful, I am lucky."

The microwave dinged, and I grabbed his plate. "Oh," I started, remembering something Lorelei had told me at work. "Lorelei said she referred someone to you. I guess I represented her current husband in a previous divorce of his."

"Monica said something about it. She set up the appointment," he stated around a mouthful.

"Good."

"Before you run off to bed, I wanted to tell you that I researched how to become a citizen."

"You did?" I smiled.

He swallowed. "I did, and Carrie's right, it takes six to twelve months. I'll have to study U.S. shit."

"Good luck with that. I'm not sure I could pass any test regarding U.S. History or Constitutions."

"You'll help me study, right?"

I walked around the bar and kissed his cheek. "Of course."

"Good. Go get naked. I'll be a few minutes."

I turned to walk to my bedroom, and he swatted my ass, causing me to jump in shock. "One of these days, baby."

I chuckled as I walked over to my coffee table to grab the remote and turn off the TV.

"Oh," I said, grabbing my open laptop. "How do you feel about Yosemite?"

He turned to slightly face me. "Yosemite?"

"Yeah, I thought that maybe for Christmas break we could rent a cabin or something."

I saw his chest rise as he sighed. "I've been meaning to tell you, but with everything going on, it slipped my mind."

"What?" I asked as I shut the laptop and put it back on my table.

"My mum and dad are coming for Christmas."

"From Leeds?" I asked. Of course from Leeds. That's where they live.

He nodded. "Yeah. I usually go there, but with the promotion on the line, they wanted to come here."

"Oh," I breathed, and realized that meant Booker wouldn't be at my place for however long they were in town. My eyes met his. "How long will they be here for?"

"They get in on the twentieth and leave on the twenty-eighth. I told them I have plans for New Year's, so they decided to return home before then."

"What plans?" I asked.

"The club, baby. They host a party every year. This year it's perfect since it's on a Saturday. Usually, if it falls on a different day of the week, they just switch the party to that date."

"Right. I need to join."

He smiled. "Yes, you do."

Booker stood and started toward the sink. "Go get in bed. I'm on my way."

After I'd stripped off my clothes, I climbed beneath the sheets and waited for him. When he came into the room, I asked, "So I won't see you for seven or eight days?"

"You think I'd let that happen?" he asked as he started to remove his tie.

"So you'll still come here?"

He shook his head and tossed his shirt onto the floor. "No, you'll stay with me at my place."

I blinked. "But ... Carrie."

He undid his pants and then stepped out of them. "My parents don't know I'm married."

"Are you serious?" I asked, my brows drawn in. "How?"

"I've never told them," he stated as he slid under the covers.

"How do you *not* tell your parents something like that?"

Booker hooked his arm over my belly and pulled me to him. "Because of the circumstances."

"How do they think you're able to stay in the states?"

"Work VISA."

"Oh, Lord," I muttered and looked up at the white ceiling.

"It's never been a problem because I usually go to Leeds."

"They've never been here?"

"Only when I was in college."

I thought for a few moments. "So you'll introduce me as your girlfriend?"

"Yeah." He grinned.

"And when they ask what I do for a living?"

"They won't understand or care that it's an issue."

"So I'll just go over for dinner a few times while they're here. I have Christmas at my parents' that's already planned since my Yosemite idea is now a no go."

"No, you're staying every night in my bed, gorgeous."

"I am not," I protested.

"You are."

"Booker," I scolded softly. "I can't be in your bed when your parents are under the same roof."

"I'm thirty-four years old. I'm sure they know I'm not saving myself for marriage."

"Still. It will be awkward."

"It will be fine."

"We aren't having sex," I stated.

Booker laughed hard and nuzzled his face in the crook of my neck. "We will, but just think, when we go to Sensation for New Year's Eve, you can be as loud as you want to be."

Chapter 21

BOOKER

I hadn't seen my parents in almost a year. I wanted to see them more often, but this whole partner business had been running its course my entire career. Therefore, I saw them when the office was closed for the holidays. One of these days I'd fly them out so they could experience a California summer. Dry heat that rarely got above thirty-two Celsius was the perfect weather, in my opinion, especially next to the Pacific Ocean.

As I drove up the ramp to enter LAX, Peyton was beside me, wringing her hands in her lap.

"Don't be nervous."

She looked over at me. "I've never met parents before."

"They're going to love you."

"That's what you said about Carrie."

"And I was right." I laughed. I'd finished work early, so I was able to pick them up. I planned to work from home when they were passed out from the long flight. No rest for the wicked, right?

"I guess, but I'm still nervous."

I grabbed her hand and kissed the back of it. "Tonight we'll just have dinner. Then they'll go to sleep, and you'll go to work tomorrow. Really you only have the day after Christmas to spend the entire day with them. You'll be fine." My parents were getting in on a Wednesday, and both Peyton and I had to work the rest of the week. Both of our offices were closed from Christmas Eve until the second of January.

After waiting behind cars and people who didn't know what the fuck they were doing, I pulled my Mercedes next to the curb where my mum and dad stood.

"Booker!" Mum cried and wrapped her arms around me when I stepped out of the car.

"Hey, mum. Have a good flight?" I kissed her cheek.

"It was nice. Fourteen hours is too long, though."

I smiled, and then wrapped my arms around my father. "Carrie has dinner and drinks at our place waiting for you."

"I could go for a beer right about now," Father boomed.

Both my parents looked as though they could sleep for days. Their greying hair was mussed, their blue eyes lined with dark circles. A beer, food, and bed were definitely in their future.

I smiled and looked to my side to see Peyton standing near the passenger door. "Mum. Dad. This is my girlfriend, Peyton."

"It's nice to meet you," Peyton stuck her hand out.

I smiled as my mum looked down at her outreached arm and then drew Peyton in for a hug. "You're even more beautiful than Booker described."

My grin widened, and I started to put their bags into the boot of my car while they exchanged pleasantries. "We better go before we get shouted at," I said, looking at the traffic guard as he eyed us chatting.

The three of them worked out who would sit where as I got into the driver's seat. Peyton argued that one of them should take the front, but they declined, and Peyton returned to the passenger seat. Once we were out of the airport and onto the 405, I grabbed Peyton's hand. She turned her head to me and smiled. Even though it was brief, I thought the meeting of my parents went brilliantly.

"So, Peyton," my mum said from the back seat. "Booker tells me you're an attorney too?"

Peyton turned her head to me sharply. She cleared her throat. "Yes, ma'am."

"Helen is fine, dear."

"And Piers is good for me," Dad said.

"Okay, Helen and Piers," Peyton agreed.

"Do you practice family law too?" Mum asked.

"I do."

"At the same firm as Booker?" Dad inquired.

"No, Si—No, at a different one."

I squeezed her hand. She was trying to be polite, and all I wanted to do was smother her in kisses. I knew she'd have no problem fitting in with my family, even if it had only been twenty minutes.

"Do you ever go against each other?" Mum asked.

"Sometimes," I answered.

We continued to talk about work, and I filled them in on running for partner. Once we arrived at my house, my dad and I grabbed the bags from the boot while Carrie rushed out to hug my mum.

"You look the same as you did nine years ago," Mum stated.

"I can't believe it's been nine years since I've seen you guys."

I went into the house with dad in tow. Peyton walked with the girls.

"If Booker would bring you to Europe with him, then it wouldn't have been so long," Mum bitched.

"If Carrie would pay her way, I would have," I shot back as I was down the hall near the guest bedroom.

"I'm sorry, Helen," Carrie said. "As you can imagine, work is busy early in your career. I mean, Booker works late hours just to make partner. I didn't realize how fast time has passed. I'll come to Leeds next year to visit."

I didn't hear Mum's reply as I passed Carrie's bedroom. Taylor was sitting on Carrie's bed, biting her nails. She was nervous. Carrie had never hidden her sexuality, but like Peyton, Taylor was Carrie's first serious girlfriend, and in a way, Taylor was meeting Carrie's parents.

"You did good, son," Dad said as he set his bag on the floor near the bed of the guest room.

"About what?"

"Peyton. She's stunning."

I smiled. "Thank you. She's quite lovely."

"Wedding bells in your future?" he asked, clapping me on the shoulder.

I rubbed the back of my neck. Even if I wanted to marry Peyton, there was still the issue of my marriage to Carrie. "We've only been dating a few months," I clarified.

"The night after my first date with your mother, I knew I wanted to marry her. I couldn't get her out of my head."

I smiled, knowing exactly what he meant. "Then maybe there are wedding bells in my future."

He nodded with a smile. "It's about time. Now, show me to your bar."

I chuckled, and he followed me down the hall. "Who's the woman in Carrie's room?" Dad whispered.

"I'm sure you'll meet her in a minute."

"Okay, dinner should be here in thirty minutes. Before we eat, I have someone for you to meet." Carrie left the kitchen to get Taylor.

My mum turned to me and silently questioned what the bloody hell Carrie was talking about.

I shook my head. "I met her over dinner too."

"Who?" Mum asked just as Carrie and Taylor stepped into the room.

"Helen. Piers, this is my girlfriend, Taylor."

I went to Peyton, wrapped my arm around her shoulders and pulled her to me, kissing the top of her head before I asked, "Are you doing okay?"

She smiled up at me and nodded.

"I'm not sleeping naked," Peyton said as she crawled into my bed beside me dressed in her PJs.

I was sitting up against my headboard with my laptop on my lap, finalizing a client's Declaration I was preparing. After dinner, my parents called it a night like I assumed they would. Carrie and Taylor went to her room, and Peyton and I to mine. My bed felt weird, foreign even, because I hadn't slept in it for over two months.

I looked over to Peyton. "No one will come in here."

She shrugged and lay with her head on her pillow facing me. "Still. Your parents are in the other room."

"They're sleeping."

"I just met them, so let me have this."

"You can do whatever you want, but it won't stop me if I want to fuck you, baby."

Her eyes widened. "No."

I grinned. "We'll see."

"How long do you need to work?" she asked, changing the subject.

"I'm almost done. Go to sleep."

"Do you ever think we can have a normal relationship?"

My hands stilled on the keyboard, and I looked down at her. "A normal relationship?"

She took a deep breath. "One where people will know we're dating. Where we can go out to dinner and not have to get food ordered in. Where we can go to the movies, maybe go wine tasting in Malibu, bowling, indoor rock climbing. At this point, I don't really care. We're either locked up in my condo or at Sensation once a month."

"Yes. In just a few weeks, that's all going to change."

"I know. It just seems to be taking a long time."

I'd been so focused on making partner that I never took into consideration how our relationship really was. Sure we were dating, but Peyton was right. We didn't go on dates. Even though I was new to having a serious girlfriend, I still knew that couples were supposed to go out and do shit together and not sit around watching TV on the weekends.

210

I closed my laptop and set it on my nightstand. I slid down until I was face to face with her. "Just a few more weeks," I said again.

"Okay," she whispered back as though she didn't believe me.

It was true. Once I made partner, things were going to change.

I woke before my alarm, hard. It was still dark outside, and when I looked over at my clock, I had thirty minutes before I needed to get up to head to the gym. As I listened, I was sure no one else was awake. I had two options. One was to go to the bathroom and use my hand, or the other was to wake Peyton with my mouth that would lead to another way to release.

I went with the latter.

She was laying on her back, her face turned out. If she were naked, this would have been a lot easier. Slowly I slid the sheet down her body. She didn't stir. I grinned and carefully rose to straddle her legs. Still nothing. I hooked my fingers into the elastic of Peyton's pajama bottoms and knickers, and inch by inch, I pulled them down her legs. She shifted a little, not touching me or waking up.

After tossing her clothes onto the floor, I slid down her body until my face was in the perfect position. With one hand, I spread her pussy. My mouth connected with her clit, and I licked. She stirred beneath me, still not waking, so I continued, my tongue slowly making circles on the bud. With each turn, the pressure intensified.

"Oh my God," she panted. "What—"

I reached up with my free hand and covered her mouth. I didn't want her to tell me to stop, and with my hand covering her mouth no one would hear us—hopefully. Peyton moaned, my tongue still working her. I slipped the hand that was holding open her slit and cupped her ample breast. Her back arched, and she moaned again against my hand.

"If you don't want them to hear, then you need to be quiet," I warned.

She groaned in response as I continued my torture on her pussy, giving her nipple a pinch that caused her to wither under me again.

"This is a better wake up than an alarm, yes?" I asked between sucks.

Peyton couldn't answer other than another moan.

I took my hand that was kneading her breast and inserted two fingers into her pussy. She was drenched, her arousal filling the air, and my dick was so hard that I was rubbing it against the mattress and giving myself pleasure. I wasn't going to last a week without fucking my woman. I didn't even make it a few hours.

As I pumped my fingers into her, curling them just right to hit that spot that I knew would bring Peyton to coming fast, her breathing quickened, and I knew she was on the verge of ecstasy. So I went faster and sucked harder on her clit. So hard that she bucked, trying to throw me off of her as she came, bowing into herself. Her cries were muffled by my hand, and if I wasn't buried in her in the next second, I was going to come on her stomach.

I didn't want that. So I rose, grabbed her hips and without a word turned her onto her belly. Peyton moaned again, this time into her pillow when I jerked her arse up and slid inside her warm, dripping wet pussy. God, she felt good. So fucking good that I forgot about where we were and started to pump into her—hard—the legs of the bed moving a little against the wood floor. I didn't care. I'd sand the floor and refinish it myself if that meant I could fuck Peyton as hard as I fucking wanted to.

Fuck the floors.

She was addicting—enticing—desirable and mine. All fucking mine. I fucking wanted the entire world to know. And I was going to find out a way to make that happen.

My thrusts quickened, sweat slid down my back and as Peyton moaned into the pillow again with her release, I followed, emptying inside of her.

Inside of her ...

Fuck!

I couldn't think. I didn't think. I was so caught up in the fact that I knew of a way to fuck her without anyone hearing, that I forgot to put on a condom. Now, as I pulled out of her and we were trying to catch our breaths, my cum was dripping from her pussy and onto my sheets.

Fuck!

I grabbed the shirt I was wearing the day before and used it to clean her up. I heard Peyton suck in a breath probably realizing *why* I was doing it.

"It's okay," I said. I didn't know if it was. I'd never gone without a condom, we'd never talked about birth control or STDs or anything that I assumed couples did before they fucked without protection. I was clean, and I knew she was clean because of Sensation.

"You didn't use a condom?" she asked.

Fuck!

"I ..." I started, still cleaning her up. "I forgot."

"You forgot?" she asked as she looked over her shoulder, on all fours.

"If you get pregnant, we'll figure it out." The plan was for me to get my citizenship and divorce Carrie. Having a baby might be before the divorce was finalized, but we'd make due. I loved Peyton, and I'd make it right.

"I'm not worried about becoming pregnant," she retorted, and spun around to sit on her arse.

"You're—not?"

She shook her head. "I'm on the pill, so it's not likely, but I thought you'd ask me or something before doing it."

My body relaxed some as I tossed the shirt onto the floor and lay beside her. "I'm sorry. I wasn't thinking."

"Clearly."

"But if you do get pregnant, we'll figure it out."

She nodded slowly, not saying a word. Then the alarm on her

phone started to chime. After she reached over and turned it off, she slid down and faced me. Mornings, before I went to the gym, were our time to talk, and had I fucking opened a can of worms this morning or what?

"I'm sorry," I said again.

She reached over and cupped my face with her warm, soft hand. "It's okay. We're clean, and I'm on the pill. Plus, we've been together for a few months now, and I trust you. I love you."

I smiled at the last three words. "I love you too, baby and it won't happen again."

"Well ..." she bit her lip. "It's fine. I'm sure it feels better for you."

My grin widened. "So good that I'm sure there are scratches on the wood floor."

We laughed.

This was apparently what it was like to have a relationship, and even though I fucked up, I loved the direction we were headed in.

Chapter 22

PEYTON

"Hey, Daddy," I greeted walking in through the front door of my parents' house in the Valley. My father was sitting in his reclining chair reading a book, dressed in a maroon sweater with a grey collared shirt under it that matched his hair.

"Hey, baby girl." He looked at his watch. "You're early."

I shrugged and sat on the couch next to the chair. "Can't I come over and spend time with you before it gets crazy in here?"

He set his book down and looked over at me, removing his wire-rimmed glasses. "Of course. We just weren't expecting you until this afternoon. Your mother could use the help cooking, though."

"I figured," I half lied.

That was, in fact, what I told Booker I was going to do. In reality, I didn't need to be at my folks' until four, but I wanted to get away from all the knowing looks I was receiving when I was at Booker's. I wasn't sure if I was getting bright smiles from everyone because I was Booker's first serious girlfriend, or because they heard us having sex a few mornings before. I didn't ask. And after tomorrow night, I would be spending forty-eight hours with his parents before they flew home, so I wanted to come to my parents' early for a breather.

My mother came around the corner. Her short brown hair was half up, and flour covered her fingers. "Peyton. Oh, thank God you're here."

I looked up to meet the same eyes as mine. "Everything okay?"

"Aunt Jessi is running late, and I'm behind on the pies."

I looked to my dad and gave him a small smile before I stood. "See. Something told me to come early."

"Sneak me a slice when the apple is done." He winked.

"She will do no such thing, Levi."

"I'm only joking, Martina."

Mother shook her head and rolled her dark brown eyes before walking back into the kitchen. Was this going to be me and Booker one day? He was at my place every night as though we lived together and I already cooked him dinner. Just call me Suzy *Homemaker* and shit.

"I'll bring you a sliver of a sliver when it's ready," I whispered. "I need to talk to you about something before everyone gets here anyway."

Tonight all of our family was coming: my aunts, my uncles, and my cousins. Tomorrow for Christmas would only be my parents and me until the afternoon when I went back to Booker's, but I wanted to talk to my dad today before everyone showed up so I had time to process his answer.

"Something told me something was on your mind. Is it about a case?"

I shook my head.

"Okay. Well, I'm here when you're ready."

I smiled and kissed his cheek. "Thanks, Daddy."

When I walked into the large kitchen, I stopped dead in my tracks. Every burner on the stove had either a pot or pan on it, both ovens were on in the double oven and flour covered every inch of the granite island. My mother knew how to cook. I'd learned from her, so I had no clue why the kitchen was a disaster.

"Did you forget how to cook?" I asked, looking around the room.

Mother tsked. "We have more people coming this year, and your aunt is running late as I've already told you."

"Who else is coming?"

"My friend Evelyn and her family."

"Okay," I said, even though I'd never heard of this friend. "I'm sure everything will be fine. What do you need me to do?"

"I'm working on the crusts for the pies. Cut those apples into slices." She pointed her flour covered finger at a basket full of green apples.

"All of them?" I asked, my eyes wide. There were about twenty apples in the basket.

"Yes, all of them," she hissed.

"Okay." I grabbed the first apple. Clearly my mother was frazzled from all the prep, so I kept my mouth shut and sliced all of the apples.

Four apple pies, two pumpkins, and prime rib later, the beginning of Christmas Eve dinner was in the making. I wasn't sure why my mother was making so many pies, but I wasn't going to ask her. We had enough food for an army.

My mom and aunt were making mashed potatoes, green beans, and rolls; again everything I thought we were eating the following day. Usually on Christmas Eve we had salad, confetti pasta which was a shrimp linguine pasta with peppers and onions, and for dessert we had cheesecake. My family had clearly lost their minds.

When I walked into the living room, my dad was watching college football with my uncle Archie and my cousin Brendan. I let out a sigh as I sank into the couch, my feet and back aching.

"Where's my pie?" Dad asked.

"Shit," I muttered. "I forgot. They're still in there making sure everything's warm. I guess Uncle Tommie and Aunt Torrie will be here in ten or so minutes."

"Something like that," he agreed. "Do you want to ask me what you wanted to know before they get here?"

I looked to my uncle, and he looked to my dad and then my cousin. "Brendan, let's go check on those pies."

I smiled and then replied with a nod to my father. "I do."

Dad sat straight and leaned toward me. When we were the only ones left in the room, he asked, "What is it?"

"When you were practicing, did any of the attorneys become ... um ... intimate with each other?" I felt the heat rise up my neck and into my cheeks as I murmured my question.

He balked before asking, "What?"

"I mean opposing counsels. Did anyone that you know of have a relationship with an opposing counsel?"

His peppered eyebrows drew together. "Are you asking because you're seeing someone you have a case against?"

I knew bringing up the question was going to make him ask me the one he'd asked. Since my father was a criminal defense attorney, and a criminal judge before he retired, I figured he didn't know any of the attorneys in family law, especially Booker. But I wanted to ask his professional advice.

I looked down at my lap. "Yes," I answered truthfully.

He leaned back in the chair, not saying anything.

My gaze turned to him. He was staring at me. "Are you mad?"

"No." He shook his head.

"Then why aren't you saying anything?"

He sighed. "Because this is going to piss off your mother, and I'll have to hear about it for a week straight."

"What?" I blinked. I had no idea what my father was talking about.

"Let's not get into that. You'll find out soon enough. And to answer your question, yes, I've known attorneys to have relationships with each other."

"Did they get in trouble?"

"With the bar you mean?"

"Yes," I answered. That was my only concern. If Chandler and Patterson found out and they had a problem with it, I could always find another job. It would suck, but it was possible. If the bar found out, they could suspend my license to practice and then I'd be screwed because it probably wouldn't be a short suspension.

"I don't know for certain, but I don't think they ever found out, and the relationship ended fairly quickly."

"Oh," I sighed.

"Let me ask you this, Peyton. Are you serious with this guy?"

I nodded. "I never thought I would be, but—I love him."

"How long has this been going on?"

"A few months."

"And you're just now telling me?"

I swallowed. "I would have told you sooner, but we've been keeping it a secret because we have a few cases against each other and he's on track to make partner. We don't want the wrong people to find out beforehand. Once he makes partner, he said he'd withdraw from the cases."

"When will that be?"

"In a few weeks."

"And if he doesn't make partner?"

I blinked at his question. Booker and I had never discussed if he didn't make partner. I assumed it would be the same scenario and he'd withdraw from the cases—or I would.

"I'm not sure," I answered honestly. "We haven't talked about it other than him withdrawing after he makes partner."

"Since you only have a few weeks and it seems that you're not under investigation which means no one has reported you, I think it's safe to say to just wait and see what happens with his career. But there are more steps that you need to do besides withdraw from the cases."

"What's that?" I asked.

Before he could answer his question, the doorbell chimed.

"Pey, honey. Can you get that?" my mother called from the kitchen.

"Yeah," I hollered back and stood.

"I want to meet him," Dad stated. I wasn't sure if he ignored my question because he didn't have time to tell me everything that needed to be done or what.

I turned to face him and smiled. "Okay." Then I went to open the door.

A lady I'd never seen in my life was holding a bottle of wine, and three men flanked her. One was around her age, and the other two were either mine or slightly older.

"You must be Peyton," she stated. "I'm your mother's friend from Book Club."

"Oh!" I exclaimed. "Evelyn."

"Yes." She smiled. "This is my husband, Fredrick, and my sons, Daniel and Dylan." They each stepped forward, and we shook hands one at a time.

"It's nice to meet you all." I gestured for them to come in. "My mom is in the kitchen and my dad—"

"Fred. Evey," Dad greeted and walked around me to shake Fredrick's hand and give Evelyn a hug.

"These are our boys," Evelyn announced, and my dad shook their hands.

I felt two sets of eyes on me when my dad was talking to his friends. *Awkward.*

"Give Peyton your coats and let's go in the kitchen. We're just waiting on my brother and his wife and kids."

"Great." Fredrick nodded, and the four of them began to unzip and unbutton their jackets.

One by one they handed them to me and then left me standing, jackets piled in my arms up to my head.

I'll just meet everyone in the kitchen.

The rest of the family arrived shortly after, and once everything was placed on the dining room table, the *kids* were able to plate their food before we ate at the breakfast table and kitchen island. I sat at the table with Daniel and Dylan, and my cousins Rylie and Brendan, while my cousins Emery and Brice sat at the kitchen island.

An awkward silence hung in the air as we shoveled our food in our mouths. It was totally weird, especially since we were all in our late twenties or early thirties. Somehow we'd been demoted to the kid's table, and now we all looked anywhere but at each other. None of my cousins had children of their own because we were all trying to become successful in our careers before we had families. At least that was my plan. I knew Rylie wanted to own her own clothing line before she popped out babies, and Brendan, Emery, and Brice were all becoming doctors. Brendan and Brice were residents at two different hospitals in LA, and Emery was still in med school.

I cleared my throat. "So, Daniel and Dylan, your parents brought you over and abandoned you to the kiddie table," I teased, trying to lighten the mood.

"Apparently," Daniel agreed.

"Any plans for tomorrow?" I asked.

"Football," the said in unison.

"Playing or watching?" Emery asked from the island.

"Watching," Dylan replied.

I looked to Rylie. "Let's switch with Em and Bri. Let the boys talk football."

I didn't even know there was football on Christmas. Maybe this year was different since Christmas was on a Sunday and that was usually when football was on TV. I actually didn't mind watching football or any sports for that matter, but I figured they'd have more in common with my male cousins than me and Rylie. Something felt weird about the entire situation too. Rylie nodded and told her brothers to switch with us.

"Wait," Dylan said, setting down his fork. "We came to meet you."

I blinked. "Meet me?"

He rubbed the back of his neck. "You don't know?"

"Know what?" I asked as I stood with my plate of food in my hands.

"Our parents are trying to set one of us up with you."

"What?" I turned my head in the direction of the dining room.

"I don't think she knows," Daniel stated.

I whipped my head back toward them. "You think?"

"We're sorry. We thought you knew."

"Well, I didn't."

"Did you say she gets to pick between you *two*?" Riley asked.

"We're both single, so my mom told us to come and see who had more chemistry with you. Her words, not mine," Dylan clarified. "But are *you* single?" he asked Riley.

"I am," she answered as I laughed under my breath.

This explained why my mother had made enough food to feed a platoon. And what was crazier about it all was these two guys had gone along with it. What if both liked me? Would they fight to the death for my hand in marriage? What the hell was the endgame?

"I'm flattered," I said, "but I'm actually seeing someone."

"You are?" Riley asked, her eyes wide.

I sighed. "It's new."

"I want details."

"Look, guys. I'm really sorry, but my mother has lost her mind. Rie and I will switch with Emery and Brice so you men can talk football."

And we did.

Going back to Booker's house was looking better and better. Or going to my condo was actually where I wanted to be.

With Booker.

In my bed.

Chapter 23

BOOKER

My family, including Carrie and Taylor, had turned our house into the Christmas spirit. There was a seven-foot Douglas fir in the front window that was decorated to the point you couldn't see the green of the tree. Our front yard looked as though Santa's Elves were about to set-up shop and start building toys. We hadn't decorated before my parents arrived because, well, I wasn't home and Carrie and Taylor hadn't planned on my mother bitching that the house wasn't decorated. So we decorated on Christmas Eve to appease Mum. And because I was extremely busy with work and trying to balance my relationship with Peyton, I wasn't able to get her a Christmas present—or anyone for that matter.

"Care," I said, rubbing the back of my neck as we ate dinner, "I have a little bit of a situation."

"What's that?"

I looked to each of my parents, Taylor, and then back to Carrie. "I didn't get Peyton anything for Christmas," I confessed.

My mother dropped her fork. "Booker! I taught you better than that."

"I haven't had time."

"It's six o'clock on Christmas Eve. I don't know what you can get her this late," Carrie replied. "Did you get any of us gifts?" she retorted.

I frowned. "I've been working fifteen plus hours a day. I think you can all cut me some slack."

"We don't need anything from you," Dad replied.

"Speak for yourself, Piers," Carrie snapped. "I have to live with this ass. The least he could do is get me a gift for Christmas."

"I'll give you your divorce papers if you want," I hissed before I realized what I'd said. I'd started the papers, but we couldn't file them until I was a citizen so we didn't put up any red flags.

"Divorce papers?" Mother asked.

"Aw fuck," I murmured.

Carrie smirked at me and waved her hand in front of her. "Have fun with that."

"What do you mean divorce papers?" Dad chimed in.

And there went the tension again. I sighed. "Carrie and I are married."

"What?" Mother gasped.

My father's eyes became wide. Taylor kept eating her pizza. I shook my head slowly and sighed again.

"Just tell them," Carrie prompted.

"We got married so I could stay in the states."

"I thought you were on a work VISA?" Dad asked.

I shook my head. "When I needed to get one, I wasn't working for Lee and Thompson yet. I didn't want to have to go back and forth until I got a job, so Carrie married me so I could stay here."

"Can you do that?" Mum asked.

I cracked a smile. "Well, we did."

Dad tilted his head slightly. "Wait. You've been with Lee and Thompson since—"

"Yes, we've been married for nine years or so."

"Oh dear God," Mum gasped, clenching her chest as though she was having a heart attack.

"We've been married that long, but it's not real," Carrie clarified.

"Right. We like the same thing if you know what I mean." I smirked at my father, and I knew he got my meaning.

"What about Peyton? Does she know?" Mum asked.

I nodded. "Yes."

"Is she why you're getting a divorce?" Dad asked.

I stared at them, contemplating my answer. Carrie asked for a divorce, but that was okay because it meant I could be with Peyton and think about a future with her. Everything seemed to be going to plan.

"I actually asked for the divorce," Carrie replied. "Book's able to become a citizen now—has for a while actually—and once he does that, we'll get divorced."

"I've already started the process," I clarified. "I should be a citizen within the next five and half months, and then we'll file the divorce papers which will take six months."

My parents stared off, obviously contemplating the bombshell I'd just told them. It wasn't a big deal. Yes, my mum had probably wanted to dance with me at my wedding, but it wasn't a traditional marriage. In less than a year I wouldn't be married, and everything would be as though it never happened at all. Though there was still the issue with Peyton and I being on different sides of cases.

"I can't believe you're married," Mum sighed.

"Think of it as though we're not." I took a bite of my pizza. We opted to have a low key Christmas Eve with pizza and beer, and my Mum was going to make Christmas Dinner tomorrow. "It's only so I can stay here and work."

"What do you need to do to become a citizen?" Dad asked.

I told them everything that I needed to do, and then we changed the subject completely.

"Amelia said she was going to stop by tomorrow after the kids open their presents from Santa."

My eyes shot to Carrie as she spoke. I hadn't seen Amelia in months.

"She is?"

"She heard your parents are in town, so she texted me and asked what our plans were for tomorrow."

"That's brilliant. I haven't seen her in a long time."

"Is she bringing the kids?" Mum asked.

"I think so. I think it will be all of them."

"Well, I didn't get the girls anything for Christmas either." And I still had the issue of what to get Peyton in less than twenty-four hours.

"You're a shitty uncle," Carrie snorted.

I rolled my eyes. "How about you try working until eleven at night, sometimes midnight and then tell me how much shopping you do."

"Have you ever heard of online shopping?" She returned.

"I don't know what you could get kids on short notice, but you can get Peyton an online gift card or something," Taylor stated, finally joining the conversation.

"Oh!" Carrie exclaimed. "That's a good idea."

"A gift card?" How impersonal was that?

"Then she can buy whatever she wants," Carrie stated.

"A gift card?" I asked again.

"I'll put your name on the gifts I got the kids," Carrie went on.

"Lovely. Thank you, *wife*."

She rolled her eyes.

I took a bite of pizza and, as I chewed the cheesy goodness, I realized what I could get Peyton for Christmas.

"I know what to get Peyton. I'll be back."

"What?" Carrie called out as I was out of my seat and moving.

I didn't answer as I walked down the hall to my room. Once I was in my bedroom, I grabbed my laptop, opened it and booked Peyton a weekend in Yosemite. It might not be for Christmas as she'd suggested, but spending a long weekend away with her was definitely what we needed.

And print!

"Carrie!" I called as I walked back toward the dining room carrying the paper. "Can you wrap this?"

She looked down at the paper in my hand once I was standing next to her. "What is it?"

"Peyton's gift."

She grabbed it.

"What did you buy her?" Mum asked.

"I booked us a cabin in Yosemite for President's Day weekend."

"You got her a gift she can't use until February?" Carrie asked.

I rolled my eyes. "Just wrap it for me, yes?"

"I can't wait until we're not married." She stuck out her tongue.

I glared at her. "Likewise."

My arm moved to the other side of the bed where Peyton was supposed to be, but she wasn't there. It was just a cold space. Too cold. Before Peyton, I liked to spread out in the middle of my bed, butt naked and fall fast asleep, but now I was staring up at the dark ceiling. It was almost midnight, and I had a half a mind to ask Peyton for her parents address so I could climb through the window of her room like a teenager and sleep with her. I grabbed my phone and texted her.

Me: *Are you awake?*

A few seconds later she replied.

Peyton: *Yes. It's weird being in bed without you now, let alone a bed I sleep in once a year.*

I smiled.

Me: *I feel the same way.*

Booker: *Also my mom tried to hook me up with her friend's two sons tonight. Awkward.*

I sat straight up and re-read the message before responding.

Me: *What? She tried to set you up with someone?*

Peyton: *Two guys. Her friend has two sons a year apart from each other, and she felt the need to invite them over to "meet" me.*

Fuck the texting.

Me: *Call me.*

The phone rang. "What happened?" I asked as my greeting.

I heard her chuckle. "Relax, Mr. Romantic. I obviously turned them down."

"Yeah, obviously," I groaned.

"I told my dad about you before they showed up, and before I knew what was happening. After they left, I told my mom we were dating."

"You did?" I asked as I lay back down on the bed, still staring up at the ceiling.

"Yeah. They want to meet you."

"When?"

"I don't know. As soon as possible. My mom is excited, thinking we're going to get married and pop out babies."

My eyes widened at her words. "Do you want that?"

There was a pause before she answered. "Well, eventually I want to get married and have kids. I'm not getting any younger, but we just started dating and—"

"Have the issue about our jobs," I finished for her.

"Yeah," she sighed.

"We'll figure it out." I felt as though I was a broken record, always reassuring her that everything would turn out fine. With everything I had going on, I had to think it would.

"Yeah," she said again, probably tired of me telling her the same shit.

"What time will you be here tomorrow?" I asked.

"Well, we practically had Christmas dinner tonight, so I think we're just going to do breakfast and a few gifts then I can head over."

"Good. You'll get to meet my mate Amelia and her family. She was a witness at my wedding."

"You went to law school with her?"

"We did. It was her, Carrie, Randy and me."

"Does she know you're getting a divorce?"

I shrugged in the dark room. "Not sure what Carrie has told her. I'm sure she has, though. Carrie and her mouth."

Peyton laughed, and it caused my dick to twitch. "She does have a big one."

"I had the big mouth tonight, though. She was running her mouth, and I asked if she wanted divorce papers for Christmas, right in front of my parents."

"You did?" she gasped.

"Yeah. Bloody nightmare."

"What did they say?"

"They quizzed me about it all, and I know my mum was hurt that we didn't tell them for nine years. It's just that on paper Carrie and I are married, but we aren't, you know?"

"Yeah. It will all be over soon."

"Not soon enough. Are you going to help me study for my test?"

"Of course."

"I study best with a naked bird in the room." I grinned.

Peyton laughed, and my dick jerked. "I'm sure you do, Mr. Jameson."

"Fine, how about this? For every right answer I get while we practice, you take off a piece of clothing."

"And every wrong answer?"

"I take off clothing."

"I think you'll benefit either way by doing that." I could hear the smile in her voice, and I realized I was grinning so wide that my cheeks were hurting.

"I think we'll both benefit, baby."

"You're so naughty."

"Only when I'm around you. You should see me at work. I don't take shit from anyone."

"Oh, I remember. I'm glad I'm not really against you anymore."

"I wish you were pressed against me right now," I countered.

"Yeah, stupid holidays."

"What are you wearing?"

I heard her shout in laughter. "Are you trying to have phone sex with me?"

"Yes," I deadpanned.

"Well, I'm wearing—nothing."

"Liar." I laughed.

"What are you wearing?"

"Nothing," I stated.

"Liar."

"It's the truth. You know I sleep naked."

"Are you hard?"

"Yes." I spoke the fucking truth. This woman made me hard almost twenty-four-seven it seemed.

"Touch yourself."

And then I did ...

I felt like a complete douche. I didn't get a single person a Christmas gift, and they each got me multiple things. My people were good, and I'd fucked them. Despite their protests, as soon as stores were open on the twenty-sixth, I was going shopping. Then Amelia and her family came over, and I was again the arsehole, but thanks to my wife, it appeared I'd at least gotten the children something.

"So, when do I get to meet her?" Amelia asked as she sat on our living room floor playing with the toys Carrie had bought for the kids.

"Who?" I asked even though I knew she was talking about Peyton. Amelia looked toward Carrie, and I rolled my eyes. "You really do have a big mouth," I said, looking at Carrie.

Carrie tsked. "Please. It's not a big deal. Plus, I'm a woman. That's what we do."

"She's quite lovely," Mum interjected.

"Carrie has told me the same," Amelia agreed.

I looked to Amelia's husband, Mark, silently asking for his help with these women. He shrugged and looked away. *Jerk!*

"She should be here soon," I finally said.

"And she knows we're getting divorced," Carrie mentioned.

Amelia and Mark turned to look at my parents.

"They know."

"Seems I've missed a lot these past few months." Amelia laughed.

"Yeah, mate, you have."

"Well, I can't wait to meet her."

I smiled and looked down at the kids. Three-year-old Emily was the spitting image of Amelia with dark, black hair, beautiful green eyes and a smile that lit her face. Eight-year-old Ryder looked more like his father, though he had his mother's black hair. As I stared at the children, I wondered if kids were in my future. I'd asked Peyton briefly on the phone the night before when she mentioned her mum wanted her to have children. She said she eventually did. I eventually did too, and I couldn't picture myself without Peyton, so that meant kids together. That was crazy to think about, but I wanted it with her.

Thirty minutes later, my girl arrived. "Hey," I said walking up to her silver Bimmer.

"Hey." She smiled as she stepped out, then wrapped her arms around my neck.

I pulled back and kissed her lips. "We have a full house. You good with meeting more people?"

"Yeah. I'm great with kids."

"Good to know."

We walked into the house and immediately Peyton's face lit up as she looked around the living room. "You guys have been busy since I've been gone." She looked around the living room at the twinkling lights.

"It didn't feel like Christmas without all the decorations," Mum said, standing and coming to hug Peyton.

Peyton smiled and returned the hug, looking at me as though she didn't expect it. It might be strange since they'd only been around each other for a few hours, but my mum probably understood how I felt about Peyton. I never made a big deal about Christmas presents or anything of the sorts regarding a woman before.

"You must be Peyton," Amelia said, standing in line for the hug.

My mum let go of Peyton, and then Amelia stepped in to give her a hug. "And you must be Amelia."

Amelia broke apart from Peyton but didn't let her go. As she held her hands on the side of Peyton's shoulders, she said, "Can I just say that it's nice to finally meet the one to make Booker settle down?"

"Let's not start this, *love*." I pulled Peyton to me and wrapped my arm around her shoulder.

She immediately looked forward and cooed. "And who are these cuties?"

"I'm Amelia's husband, Mark," Mark said and stuck his hand out for Peyton to shake.

Everyone looked over to where he was sitting off to the side.

"Don't think she's talking about you, mate." I laughed.

Peyton chortled. "I wasn't, but it's nice to meet you as well." They shook hands.

"This is my daughter, Emily and my son, Ryder," Amelia introduced.

The kids looked up from their toys and Peyton bent to their level. "Hi, guys. I'm Peyton. Can I play with you?"

Both kids glanced at Amelia and then back to Peyton. Without a word, they both smiled and nodded.

"Great. What are we playing?" Peyton asked.

"Transformers," Ryder replied.

I sat on the couch next to my dad as I stared at Peyton. Yeah, I could totally see this woman with our kids.

"Transformers, huh? That's so cool. Which one's your favorite?"

Ryder grinned and picked up the red and blue truck. "Optimus Prime!"

Peyton smiled. "He's cool. Want to know my favorite?"

Ryder nodded. "Yeah!"

Peyton reached over and grabbed the yellow Autobot that wasn't in car form. "Bumblebee."

"I like him too."

"I like him because he turns into a cool car and plays music."

Ryder grabbed the action figure from Peyton and started to make it into a car. Peyton turned to Emily. "And what are you playing with, Emily?"

The three-year-old that not only would have a big brother to protect her, but an uncle too, smiled. "Barbie."

"Barbie?" Peyton gushed. "Did she come with Ken, too?"

Amelia, Carrie, and Taylor all snorted. All eyes in the room looked between the three as Emily replied that Ken was at home. Then Peyton started laughing.

"What?" I asked.

"Nothing," Carrie replied.

"Why was that funny?" Mum asked.

"It's a joke," Amelia shared. "Ken doesn't have the parts to make Barbie ... you know."

"I didn't even mean it like that," Peyton said, still laughing.

I shook my head. Yes, Peyton was going to fit right in.

Chapter 24

PEYTON

A fter I had played with Amelia and Mark's children for a few minutes, Booker handed me an envelope. "What's this?"

"It is Christmas," he stated.

I looked around the room. Was I supposed to get everyone a gift? Was this a thing and I had no idea? I wasn't expecting to exchange gifts with Booker in front of everyone.

"I ... I left yours at home."

He smiled. "I don't need anything. Just open it."

This might be true. Though, I knew he'd be excited about what I'd gotten him. Coincidentally it could fit in an envelope too.

The room fell silent except for the children playing with their toys.

I flipped the envelope over to open it and Booker spoke. "I'd asked Carrie to wrap it, and she put it in the envelope."

"It's fine, Booker," Carrie groaned.

I shrugged. "Whatever it is, I'm sure I'll love it."

I broke the seal and then pulled out the white folded paper. It was a printout of a cabin. I immediately sucked in a breath then gushed. "We're going to Yosemite?"

"In a few months," Booker clarified.

"When?" I asked for more of a clarification. There was no info on the paper except for a picture of a snow-covered log cabin.

"President's Day weekend when we have three days off."

I looked over at him. That was after he'd make partner and we would be out in the open. "I get you all to myself for three days?"

He smiled. "Yeah, gorgeous. I won't even bring my laptop."

I stood and rushed to where he was sitting on the couch to hug him. "I can't wait ..."

Booker turned his head and whispered into my ear, "And no one will be around to hear you when you come."

Or at least it wouldn't be Booker's parents and I wouldn't care.

Tonight was New Year's Eve.

For the past several days, I'd been spending time with Booker and his family. I never thought the cocky attorney I used to hate seeing in court would have a playful side. Sure we *played* in bed, but watching him with the children made my heart and stomach do things that I was sure shouldn't be happening so soon in a relationship.

I'd definitely fallen in love with the most unexpected person at the most unexpected time.

Unlike the last time we attended Sensation, Booker got dressed at my condo. The gang was picking us up in a limo, and we were all riding together like the first time Lorelei went to Sensation. This time she wouldn't be a *virgin*. Randy and Lorelei were hitting it off. So much so that I hadn't seen much of Lore in the week off. Usually over the winter break we'd go shopping for after Christmas sales or whatever, but not this year. She was with Randy, and I was with Booker and his family. They did stop by before Helen and Piers left to go back to Leeds. It was only for an hour or so, and not long enough for Lorelei to gush about her relationship with Randy.

I knew it would happen once Lorelei went to Sensation, and sure enough she was also thinking about joining the club, which I officially did before Christmas. It was my gift to Booker and was going to cost me two thousand dollars a month. It was a big price to pay for entertainment, but totally worth it. It might be weird to gift something to him that was essentially for me, but Sensation was a part of him. It was something he enjoyed, and I enjoyed it too. It was a place to leave my inhibitions at the door and be the person I truly wanted to be.

I wasn't the attorney who needed to be on her game.

I wasn't the best friend who laughed while talking about sex.

I wasn't the girlfriend who cooked her boyfriend dinner every night.

I was confident, sexy, and I finally had no embarrassments when it came to anything I did or saw the moment I walked through the black velvet drapes.

Booker, of course, was still a Diamond member, but I opted for Pearl. Since I was with him, I could do it all and didn't need to purchase anything more.

"Is tonight special?" I asked, walking into the bedroom to find my heels.

"The only difference is a champagne toast at midnight," Booker replied, fixing his bow tie in the floor length mirror.

"Oh."

"But not with champagne flutes."

"What?" I turned to look at him through the reflection.

"Well," he grinned, "they have flutes, but people tend to use each other's bodies to drink it."

"Really?"

"It tastes better that way." He winked.

"You're so full of shit." I laughed.

"Try it tonight. I bet you'll taste the difference."

"Anything off your abs would be delicious," I countered.

"That can be arranged for every meal."

I threw my head back and laughed. "You're too much."

"But you love me."

I walked up behind him and wrapped my arms around his waist. "I do."

"Good. Randy texted they were almost here, and all the members tend to come on New Year's Eve, so I don't want to wait in the queue all night."

As we walked into the mansion, first thing was first; we had to get a drink. Even though I was being carefree, I still needed a little liquid courage. Booker ordered me a vodka cranberry with the *good* stuff and a vodka and water for himself. After we had our drinks, we walked through the house, people watching. I had no idea where our friends ran off to. Nor did I care. Lorelei told me about her and Randy doing it against the wall in a part of the mansion, and that was enough of a visual.

As we strolled, my gaze landed on none other than Jason Black. I hadn't seen him for a long time. After the last incident, I had no desire to ever speak to him again. It was sad to realize that your celebrity crush was a date-rape-drug-slipping-asshole, and it still baffled me to think that was how he got laid. If he had his kink of wanting to double penetrate a woman, then there was a better way of going about it. A hooker might be cheaper than Sensation.

Booker and I walked toward the window by the pool. "I bet the pool is nice in the summer," I stated, looking at the illuminated water.

"It's nice year round."

"Really? Isn't it cold?"

"It's heated," he confirmed, taking a sip of his drink.

"Aren't you cold when you get out?"

"Only briefly. They have warm towels, and there are heat lamps by the loungers."

"Fancy."

"Want to go out there?"

"Sure."

As soon as we stepped through the French door, a chill washed over me. It may be So Cal and not somewhere that snows for the entire winter, but it was still cold to me, especially in a dress.

"Want to get in?" Booker asked.

I looked up at him and then back to the pool. People were in there doing *stuff*. "I'm good for now."

Booker stepped closer to me. "You know I'm going to break you, and you'll enjoy receiving pleasure in front of people one day." It wasn't a question.

Would I? Sure everyone around me didn't care, and I thought I'd left my inhibitions at the door, but when it came down to it, could I not care if people watched? When we were watching the Shibari show, the room was almost dark, and I felt as though people couldn't see me. But now, even though it was dark outside, there were lights.

"Come on," he said and grabbed my hand, leading me to a lounge chair.

Most of the white chairs around the pool had blankets on them and a standard heat lamp behind them. We took a seat, and Booker set my drink on the small round table next to his chair.

"I think we should start off small."

My gaze turned to him. "What do you mean?"

"We should make out." He grinned.

Kissing in public wasn't a big deal. "You want to make out with me?" I teased.

"I want to do more than make out with you."

"Tell me."

"I want to kiss your neck while my hand runs up your bare leg." His hand turned to velvet as it glided over my skin.

"Uh-huh," I said, tilting my neck to the side to give him better access.

"While I taste your skin, my hand will move up and slip under your black dress to discover—" he pulled his head back and grinned, "you're not wearing any knickers."

I swallowed, his finger grazing my center.

"Then I'll get you dripping by rubbing your clit. You'll spread your legs, and if the people in the pool look over, they'll have a view of your pussy."

My eyes snapped to the people in the pool while my legs betrayed me and spread for Booker.

"I'll inch your dress up with my free hand. Once your warm pussy feels the cold breeze, I'll slip two fingers inside you, making you moan."

And I did.

"Then, as my thumb rubs your clit and my fingers thrust inside you, I'll make out with you until you're on the verge of coming."

And he did.

His tongue worked in sync with his thumb, causing me to pant. It felt good. So fucking good as the breeze blew across my bare skin, cooling my arousal and sending a shiver racing up my spine. Just as I was about to fall apart from his touch, Booker stopped. My eyes fluttered open.

"Booker—"

He moved onto my chair, took my legs and hooked them over his shoulder as he descended his face between my thighs. I wondered if the people in the pool were watching—getting off to Booker pleasuring me with his mouth, but I didn't open my eyes to see. Instead, I relinquished the feeling of his tongue licking and sucking.

I began to moan, unable to control myself. His tongue really was wicked. And then he did something he'd never done before. He bit my clit. It wasn't hard. It wasn't soft. It was just right, and made me suck in a deep breath and groan my release.

My pussy pulsed from the orgasm as I watched Booker move back to his chair. Then I looked to the pool, and only a few people were watching. I thought I'd feel embarrassed, but I felt—*sexy.*

"That wasn't so bad was it, baby?"

I looked back into his baby blues and grinned. "No."

"Next time, we'll get you completely naked."

My eyes widened, and he winked.

We decided to get another drink before heading up to Booker's room. As we stood at the Diamond member's bar, Jason walked up. He didn't look at us, didn't say one single word. Instead, he ordered two drinks.

Booker looked down at me as we waited for our own and I gave a tight smile. "Are you happy about your decision?"

I didn't need to know what he was referring to. "That's debatable," I teased.

He grinned, knowing I was only messing with him. Instead of responding, he grabbed my face and planted a firm, hard kiss on my lips. I melted into him, moaning as our tongues danced together. When we pulled apart, I grinned up at him.

"That's one way to persuade me."

We both laughed. The bartender placed our drinks in front of us, and Booker thanked him. Just as we were about to turn to walk away, we stopped, letting Jason go in front of us. From the sliver of view, I saw Jason drop something in the cola colored drink. Without thinking, I moved and grabbed his arm, making him spin around.

"Putting Rohypnol in someone's drink again?"

He snorted. "Shut the fuck up, bitch."

Booker stepped up and got in Jason's face. "Watch your fucking mouth."

"Tell her to mind her own fucking business then."

"Do you know what I do for a living?" Booker asked him, inches from Jason's face.

Jason blinked at Booker's question. "Divorces."

"Right, but I also know a lot of celebrities who have ties with *Star Nation*, and once they find out about your habit, you'll be up shit creek, mate."

Star Nation was the hottest celebrity news television show. If you wanted to know what happened day to day in the life of your favorite celebrities, you'd watched the show.

"If you tell, then you break your confidentiality agreement with Sensation," Jason spat back.

"You're already breaking it."

"What's going on?" I watched as Gwen Walters walked up to us. She was an up and coming actress. I couldn't say that I'd seen anything she starred in, but I knew who she was.

"Nothing. Let's go," Jason responded.

"Did you ask him to get you a drink?" I asked Gwen.

"Yeah, why?"

"He has a habit of slipping something in them. Be careful," I answered. "He tried to do it to me not too long ago."

Her green eyes flashed with confusion, and then she turned to Jason. "Is this true?"

"Of course not," he lied.

"I'm not lying to you," I pleaded and reached out to touch her arm.

Gwen looked to Jason and then back to me and then back to him. "Get me another drink."

"Nothing's wrong with this one."

He went to hand her the beverage, but Booker grabbed it.

"Like I suggested last time, why don't you take a sip first?"

I didn't notice that a crowd had formed around us, but then I noticed *him*. Savior was walking toward us, the unmistakable one in a mask, but Jason didn't see because his back was facing that direction.

"I'm not taking a sip, asshole. This is Gwen's drink."

Before Booker could respond, Savior did. "Do we have a problem?"

His voice was like thick caramel: rich, smooth and luxurious. No wonder he was Mr. Sex.

Booker looked at Jason and spoke to Savior. "Since you ask. I think it's pertinent to know what Mr. Black has been doing." Jason's eyes widened as Booker continued. "He fancies slipping roofies in women's drinks."

"Is this true?" Savior asked.

"No," Jason lied again.

"I saw it with my own eyes, Savior," Booker agreed. "And Peyton just saw him do it again with Gwen's cocktail."

Savior snatched the drink from Jason's hands. "I'll have my lab test this. After the results, I'll make a decision regarding your membership. For now, it's best you leave."

"Savior!" Jason protested.

"Get out, or I'll call Luke to throw you out."

Jason glared at Booker then looked at me. I glared right back.

"You heard him, mate," Booker snapped.

Jason turned, not saying another word.

"Thank you," Gwen said to me.

I smiled warmly. "Girls need to watch out for each other."

"Never thought it could happen at a private club." She sighed.

"It's against all the rules," Savior responded. "I'll comp your membership for a month, the three of you."

"That's not necessary," I responded.

"It's my pleasure, and please, let me know if you ever need anything. You have a great guy here." He slapped Booker on the shoulder. "I've watched him turn into a man, and I have to say that love looks good on him."

A lump formed in my throat. Booker *was* a great guy.

The best.

Chapter 25

BOOKER

I woke up before my alarm. Today was the day I'd find out if I made partner. I'd never worked so hard for something in my entire life, and my nerves were getting the best of me. While at the gym, I caught myself staring off into space instead of lifting. I also ran for ten minutes longer than I normally did on the treadmill, which caused me to run late. Luckily I'd remembered my suit for work, though I had replenished my back up one in my locker.

"Would you like a cup of tea?" Monica asked as I walked past her desk.

"I need coffee this morning."

She blinked. "Okay."

"One *Stevia* and a splash of cream, please," I added as I walked into my office.

After hanging my jacket on the coatrack, I pulled my mobile from my trousers and saw that I had a text from Peyton.

Peyton: *Good luck today, baby. I know you're going to be the best partner L&T has. I love you.*

I smiled as I read her text and replied back.

Me: *Thanks, gorgeous. I love you too.*

As I set the mobile on my desk, another text chimed.

Peyton: *Call me when you know.*

Me: *I will.*

"Today's the day."

I looked up from my mobile to see Randy walking in my door. Behind him was Monica with my coffee.

"Thank you," I said to Monica as I took my coffee from her.

Randy sat in the chair in front of my desk, and I took my seat then took a sip of the java. "So, you buying lunch to celebrate when you make partner?"

"Shouldn't you buy me lunch?" I countered.

"You'll get a pay raise. Only fair you buy."

"I don't think it works that way." I smiled.

Even though Randy and I had been at L&T for almost the same amount of time, he wasn't set on making partner. He had no desire to become one. He was happy with the cases he was pulling in and going home at five-thirty every night. Especially now that he and Lorelei were seeing each other.

"Fine, I'll buy you lunch."

I smiled. "That's how it should be."

"Well, meeting should start soon. Are you ready?"

I lifted my coffee cup and quickly drank the lukewarm liquid. "Yeah, let's go."

People clapped me on the back as we made our way to the conference room. When I saw Clint, I glared, not saying a word. He didn't either. I didn't understand how he felt he'd make partner over me. I'd worked until my eyes felt as though they were bleeding while he went home to play house.

We all gathered around the wood table, and when Mitch came in, he started the meeting. "I hope everyone had a nice Christmas and enjoyed your week off."

No week off for me, Mitchy.

After he went over cases and what the plan was for January, he said, "Our ladies in billing came in early this morning to run the numbers for Booker and Clint. They knew we'd want to announce who made partner during this meeting, so the person I'm about to announce should really give Nicole and Bridgette something special. Plus, as you know, they cut the paychecks."

Laughter filled the room as my leg bounced up and down.

Hurry the fuck up, Mitch!

"So, I looked over the numbers before coming in here, and it appears that this past week sealed the deal for one of you. I'm proud to welcome Booker as partner."

I smiled, cheers erupted, and Randy pulled me from my seat and gave me the tightest hug I'd ever received in my entire life. *I did it. I fucking did it!* Hugs, handshakes and slaps on the back commenced until it was Clint and I face to face.

"You worked over Christmas break?" he asked.

I nodded. "I did. I had to make partner," I clipped.

He sighed with a slight nod. "I thought you'd take it off with your parents in town and all."

How'd he know my parents were in town?

"They understood," I clarified.

"Hey, I have a conference call with a client. I'll meet you at noon at your office for lunch," Randy said, patting me on the back as he walked passed Clint and I. Once he was out of the door, Clint and I were alone. I hadn't realized everyone had left, but here we were.

"It's funny." Clint crossed his arms. "I expected you to enjoy the holidays with your folks and your *girlfriend*."

My body went ridged. "Girlfriend?"

He looked toward the open door and then back to me as he took a step closer and whispered, "Yeah, Peyton Winters."

What. The. Bloody. Fuck?

"Peyton? I'm not dating Peyton Winters."

"Oh, so you're just fucking her?"

I officially wanted to throttle this wanker, throw him against the wall and beat the shit out of him. But then it would prove he was right. The weird thing was how did he know? The only time Peyton and I were out in public together was when we went to Sensation. Every night I went over to her apartment at the wee hours of the morning or late at night like some love struck teenage boy looking to get laid. Of course that wasn't true, but we were careful.

I thought.

"I don't know what you think you know, mate, but you have it all wrong." I crossed my arms and spread my legs a little to stand my ground.

He grinned. "You see, that's what I thought. I knew I lived in the same building as that hottie, and when I saw you the first time, it didn't even register that she was the one you were going to see."

"You don't know what you're talking about," I clipped.

He continued. "But then I saw you again and again and again. You see, I take my dog for a walk before bed, and sometimes I'd see you pull into the garage and then I'd put two and two together."

"I was visiting my mate."

"Peyton?"

"No, my mate, Sam." I thought of that guy quickly as my cover. Thankfully I "knew" someone else in that bloody building.

Clint threw his head back and laughed. "Right. So you're telling me that you go to a guy's house that late at night?"

I glared daggers at him and thought more of a cover. "Do you know Sam? Do you know what goes on behind his closed door?"

"Enlighten me."

I chuckled and leaned back to sit on the edge of the table, my hands beside me as they curved around the edge. "Walk by his apartment at night. I'm sure you're bound to hear the women screaming."

I knew I could.

"So you go over there to have orgies?"

I laughed again and stood, clapping him on the shoulder. "I'm not the one married. What I do in my free time is my business." I didn't care if he thought I was having orgies. I was protecting my girl. He didn't need to involve her in anything because he was upset he didn't make partner. I went to move passed him to walk back to my office, but his words stopped me in my tracks.

"So when I saw you getting into a limo last month with Peyton, Randy, and some other woman, it was only a coincidence?"

I whirled on him and hissed, "Why do you care?"

"I don't," he retorted. "But the California State Bar will."

Everything Peyton had feared was starting to come to a head, and it was because of me.

I was the selfish one who wanted a relationship with her.

I was the one who convinced her that no one would find out about us.

I was the one who thought no one would care.

And I was the one who was following my dreams and jeopardizing hers in the process.

"So you're going to report me for something you aren't one-hundred percent sure about all because you didn't make partner and I did?"

It didn't matter if he tried to report us. I was going to withdraw from the cases before he could file his paperwork.

"I worked hard to get the promotion—"

"I worked harder," I returned.

He continued as though I didn't speak. "And I have a family to take care of. It's not my fault you're breaking the rule of professional conduct."

"Like I said, you know nothing. You're only speculating. If you think you saw me with her, it wouldn't be in a romantic sense. I do have cases against her." I was running out of lies to tell him and ways to deflect him. He clearly had it out for me, and wouldn't stop unless I gave in and told him he was right. Then he'd walk back to his office and file the complaint.

He chuckled and before he could respond, I did. "I don't know what you think you saw, but if you want to file a complaint against me, then go ahead. I have nothing to hide because I'm not dating her." I practically lived with her was the truth.

"I already filed a complaint against both of you."

Fuck ...

If I asked him when, he'd know that he was right. I thought we could get ahead of this, but maybe we couldn't. If we withdrew from the cases, I wasn't sure if that would be enough to ward off an investigation.

"Whatever, mate. I made partner fair and square. I'll tell the bar exactly your motives, then I'll tell Mitch and the other partners, and you'll be without a job."

"And so will you."

I was done.

As I walked toward the door, I said, "If you want to start this fight, go ahead, but remember your family. If you try to take me down for something I'm not doing, then my wrath will be a million times worse." I said those words in hopes he'd tell the bar he got it wrong about my relationship with Peyton. It was a lost cause though because he was out for blood.

As I walked back to my office, everyone that I saw stopped me to congratulate me. I had to put on a smile and thank them, when in reality I wanted to jump from the window. No, I wanted to push Clint out the window. *Fucking arsehole.*

When I finally made it to my office, I closed the door behind me, needing a break from everyone. I should have been over the moon jumping with joy. I pulled up my calendar on the computer and confirmed I didn't have anything scheduled. I didn't care that it was the second day of the year, or that most people were now back in the office after being off a week. I worked, and therefore, I decided to take the rest of the day off.

I needed to leave.

I needed Peyton.

I wanted to pick up the phone and call her to tell her my good news and to also see if she could take the day off. But I didn't know if Clint had ears on me or what, so I decided to text her.

Me: *Hey, can you meet me at my place?*

A few seconds later she texted back.

Peyton: *Your place?*

Me: *I need to see you.*

Peyton: *Did you make partner?*

Me: Just meet me at my place, okay?

Peyton: *Now?*

Me: *Can you?*

I stared out my window at the sunny view as I waited for her to respond. A minute later she texted back.

Peyton: *Yeah. I'm clear the entire afternoon.*

Me: *Me too. Take it off. I need you.*

Peyton: *You're scaring me.*

Me: *I'll explain when I see you.*

Peyton: *Okay, see you in thirty.*

I grabbed my jacket and headed to leave. "Monica, I'm taking the rest of the day off."

"To celebrate?" She smiled.

I gave a tight smile back. "Yeah."

"Congrats. You deserve it."

"Thank you."

On the way to the lift, I texted Randy.

Me: *Raincheck on lunch. Clint knows about Manning.*

When I got out of the lift, I noticed Randy had texted back.

Randy: *How?*

Me: *I don't know. Keep an eye on him. He's threatening me, saying he filed a complaint with the bar.*

Randy: *Fuck!*

My thoughts exactly.

Me: *I'm going home to tell her.*

Randy: *Good luck!*

I wasn't sure luck was going to help me.

Chapter 26

PEYTON

Booker asking for me to meet him at his house was odd because my place was closer to both of our offices. The only thing I could think of was that he didn't make partner and he went home because he was upset. But why his house? He had a key to mine, and that was where we spent every night.

I pulled up in front of his house, and before I could make it to the front door, he opened it, clearly waiting for me. I took in his face, searching for any sign that it was good or bad news. He looked—worried. He was in his work slacks, and the crisp white dress shirt he wore with his suit was unbuttoned and hanging open, showing his undershirt. This wasn't like the man I knew. He was always presentable, even late at night after working all day. The only time I saw him without a tie was on the weekends.

"What's wrong?" I asked, not wanting to jump to any conclusions that he didn't make partner.

"Just come inside." He gestured for me to walk inside. Yes, he was clearly upset.

No hug.

No kiss.

No hello.

He shut the door and turned, running his hands down his face as he sighed.

"Did you ... Did you not make partner?" I couldn't take the suspense.

"I made partner," he answered without a smile, without emotion.

I blinked. "You're upset—"

"Not about that."

"What about then?" I asked, taking a step closer to him only for him to take a step back. I stopped, my heart stopped, and so did the world.

"You might want to sit down." He motioned with his head for me to sit on the couch. I didn't.

"Why? Just tell me what's going on. You made partner, and now you're acting like I repulse you."

He shook his head slightly. "You don't repulse me."

"Then why won't you touch me? Why haven't you kissed me?" I inquired.

"I want to do nothing but that, gorgeous."

"Then do it!" I cried.

"I can't."

"Why?" My chest rose up and down as I waited for his answer. I was freaking out. This was nothing like him.

"Because I was wrong."

"Wrong about what?"

"Us." He sighed.

My world started to spin again, spinning so fast that I felt as though I would fall.

"You're breaking up with me?"

"I don't know." He ran his hand along the back of his neck.

"You don't know? What does that even mean? How can things be good this morning, and you make partner, but now you don't want to be with me? Was I just there to satisfy you? To help you relieve the stress from working crazy hours, and now that you've made partner you don't need me?"

"No, it's not like that." He took a step toward me, but it was my turn to retreat.

"Just tell me what the fuck is going on. If you want to break up with me, I'll leave and never look back."

"I don't want to break up with you, but you will want to break up with me when I tell you—"

"You cheated on me?" I asked, cutting him off.

"No! God no!"

My head seemed to become lighter as though I was going to pass out and tears pricked my eyes. "I don't understand."

"Please, baby. Sit down."

"Touch me," I retorted, needing him to show me he still wanted me.

He did. He rushed to me, cupped my face and pressed his lips to mine. I melted against him, and as our mouths worked together, I realized he was slightly carrying me to the couch. He pressed his body to mine, and I fell onto the soft surface, him on top of me. It didn't feel like a goodbye kiss, though at this point I wasn't sure.

"Baby, I never want to stop touching you or kissing you or loving you. But something happened about an hour ago that—"

"Just tell me," I said as he looked down into my eyes.

He sighed. "Clint knows about us."

"What? How?"

"He said he lives in your building."

My heart stopped again. "He does? I've never seen him, and when he asked me to get drinks with him, he's didn't mentioned it. Plus, he has a wife and a baby, but I did always get the vibe he had a thing for me."

"Right." Booker sat up, and so did I.

"He's a jerk who's made advances toward me when we've seen each other in court."

"Like that day in the stairwell?"

I shuddered. "Yeah. He wasn't taking no for an answer, but luckily you walked up the stairs and I could make my getaway."

"I'll kill him."

I smiled softly for the first time since arriving. "Nothing will ever happen with that guy."

"He clearly has it out for me, and now that I'm with you, he won't stop. I'm sure of that."

"He's married and has a baby," I said again as though that would stop a sleazeball.

"Obviously that didn't stop him from hitting on you."

"True," I agreed. "So what do we do?"

Booker's piercing blue eyes turned to me. "I don't know. He said he already reported us to the bar."

I sucked in a breath. This wasn't the plan. The plan was for Booker to make partner, withdraw from the cases, and then we'd live happily ever after. Now that the bar might already know we're an item, they still might suspend us or even take our licenses away.

I thought for a moment, trying to think of what to do. "I talked to my dad about us when I told him we were dating. He was a lawyer for twenty plus years, and a judge for ten or so beyond that. He said we should be okay if one of us withdraws."

"That's all he said?"

"Well, we got interrupted, but yeah."

"I don't think it's that simple."

"I'll talk to him again. I'll go over there right now. *We* could go over there right now," I suggested.

"You want to do this. Want to risk your career if the bar investigates us?"

"You don't?" I asked, fearing his answer.

"Of course I do. I've wanted to be with you for five years. If we have to start our own firm, then I'll do that."

I smiled again. "And I never knew I wanted you, but now that I have you, my heart doesn't want to let you go."

"Then let's go figure out how to fix this mess."

We stood, and I wrapped my arms around his waist, leaning my head on his chest. "I'm so proud of you for making partner, though."

He kissed the top of my head. "Hopefully we can celebrate tonight."

"We'll definitely celebrate." I winked up at him.

After I had called my dad to make sure he was home, Booker drove us to my parents' house. I hadn't brought a guy home since my senior prom. And that wasn't even me bringing a guy home. Jonathan was just the kid who asked me to be his date, and because I wanted to go to prom, I said yes. After high school, I went to college and then law school. I didn't have time for boys. Sure I dated, but nothing was serious enough to warrant bringing someone home to meet my parents.

Until now.

"Nervous?" I asked as we pulled up to the two-story house.

"Should I be?"

I shrugged. "You're the first guy I've dated who will have met them."

"Really?" Booker grinned.

"No one was worthy enough."

He leaned across the center console. "I'm honored, gorgeous." Then he kissed me. He kissed me in front of my parents' house with them home and probably my dad watching from the front bay window. It was definitely something I'd wanted to do since high school but never got the chance.

We walked up the front walk and straight into the house. Dad was sitting in his favorite recliner, and when he saw us, he stood.

"Judge Winters," Booker greeted, sticking out his hand.

"That ship has sailed, son. Levi is perfectly fine, Booker." My two guys shook hands. "You two want to go in the kitchen? Your mother can make us some coffee or tea."

"Where is she?" I asked as we started walking toward the kitchen.

"Upstairs primping or something."

I rolled my eyes. I was positive my mother had been waiting for this day since I was eighteen. The guys sat at the breakfast table that had a view of the backyard while I started making coffee and tea. No telling how long Mother would be.

"Thank you for talking with us," Booker said.

"I'd do anything for my daughter," Dad replied, and I smiled.

"I would too. That's why we need a solution."

I turned my head and smiled warmly at Booker.

"What's going on?" Dad inquired. When I called to see if he was home, I didn't give him any details. I'd only told him that we needed to talk to him.

"A bloke at my firm says he reported us to the bar for dating," Booker responded. "And we don't know what to do."

"I see," Dad responded. "Well, there are two options. You either stop dating, and then when they investigate you, you have nothing to hide. Or one of you withdraws from the current cases you have against each other and inform the judge with a letter of your relation-ship. Whoever withdraws can just have another attorney at their firm take the case, but promise to never discuss the case again, especially with each other. You'd also need to tell your employers."

Booker turned to me then back to my dad. "It's as easy as that?"

Dad nodded. "It is. The question is which one of you are going to withdraw from the case?"

My eyes connected with Booker's. "I should be the one like we talked about," he stated. "If it wasn't for me making partner, I don't think this would be happening."

"But you need the clients for billable hours, or they'll ask you to leave and give you a severance package. Then I'll be the bread winner," I teased, trying to lighten the mood. When you became a partner at a firm, they couldn't fire you per se. They could, however, ask that you leave, and you'd be given a severance package.

"I'll make it work," Booker stated.

"My suggestion," Dad cut in. "Just tell them that you started dating over the Christmas break. They won't have proof otherwise except for that man at your work, Booker. And even then, if you with-draw and do all the formalities, you should be in the clear because they won't have a reason to investigate you."

Booker nodded. "Thank you. I will."

Mother decided it was then that she should make her appearance. "Peyton," she greeted warmly. "Are you going to introduce me?"

I turned to face her. "Hey, Mom. This is Booker. Booker this is my mother, Martina."

Booker stood and stuck out his hand. "It's nice to meet you."

"Likewise," Mother said.

"And, if I might add," Booker said, and my eyes shot to him. "There's no need to set Peyton up with anyone ever again. I'm not going anywhere."

I smiled as my heart squeezed in my chest.

"Duly noted. Now, Peyton, be a dear and get me a cup of coffee too." She walked over to the table. "With half and half."

"And the name?" I joked, pretending I worked at a coffee shop and was a barista. Somehow I'd turned into one the moment I walked into the kitchen.

"We have celebrating to do," Booker said as we pulled away from my parents' house.

"What do you want to do, big shot partner?"

He smiled and squeezed the hand he was holding. "I want to take my girlfriend to dinner."

My eyes widened. "Really?"

"Really. We have a solution, and there's no need to hide anymore. I'll withdraw in the morning."

"Okay." I smiled. "Where do you want to go?"

"I'm happy going wherever as long as you're with me."

After the afternoon's events, it was clear that Booker and I were stronger together than alone. Clint might be hurt that he didn't make partner, but my man deserved it.

We deserved to be happy.

Chapter 27

BOOKER

My first full day as partner was going to be brilliant.

First thing first was telling Mitch about Peyton and me. I knocked on his door, and after he told me to enter, I did. "Got a second?" I asked.

"Everything all right?" he asked, setting his pen down.

"I think so. I *hope* so," I responded, closing the door. I sat in the chair before his desk.

"What's on your mind?"

I took a deep breath, crossing my leg over my knee. "After you made me partner yesterday, Clint threatened me."

"He what?" Mitch snapped.

"Not physically, though I was tempted to make it physical."

"What did he say?"

"I'm no snitch, and I wouldn't tell you if I didn't have to because it's not something you need to get involved in."

"Spit it out, Booker."

"Right, so I've started dating Peyton Winters."

"From Chandler and Patterson?"

I nodded. "Yeah."

"Okay. And how is Clint involved?"

"He's bitter he didn't make partner and wants to get me fired. He said he reported us to the bar."

Mitch closed his eyes briefly as though he was trying to process the drama.

"But you said you just started dating her. How recent is this, and when did he report you?"

"We started dating over Christmas break. He said he saw me at her place cause he lives in the same building." I was only half lying to my boss. "But I've decided to withdraw from the cases I have against her, give them to Randy, and also tell the judges on the cases. Then, if the bar investigates us, there's nothing to investigate."

"By doing this, you know you can't *ever* speak of *any* of the cases we have against her or her firm?"

I nodded. "I do, and it won't be a problem."

"Well, we can't tell you who you can and can't date, and I trust you'll do the right thing. You've been with this firm far too long to jeopardize your career over some woman."

I bit my tongue. Peyton wasn't some woman. I loved her. I wanted to tell Mitch that, but since I was pretending we just started dating like a week ago, I kept my mouth shut and only nodded my agreement.

He nodded in return. "Thank you for coming to me. I'll deal with Clint, and you do the Sub of Attorneys for Randy to sign plus the letters to the judges."

"Actually..." I'd just remembered Randy couldn't take the cases either because of Lorelei, and I briefly wondered if he withdrew from the cases he was on against Peyton. "Randy shouldn't have the cases either. He's dating Peyton's assistant."

Mitch threw his head back, looking at the ceiling and sighed. "I don't want to know. Just handle it."

"Already in the works."

Over the next few months, everything was perfect. Clint was put on probation, I withdrew from the cases against Peyton, and we never talked about them. The bar never came knocking on our door so maybe somehow they got wind that we took all the steps needed before they'd opened an investigation. Whatever it was, I was happy. Being able to go out in public with Peyton was the best feeling in the world. For Valentine's Day, we went to Malibu, had dinner at a restaurant that overlooked the ocean, and enjoyed being a normal couple.

President's Day weekend, we drove up to Yosemite where the snow was still on the ground and beautiful. We took a walk around Mirror Lake, drove to Bridal Veil Falls and took pictures at the scenic turnoff that had Half Dome in the background. When we weren't taking in the park, we were in our cabin doing other *things*.

It was then I'd realized I wanted to marry her. I knew I loved her, knew I wanted to wake up with her every morning and knew my world would be crushed if something were to ever happen to her. There was nothing I wasn't more sure of.

Therefore, I couldn't let more time slip away without making things permanent. We practically lived together already, and my divorce from Carrie would take as long as it needed for Peyton to plan our wedding.

My *real* one.

But first, I had to become a U.S. citizen. I would still be a citizen of the UK, but now I'd be in the States more on a not-breaking-the-law status. I had my biometric appointment with the United States Citizenship and Immigration Services (USCIS), and I was currently waiting for the FBI to perform a background check on me before they scheduled my naturalization interview where they'd ask me a bunch of questions. I'd then take the civics test, pass and wait to take the Unites State's Oath. It was no wonder it took at least six months to become a citizen.

"What's the name of the current Speaker of the House of Representatives?" Peyton asked, holding up a flashcard to help me study for the test and then she listed four names.

"D," I answered.

She smiled. "Correct." She flipped to the next card. "What did Susan B. Anthony do?" More multiple choice answers.

"She fought for women's rights."

"Correct." Peyton smiled again. "Why does the U.S. flag have fifty stars?"

"That's easy. One star for each state."

"Correct."

"Shouldn't you be taking off clothes for all my right answers?"

Peyton chuckled. "You'll get too distracted and get the answers wrong."

"No, I won't," I stated.

"There are twenty practice questions. I'll be naked before you answer all of them."

"Exactly."

She rolled her eyes. "Booker! Come on—"

I stopped her mid-scolding by throwing her into a fireman's hold.

"What are you doing?" she screeched.

"It's been a long time since you've rolled your eyes at me, baby. Now I need to punish you."

"Punish me?"

I threw her on the bed and started to work my belt free.

"You're kidding?"

I shook my head. "I'm not."

"You're going to spank me with a belt?"

"Not hard."

"But you're going to spank me."

I tore the belt from the loops of my trousers. "You're going to be drenching when I'm done."

"With what? Blood?"

I took her ankles and flipped her on to her stomach. "With your cum."

She stopped protesting, and I yanked her leggings and knickers down, revealing her bare arse. I decided I didn't want to use my belt as I spanked her. No, I wanted to use my hand, needing to feel her skin beneath my palm as it tingled when it made contact.

"Lift your hips." As soon as she did, my hand came down and she hissed. "Did it hurt?" Peyton shook her head, and I did it again. As I made contact with her arse, lust tore through my entire body. This was my girl. No matter what new thing I exposed her to, she trusted me.

"You like that?" I asked.

She nodded.

"Tell me what it feels like." *Smack.*

"It's ... It's making my pussy tingle," she panted.

I ran my hand through her slit. "And you're wet, baby."

She moaned in response, and I spanked her two more times before I pushed my trousers down to release my dick, and then slid into her. Images of the first time we were together entered my mind as I grabbed a fist full of her long, chestnut hair. This time she wasn't bound to restraints, but I still wanted to plow into her hard. She titled her head back, her back bowing, and the red mark on her arse made me go wild. I thrust into her, the bed creaking as it slammed into the wall. Yeah, I definitely wanted to do this for the rest of my life. My pace quickened, and before I knew it, we were both coming, groaning our releases and left sated.

"Are you going to roll your eyes at me again?" I asked, pulling out.

"Maybe." Peyton smirked, looking over her shoulder at me.

"Good because I love your arse." I watched as my cum leaked from her pussy, and it did nothing but make me hard again.

"I hereby declare ..." I started, holding my right hand up and not lowering it until the oath was complete.

After all was said and done, and I had my very own U.S. flag on a stick, we left to celebrate. It was definitely a big day. For years I felt as though I was a citizen, but now I was a permanent one and I no longer needed a Green Card. I felt—relieved. Thankful, grateful and happy. After the ceremony, we all went to dinner at a steakhouse in Beverly Hills, ordered the best wine and laughed until our cheeks hurt.

Definitely a good day.

"So, since Booker's a U.S. citizen now and we're all here," Carrie announced. "Taylor and I have some news."

I looked to Peyton who was sitting next to me, and then back to Carrie as she and Taylor stood.

"Of course, this will be later once everything is finalized with Book, but," Carrie raised her left hand from her pocket. "Taylor and I are getting married!" Peyton, Amelia, *and* Lorelei screeched and rushed to her.

I watched as the five women all exchanged hugs, and then I made my way over to Carrie to congratulate her. "Congratulations, *wife*."

"Thank you, *husband*."

"Since I *am* your husband, it's only right for me to give you away at your wedding."

Carrie's eyes were glassy. "I'd like that."

Chapter 28

PEYTON

B eing in court was second nature to me. Get in, get out, see you later. And that was how it went most days I had hearings, but today I was stopped by Clint in the stairwell—*again.*

Even though he was still on probation at Lee and Thompson, he still had cases he was the attorney of record for. His probation was strictly in regard to his employment at L&T.

"Hey, Peyton," he called, but I kept walking, pretending I didn't hear him. "Peyton! Wait up."

I stopped, sighed, and turned around with a big, fake smile on my face. "Oh, hey, Clint. What's up?"

"Marriage of Waterford, you ready to talk settlement?"

"I'm always ready to talk settlement. Email me a draft agreement, and I'll run it by my client."

"I was thinking we could go for that drink and I'll tell you what my client's proposing."

It really didn't work that way. An email would do just fine. Unless he was Booker, and then he'd storm into my office with an agreement and a hidden agenda. Clint had to know I knew he'd said he reported us. Though, we never got a letter from the bar saying they were investigating us.

"You know I can't do that." *Won't* was the real answer. It didn't matter if it was on a professional basis. There was no way I would go anywhere with this asshole.

"Because of Booker?"

I stared at him, not responding. The door on the second level opened, and I prayed it was Booker. It wasn't. "Not only because of

Booker, but there's no reason for us to do anything outside of work. I'm not interested." I was done being nice to this jerk.

He stepped closer, and I stepped back only to hit the railing against the wall. "How long have you been dating that fucker?"

"That's none of your business."

He stepped even closer, and everything in my entire body was on alert. I didn't know if Booker was at the courthouse or not because we didn't talk about cases.

"What if I told you that he's not the man you think he is?"

I rolled my eyes. "Do you think I care what you think?"

The second-floor door opened again. No Booker, or anyone for that matter. People were going down, not up to us on the third floor.

"I think you'd care about the information that I have."

"Let me guess? He killed someone?" I joked sarcastically.

He grinned. "Clever, but not that I know of."

"So you don't know everything about the man you want to be?"

He narrowed his eyes. "I don't want to be him."

"No, you just want to harass him, stalk him."

"I'm not stalking him."

"But you have this "information" about him?" I asked, using air quotes.

"Look, I'm trying to help you."

"I don't need your help," I replied and tried to step around him. He didn't let me.

The third-floor door opened. "What the fuck is going on!"

My eyes snapped to Booker. He had fire in his blue eyes, but it wasn't the lust I was used to seeing. This was rage. He was pissed.

Clint stepped back. "I was just about to inform your girlfriend that you're leading a double life."

"What?" Booker and I both said at the same time.

"I was doing research for a client, and came across something our sweet Peyton needs to know."

"My girlfriend is none of your business," Booker snapped and stepped up a few stairs to get closer to Clint.

"Maybe so," Clint agreed. "But if I can crush your world like you did mine, I'm doing it."

"Well, spit it out, mate. I'm curious what you think you know and Peyton doesn't."

I had to admit, I was curious too. I thought for sure I knew everything there was to know about this man.

Clint turned his attention back to me. "Your boyfriend here is married."

I looked to Booker, him to me, and after we stared at each other for a few beats, we burst into laughter.

"You're laughing?"

"Yes, we're laughing, you bloody wanker. Peyton knows I'm married."

"You do?" Clint asked.

I nodded, still chuckling.

"Good try, mate. And just so you know my entire life's story, and you can fuck off after this, I filed for divorce. Don't try and fuck with me again. You won't win." Booker clapped him on the shoulder and then grabbed my hand, lacing our fingers. "I'm not going to tell Mitch about this, but do yourself a favor and give up."

And then we walked down the stairs and left.

It was the monthly Sensation party night. Booker and I were getting ready to drive into the hills of Beverly Hills and *play*. It almost felt like any date night, though when we got there, it was anything but: no dinner, no movie, no long walk on the beach. Just right to the sex—or foreplay at least.

I slipped on my Louboutins that I wore each time. They were comfortable and sexy, both things I needed while attending Sensation.

Lorelei and Randy were both coming of course. We all rode together either in Booker's car or a limo if Carrie and Taylor wanted to come at the same time. Sometimes they went on their own so they could leave whenever they wanted. Lorelei had become a Pearl member like me since she and Randy were still going strong. I hadn't heard the L word from either of them, but I was sure it was coming soon.

The entire way, I noticed Booker would look into the rearview mirror at where Randy was sitting, but they never said anything. They'd just listen to Lorelei talk and talk about random ass shit. That was what we did when we were together. I wasn't her boss outside of work, and we told each other everything.

Booker pulled into the circular drive and when we finally made it to the red-carpeted steps, Booker pulled up, and the valets opened our doors. Lorelei tugged me up the stairs, not waiting for the guys. After Luke had checked us off, we waited for the guys just inside by the coat check.

"Any plans for tonight?" Lore asked.

I shrugged. "Not sure. I think we've done almost everything we can alone."

"Maybe you should try not alone?"

"That's not Booker's thing."

"Is it yours?" She winked.

Booker walked through the French doors, and I thought about sharing him. "No, not my thing either."

"What's not your thing?" Booker asked, smiling.

I returned the smile. "Sharing you."

His grin widened. "And this is why we're good together, baby." He kissed my lips softly, and Randy cleared his throat.

"I know we're at a sex club, but you two can wait until we get past the black velvet drapes."

"Leave them alone," Lorelei scolded. "We'll see you two when it's over." She grabbed Randy's hand, and then they disappeared passed the drapes.

"Shall we?" Booker asked, and hooked his arm out for me to slip mine inside.

"We shall." I smiled. "Any plans for tonight?"

"Only a few."

"Oh?" I asked, tilting my head up to his as we walked into the red-tinted house.

"First, let's get a drink. Then I thought we could watch Savior for a while. Get some ideas."

"You want to chain me up tonight?" I teased.

"Something like that."

We grabbed our drinks and made our way toward Savior's chair. People had already gathered around. A man with two women were on the couch not far from us. He was laying down, stroking his cock as one of the women had her back against his side, her legs spread, and the other woman was licking her pussy. I watched as he reached around the woman getting pleasured and started rubbing her clit while the other woman stuck two fingers in her.

I then turned my head to a nearby wall and saw two attractive, muscular men kissing and rubbing on each other. I hadn't recalled seeing any guys together before tonight, and I had to admit it was fucking hot.

Savior came into the room, and my attention turned to him. His scene wasn't instructional but for us to observe and maybe gain ideas. If you wanted instructions, you booked an appointment with him to learn, *if* you were Sapphire or Diamond, of course.

After he had taken his seat, a woman from the crowd stepped forward. At first, I thought she was only a member, but then it became clear that she was his pet because as she rubbed against his lap, he didn't push her away. Instead, he grabbed her wrists and brought them behind her back as he cuffed them.

"We know you like to be cuffed," Booker whispered into my ear.

I nodded. I did like cuffs, and remembered how Booker had strapped me to his bed upstairs. My pussy became wet at the thought as I continued to watch.

Savior cuffed each wrist and then stood, grabbing two more cuffs and fastening them around the redhead's ankles. He grabbed the woman's neck and kissed her. The woman moaned as his tongue thrust into her mouth. With a harsh pull, he pulled away. Before I realized it, Savior had pulled a ball gag from the back of his pants and placed it in the woman's mouth.

"That's one way to get her to not talk," Booker teased in my ear.

I jabbed him with my elbow and said, "Shhh."

In response, Booker reached up and placed his arm across my upper chest and tugged me against him. The moment my ass touched his crotch, I felt *him*.

I watched as Savior started to strip the woman, leaving her naked. He took her cuffed wrists, brought them behind her back again and then secured them together with a small chain. Savior reached for a chain attached to the ceiling above them and hooked her bound wrists to it. I knew what it was like to be restrained so I couldn't touch Booker, and I was curious how Savior was going to make it different. Savior then took a spreader bar, pushed the woman's legs apart, and hooked the ankle cuffs to the bar securing it with the chain from the ceiling.

"Do you want to use a spreader bar?" Booker asked in my ear.

I wanted to do anything with this man. "Yes," I answered honestly.

Booker kissed the slope of my exposed neck causing me to shiver. "Good."

Savior took the chains that were hanging from the ceiling and started hoisting her off the ground. My eyes widened as I watched this gagged, naked women start to lean face down toward the floor.

"It's kinda like when we watched the Shibari demonstration," I whispered as I turned my head slightly to Booker.

"Yeah," he agreed. "But this one is more for his pleasure." He kissed my neck again.

Once the woman was at Savior's waist height, he stopped bringing her up and secured it to a hook on the wall not far from his chair. I'd never seen Savior do anything except sit on his throne and have women rub on him, so I expected him to sit back down in his chair and leave the poor girl hanging from the ceiling for the rest of the night. Instead, he ran his hand up her spread leg and cupped her. She moaned against the ball gag, and if I were closer, I was certain I could see he was fingering her.

Instinctively I stepped into Booker more and rubbed my ass on his cock. "This turning you on, baby?" he whispered again into my ear.

I nodded, still rubbing and not using my words.

"Me too," he agreed. "I'd love to bring you upstairs and have my way with you."

"Do it," I replied.

We made it to Booker's room, and I half expected him to maul me as soon as the door was closed. He didn't. Instead, he sat on the bed, his arms behind him as he leaned back and watched me.

"What are you doing?" I asked, standing between him and the fireplace.

"Just admiring you, gorgeous."

"Don't you want to admire me naked?" I was burning with need, my pussy throbbing so bad, wanting to be touched.

"I do, but first I want you to tell me what we're doing."

I blinked at him. "You want *me* to tell *you* what we're doing?"

"Don't you want to be in control, baby?"

"Like a Dom?" I laughed, but then it died off because I was questioning if he really meant that. Did he want to be dominated?

He grinned. "No, not like a Dom. I just want you to choose something you truly fancy."

"I've liked it all," I retorted, crossing my arms over my torso.

"But we haven't done it all."

"I know that," I snorted with a smile.

"Why don't you open the top drawer of the dresser and pick something you want to try."

"Like a toy?"

He nodded with a grin. "If that's what you choose."

"What else is in there?"

"Floggers, handcuffs, anal plugs, anal beads, vibrators, cock rings—"

"I'll just look in the drawer."

When I got to the dark wood dresser and opened it enough to see in, I went left to right analyzing the contents. First was what appeared to be a butt plug with a tail at the end of it. Like a fox tail. Then there were two black, glass balls that I knew were Ben Wa balls, though I'd never tried them. I'd read about them in a popular erotic trilogy years ago and had always wanted to try them. As I reached in, my gaze landed on a black, velvet box in the center of the drawer. Curiosity got the best of me.

"What's in here?" I asked as I spun around to Booker with the box in my hand.

He wasn't on the bed. No, he was kneeling before me on one knee.

My breath hitched, and I could have sworn to everything holy that my heart stopped.

"Hand me the box, beautiful."

Booker reached out his hand, and without saying a word, I handed it to him. I wasn't even sure I could speak. Was he doing what I thought he was doing?

I stared into his crystal blue eyes that held so much love and passion. He cleared his throat, took a deep breath and then his gaze returned to mine.

"That night you left me here without a goodbye, was the night I knew I wasn't going to ever let you go. I wasn't going to give up fighting for you. I got my first taste of you, and I was addicted. You were everything and then some from my fantasies of you. And then you gave me a chance. You let me in.

"When Clint told me he'd reported us, I was prepared to do everything to protect you. I loved you enough to let you choose work over me. I only wanted you happy. Luckily, your dad had better news for us because I don't know what I would have done if I were to wake up without you next to me. I look forward to you kissing me awake, that sleepy look in your beautiful brown eyes when I know you're tired, but you'd rather wish me a good day at work than get a few extra minutes of sleep. Those are the moments that make me realize you're the love of my life. You do things to my heart. You make it beat, you make it have a purpose."

Tears fell from my eyes as I listened to him.

"So what I'm trying to say…" He lifted the lid, and my eyes dropped to a sparkling, solitaire, round diamond on a silver band. A sob escaped my throat as I watched the diamond radiate from the light of the room. "Peyton, gorgeous, will you marry me?"

I was nodding before he'd said the final word. I rushed the two steps to him and tackled him to the floor.

"Is that a yes?" Booker asked as I looked down into his eyes.

"That depends. Does this make me a Diamond member too?"

"You've been a Diamond member from the second I laid eyes on you in court. You just didn't know it yet."

Another sob hitched in my throat. If Booker hadn't been a Diamond member of Sensation, he never would had dragged me up the stairs that first night and I wouldn't have started anything with him downstairs. Booker's room was our sanctum; a place that held our secrets, our firsts and the place he first told me he loved me and now the place I agreed to be his wife.

"Then yes, Mr. Romantic, I'll marry you because, without you, my heart wouldn't have a reason for beating either."

Chapter 29

BOOKER

A part of me thought Carrie was moving too fast with Taylor. They'd been dating for such a short amount of time before announcing they were getting married. But it didn't matter the length of time someone was with a person. It mattered what they felt for each other. And that was no different from how I felt about Peyton.

There wasn't a day that went by that I second guessed our relationship and I decided I wanted it to be permanent too. So one day during lunch, I went ring shopping.

I returned from lunch and went straight to Randy's office. When I was at court and saw my woman doing her thing with her cases, a thought hit me. A thought my father had told me about my mum when they'd first arrived from Leeds over the Christmas holiday. "I knew I wanted to marry her. I couldn't get her out of my head." And that was true for me too. So instead of heading back to the office to see if Randy wanted to grab a quick lunch, I'd gone to the nearest jewelry store.

Now I had the ring in the pocket of my trousers as I walked to tell my mate what I wanted to do. "Hey." I knocked on his open door. "Do you a minute?"

He looked up from his computer screen. "Yeah. I don't need to be in court until three."

"Good," I said and moved to sit in the chair before his desk. Before I sat, though, I dug into my pocket and pulled the velvet black box out and set it in front of him.

Randy looked from the box up at me and as I sat he asked, "This for me?"

I chuckled. "No, you bloody wanker, it's for Peyton."

He lifted the lid. "Holy shit!"

I smiled.

"Are you sure?" It was a valid question given the length of time Peyton and I had been together, and what Randy and I did for a living.

"Yeah, mate. Deadly sure."

"When are you going to do it?"

I reached for the box, and he handed it to me. As I stared down at the shiny diamond, I said, "Soon."

"How soon?"

I thought for a moment. "Would it be weird to propose at the club? I mean, it's a beautiful backdrop off my balcony."

"With the moans of women coming in the background?"

"Right," I agreed. But something was telling me that it was right to propose at the place we started at. "What if I do it in my room with the door closed?"

He nodded. "I think that would be okay if you're really set on doing it there."

"I'm going to need your help then."

"Okay, tell me what you need me to do."

The plan was set.

I'd given the ring to Randy when we arrived at Sensation. Lorelei dragged Peyton inside without us because that was her job in *the plan*. When we were all inside and went our separate ways, I knew that Randy and Lorelei went up to my room and put the box in the drawer as I'd instructed.

Then I pretended it was like any other night at the club. We usually spent an hour or so looking around after getting a drink so I couldn't rush going up to the room. Though it was killing me.

When Peyton finally opened the top drawer, my heart was pounding so hard that I was positive she could hear it. The wait felt like hours as I watched her examine a few of the toys. Her gaze finally landed on the box, and when she reached inside the dresser, my heart stopped. I quickly got off the bed and knelt in front of her.

And my speech wasn't planned. I'd planned to just pop the question so to speak, but then looking up into Peyton's mocha eyes, I knew I needed to express how I felt about her. I wanted to tell her every thought I had about her from the first day I saw her until that moment. But instead, I voiced my fears and told her how I never wanted to be without her. Luckily she never wanted to be without me either.

The other big news was my divorce from Carrie was fast approaching. I never thought I'd be excited to divorce her, but I was. Our lives were changing for the better and working out better than I could have ever hoped for.

"We decided to have a beach wedding," Carrie stated as we ate cheeseburgers at the dining room table.

I was slowly moving my stuff out, and Taylor was slowly moving her belongings in, but it didn't stop us from having weekly dinners together. Carrie was still my best mate. Now that Peyton and I could go out in public, it was an entirely different ball game. Being able to walk out in the daylight with my fiancée was bloody brilliant. We also saw a lot more of Sam as we came and went. Even though things had started off rocky with that wanker, I think he was finally starting to realize I wasn't going anywhere. It didn't stop him from banging on our wall a few nights a week, but Peyton and I found ways to tune him out. Like using her dining room table with cuffs or taking a shower together that lasted a really long time. Or we just left, took a walk, did *normal* things.

"That's going to be so beautiful," Peyton exclaimed.

I wondered if she wanted to get married at the beach too. I had an idea of where I wanted to get married that I needed to ask her about.

"At sunset," Carrie clarified.

"I can*not* wait. You both are going to look stunning," Peyton stated.

"You will too on your big day," Taylor said.

Peyton looked over at me.

"You'll be the most beautiful bride I've ever seen," I told her.

"Hey," Carrie protested.

My eyes cut to her. "Sorry, *wife*, but it's true."

"We're all going to be beautiful brides," Peyton countered.

This was true, but I only cared about the one who had my heart in the palm of her hand.

I was legally a single man. My divorce with Carrie was finalized and filed with the Beverly Hills Superior Court. The easiest divorce I'd ever done. We filed the petition, the response, and all other documents needed. When we met with the judge for our first hearing, I explained we'd come up with a settlement agreement. I was probably the easiest propria persona (pro per or pro se) case Judge Brown had ever presided over.

Unlike normal divorces, Carrie and I went to celebrate with our friends. It was more or less a divorce party, but both of us were there.

And today my ex-wife was marrying her girlfriend.

I never thought it would happen. Granted, I didn't think a lot of stuff that was happening was ever going to happen. But since I'd first met Carrie, I knew she wanted the dream wedding. It's a shame that society and the law still frown upon same-sex couples getting married in some states and countries. When would love be enough?

That was what I admired about Carrie. She wasn't just my best mate who liked pussy as much as me. She was an attorney fighting for the rights of her fellow peers facing the same hardships as she. I was positive that one day no one would bat an eye at two women or two men getting married.

"I'm going to go find my seat," Peyton said behind me.

I turned from the floor length mirror in our hotel room. "Let me escort you."

"You have someone else to escort." She smiled.

"I do, but they won't start without me," I teased. "By the way, baby, you're beautiful tonight."

She smiled, and a blush flushed her cheeks. The same color as her pink, strapless dress. Her hair was up in some sort of twist. A twist I couldn't wait to take apart and watch her hair cascade around her shoulders as I made love to her. We were in a hotel, at a wedding—a wedding where I was giving away my ex-wife—and getting laid was what happened at weddings. It was tradition.

We walked out of the white beachfront hotel and down to where the sand met a walkway. Peyton slipped off her silver, strappy heels and handed them to the attendant collecting shoes. She turned to me. "You're not taking yours off?"

"I'll empty them after I walk Carrie down the aisle."

"You know she'll be barefoot, right?"

"It's her day, baby. I'm just here to give her away."

Peyton gave me a warm smile. "For what it's worth, I think it's special that you are since her father is no longer with us."

I stuck out my elbow for Peyton to slip her arm in and we began walking toward the white, cushioned, bench-style seats. "I told her years ago that I would. No matter what happened between us, I wasn't going to miss this day."

She leaned her head on the side of my shoulder was we walked, not saying a word. The sweet gesture was all I needed. This was a big deal. One I would cherish for the rest of my life.

We made it to the four post, wood arbour that had various white flowers wrapped around the legs. The benches for guests were in a circle instead of the traditional bride's side and groom's side. Carrie had wanted everyone to have the best view of her getting hitched, and I have to say it was a brilliant idea.

I lead Peyton to a bench closest to one of the sides of the arbour, kissed her goodbye and then started to walk back to get my ex-wife. People passed me as they made their way through the sand, and once I was on cement again, I emptied my shoes. There was no way I would be able to walk ten feet with the amount of sand that was in my shoes. *Apparently, my fiancée was right.*

As I entered the hotel, my parents were walking out. "Peyton saved you a seat," I told them.

"This is going to be a beautiful wedding," Mum gushed. "It's about time I see California in the summer."

"Yeah, Mum. You'll have the perfect view of the ocean," I agreed.

"Go get Carrie, son. We'll find Peyton," Dad said, and then he and my mum walked the opposite way.

I found the room Carrie was getting ready in, knocked and waited. The door opened and Amelia stood, grinning at me.

"Can you believe our girl's getting married?"

"Not the first time," I joked.

Amelia slapped my arm. "The first one to count."

"True," I agreed, and my eyes found Carrie in her white dress. Her blonde hair was pulled up into one of those twist things, and her gown was lovely. She looked like a princess.

"Why didn't you look this good when we got married?"

Her blue eyes lifted and she glared. "Because you made me get married at the courthouse."

"You made me marry you."

"Will you two stop?" Amelia cut in.

"We're only joking around, *love.*"

"Don't love me. I know you only say it to be rude."

I lifted a shoulder. "And?"

"Do you want to babysit my children? I can make that happen."

"You wouldn't," I protested.

"I'm sure I can talk Peyton into it."

"All right, I'll play nice."

"Good. Now take our girl's hand and give her away once and for all."

"With pleasure." I stuck out my hand for Carrie to take it. "Come on, sweetheart. It's time to make an honest woman out of you."

Chapter

PEYTON

"I want you to have this."

I looked up to see my mother walking into her kitchen. Lorelei and I were sitting around my parents' breakfast table, finalizing everything for my upcoming wedding in a few weeks.

"What's that?" I asked, looking at the folded baby blue cloth in her outreached hand.

"This belonged to my mother and father, and I've been saving it to let you borrow it for your big day. I know they'd want to see you walk down the aisle if they were still with us." A lump started to form in my throat. I wished they could be there too, but God needed them more than us.

"It's a handkerchief that belonged to your grandfather," she went on. "But my mother kept it after he passed and carried it in her pocket."

"I remember," I whispered and took the cloth from her. I hadn't seen the handkerchief in—well I couldn't remember how long, but it had been a long time since my grandmother passed away.

"You can stuff it in your bra," Lorelei cut in.

I snorted, and my tears started to slip away. "I'll do that."

As we continued to finalize the seating chart, catering menu and various other things I was stressing about, I thought about Booker's grandmother. He hadn't said anything, but I knew deep in my heart that he wished she could be there for our big day too. So, I needed to figure out a way.

Today was the day that I'd waited my entire life for. I never thought it would happen because I was the single, divorce lawyer who men were scared to get serious with.

Until Booker.

We were on the same team. We knew what went on in divorces, and even though he was a divorcé himself, we knew what not to do in a marriage to make it work since we'd practically seen or heard it all.

Booker had asked me what I thought about getting married at Sensation. I thought it was perfect. When we met with Savior to ask him if we could use his home because that was where our relationship started, he was delighted to help us.

And free of charge, though for as much as we paid to be members, it should be a wash.

It was truly a blessing and Savior was the sweetest man—besides my fiancé, of course. I'd always thought that people who were into BDSM must be assholes. But what I'd discovered was that being into BDSM didn't mean that their desire emerged from abuse or domestic violence, and engaging in it didn't mean that they enjoyed abuse or abusing. Instead, enjoying BDSM was just one facet of someone's sexuality and lifestyle, and slowly I was starting to learn that I liked the bondage aspect, as well as a being a little submissive.

When I told my family where the wedding was being held, they asked me how we were able to secure a mansion in Beverly Hills. There was no way in Hell that I'd tell them the exact truth, so I'd told them that Booker knew people. It was true.

"Ready?"

I turned to see my dad had walked into the room. It wasn't Booker's room, but Carrie's down the hall. She was letting me borrow it while I got ready. And Booker was getting ready in his.

I smiled at my dad. "I am."

I expected him to hook his arm out for me to slip my hand in the crook. Instead, he placed both of his hands on my shoulders and looked down on me. "Today's the day I officially give you to someone else. There's not a doubt in my mind that Booker will keep you safe and treat you how a man should treat a woman. You did good, kid."

Tears started to prick my eyes, but I fought them. I couldn't cry before I walked down the aisle. I couldn't cry at all. My makeup would turn to shit, and then I'd be late to my own wedding.

"Dad," I whispered, but he kept going.

"I know I'm supposed to give my speech later, but I just want to talk to you alone for a minute."

I nodded, still trying to hold my tears at bay.

"I'm not always going to be here for you, and as you got older your mother and I hoped you'd find that one person who would look at you like you were their world. When I watch Booker with you, I know that's what he's thinking. You're not just a woman to him, you're his everything. And I don't need him to tell me that. I see it."

I nodded again, a tear slipping from my eye. I wiped it away and took a deep breath so no more would spill over.

"What I'm trying to say is that I'm comfortable giving you over to him because I know he'll treat you like the princess you are. I love you, baby girl."

"Thanks, Daddy." I wrapped my arms around his waist, no longer caring if I messed up my hair or makeup. My dad would always be my first love.

"Let's go get you married."

I nodded and pulled back.

As we walked down the stairs and made our way to the doors that led out to the pool, butterflies fluttered in my stomach. I was about to marry Booker. Booker Jameson. I was about to become Peyton Jameson. The thought made me realize that if you gave someone a chance, they might become what you always wanted—who you were always missing.

I was missing Booker all those years.

My dad and I stopped just before exiting the doors. Lorelei was there with Randy because they were walking down the aisle before me. Even though we were having a small, intimate wedding, we wanted them to be a part of it. Amelia's children were the flower girl and ring bearer, and Carrie was officiating. Yes, Booker's ex-wife who he gave away at her wedding was marrying us.

"You look so beautiful," Lorelei beamed.

I looked down at my princess style wedding dress with sequins on the skirt. I felt beautiful. "Thanks, babe."

Randy stepped up and gave me a side hug. "If Trent Inglewood was my client and not Booker's, would we be getting married instead?"

I pushed him away as Lorelei hissed, "Randy!"

"What?" he asked with a shit eating grin. "That's how they started."

"You better knock it off, or we're—" Her gaze moved to my dad's, and she smiled then turned back to her boyfriend. "Just knock it off."

"You love me."

"I don't love you hitting on my best friend."

I shook my head, chuckling. These two were made for each other and yes, in love. Randy had confessed his love for her after Carrie's wedding three months ago while they'd walked on the beach. Seemed my man wasn't the only romantic one.

"If you two are done, I think it's time," Dad stated as the music started to play.

I watched Randy escort Lorelei down the aisle that was just to the right of the pool. Evening had started to descend, casting a yellow hue across all of our family and friends. I made it a point to not look at the front so I didn't see Booker. I wanted to wait until I got to the far end of the walkway and then look to find him. I wanted to look directly at him as I made my way to my forever with him.

Amelia stepped up, smiled at me and then told Ryder it was time for him to go find Uncle Booker. I smiled back and then watched as she gave Emily a basket with red rose petals inside. Not only were the roses the first flowers Booker gave me, but they symbolized Booker's grandmother because they were her favorite. She'd obviously meant so much to him for him, and I felt that she should bring a little beauty to our day.

"Ready?"

I nodded, and my dad and I started to walk as Lennon & Maisy's version of *Boom Clap* started to play. I kept my eyes looking down at the bouquet of red roses in my hand as we walked toward the end of the aisle. Our guests probably assumed I was embarrassed since I didn't meet any of their eyes, but if they only knew what I'd done by this pool, it would blow their minds.

I stopped just at the last row of chairs and waited for the second verse to start. When it did, I looked up and my eyes met Booker's just as the words being sung talked about the person being the glitter of her world. Booker was definitely my glitter in my darkness.

Booker smiled.

I smiled.

And everything and everyone around us disappeared as I walked closer to him because he was my guiding light in a world that was empty before him.

Booker and my father shook hands, and then dad turned to me, kissed me on the forehead, and found his seat next to my mother. I turned and looked up at Booker. He had tears in his eyes. For the past fifteen minutes, I'd been trying not to be a sobbing mess, but seeing this cocky man crying made me shed my tears.

"I'm glad you showed," he teased in my ear.

I chuckled through my tears. I knew he was only saying it to lighten the mood. He was truly meant for me.

We held hands, and Booker mouthed, "You're beautiful."

I knew that my father was right. Booker saw me as his world, and not just some woman in it.

And to think ...

It had all started with an invitation.

the end.

*Keep reading for a sneak peek of *Angels & Whiskey* by Kimberly*

A note from the AUTHOR

Dear Readers,

I hope you've enjoyed *By Invitation Only*. If you would be so kind to leave a review where you'd purchased this book as well as Goodreads and Bookbub, I would greatly appreciate it. Honest reviews help other readers find my books and your support means the world to me.

Please subscribe to either my blog, newsletter or both to stay up-to-date on all of my releases. You can find the links on my website at www.authorkimberlyknight.com. You can also follow me on Facebook at: www.facebook.com/AuthorKKnight.

Until we meet again, friends.

xoxo,

Kimberly Knight

ACKNOWLEDGMENTS

I always start with my husband because he's the one that has supported me through this journey. Over the years, we've faced many challenges and without him, I wouldn't be as strong as I am today. Thank you for everything you do for me and for all your love. I love you, you know?

To Jessi Gibson: I dedicated this book to you. You gave me the push to keep going and without you, I wouldn't have continued to believe in myself. Thank you for all the brainstorming we did and being there when I needed you. So happy to call you my friend.

Andrea Long aka Andie M. Long: Mate!!! Thank you for helping me give Booker his British voice. Now when I visit you and we go to that bar with all the balls, I'll be speaking the language! Keep fighting, Wonder Woman.

To my editor, Jennifer Roberts-Hall: Thank you for always being the one to make sure my books are perfect. There's not a day that goes by that I'm not thankfully we met that one day in the Vancouver airport and became fast friends.

To my best friend, Lea Cabalar: You're my yin to my yang. My ebony to my ivory. I appreciate all you do for me and truly being my best friend.

Jennifer Severino: Thank you so much for being my attorney in this matter. Haha, but seriously, thank you for all the help to make sure that these two attorneys in this book got their story straight. You rock, and one day I'll take you up on your *Werther's Originals* offer.

Renee Reigles: I know life got in the way, but I still love you. Hope Booker was up to your standards ;)

To my betas: Rachel Adams-Burgess, Helena Cole, Kristin Jones, Maureen Mayer and Kerri McLaughlin. Thank you for being my eyes and making sure this story made sense. You ladies are amazing and I'm lucky to have you willing to help me out. Thank you so much.

To all the bloggers who participated in my cover reveal, release day blitz and review tour, thank you! Without bloggers, I have no idea where I would be. You've all taken a chance on me and my books time and time again, and I can't tell you how much I appreciate it.

To Liz Christensen of E. Marie Photography: This makes number eleven!

And finally, to my readers: Thank you for believing in me and taking a chance on my books again and again. Without you guys, I wouldn't still be writing and living my dream!

www.facebook.com/E.MariePhotographs
emc33photos@gmail.com

Models:
Amy Belle Reusch and Bailey Lee

Books
BY
Kimberly Knight

Club 24 Series – Romantic Suspense

Perfect Together – The Club 24 Series Box Set

Halo Series – Contemporary Romance

Saddles & Racks Series – Romantic Suspense

Use Me – Romantic Suspense Standalone

Burn Falls – Paranormal Romance Standalone

And more ...

Kimberly Knight is a USA Today Bestselling author who lives in the mountains near a lake in California with her loving husband, who is a great *research* assistant. Kimberly writes in a variety of genres including romantic suspense, contemporary romance, erotic romance, and paranormal romance. Her books will make you laugh, cry, swoon, and fall in love before she throws you curve balls you never see coming.

When Kimberly isn't writing, you can find her watching her favorite reality TV shows, binge-watching true crime documentaries, and going to San Francisco Giants games. She's also a two-time desmoid tumor/cancer fighter, which has made her stronger and an inspiration to her fans.

KIMBERLY KNIGHT

www.authorkimberlyknight.com

f facebook.com/AuthorKKnight

🐦 twitter.com/Author_KKnight

📷 instagram.com/authorkimberlyknight

P pinterest.com/authorkknight

BB bookbub.com/authors/kimberly-knight

SNEAK PEEK OF

USA Today bestselling author

Kimberly Knight

ANGELS

& Whiskey

A Saddles & Racks Novel

PROLOGUE
Gabe

March 9th

I never thought I'd see a day where my world was more consumed by one person than by serving my country.

My life was set to follow in my grandfather's footsteps. It was my destiny. I'd forgotten he'd met my grandmother while serving in Vietnam, so I should have known I would meet my future wife while serving in Afghanistan.

"You gotta girl back home we don't know about, Cap?"

I glanced from the computer screen to First Lieutenant Paul Jackson as he spoke and then to Cochran, who was sitting across the room. The moment I'd laid eyes on Cochran when she joined my crew, I had no idea she'd become my first love.

For a few seconds, I watched as Cochran laughed with Stone, her fellow medic. "Something like that," I murmured, turning back to the website on the computer that was allowing me to *secretly* design an engagement ring for her. I was Specialist Cochran's Captain, and because of military regulations, no one could know we had been dating for nine months and that I wanted to make her my wife.

My life's plan had always been to work my way through the ranks until I was no longer breathing. But now I wanted to be with Cochran and spend the rest of my life making her happy. It was hard not being able to kiss her whenever I wanted—to touch her as she walked by or hold her hand. I felt like a stalker; always secretly watching her.

"Why are you designing an engagement ring?" he asked, interrupting my thoughts.

I looked over my right shoulder at him. "Are you a moron, LT?" I chuckled.

"I just didn't know you gotta girl is all." He shrugged, still peering over my shoulder and looking at the computer screen.

"Well, I do." I glanced to Cochran again and then back to the computer before Jackson noticed. "Get out of my hair and go check your gear before Major Dick rips you a new asshole."

"You don't have any." He laughed, looking at my bald head.

"I like it that way, Lieutenant. Now fuck off." I ran my hand over my bald head. I'd been losing my hair for a few years, so I finally said fuck it and shaved it all off. Cochran thought it looked sexy on me. I was his Captain, but we were like brothers and even had that brotherly banter. Honestly, he was the closest friend I had on base, so it was no wonder he was questioning me about my love life.

"You know I'm going to get you to show me naked pictures of her."

"In your dreams, P.J. Now really, fuck off."

"All right," he huffed. "By the way, the gear's good, Cap. But I feel ya. I'll leave you to your girly shit." He laughed again then slapped me on the back and left to join the rest of the crew. They were binge watching *Lost* while we waited for any MEDEVAC (medical evacuation) calls.

I was tired of the war. I never thought I'd say that. For as long as I could remember, I'd wanted to be an American hero. Not anymore.

I'd already completed two tours and as soon as my third was done, so was I. I didn't want to be in the sand anymore. I didn't want to hear gunfire in the distance twenty-four-seven. I didn't want to have that sinking feeling in the pit of my stomach on a MEDEVAC call as we potentially stepped into the line of fire.

I wanted Alyssa Cochran—on a beach in Hawaii.

I wanted to wake up next to her and see her blue eyes sparkle while the sun rose.

I wanted to see her blonde hair fanned across my pillow.

I wanted to be with her openly.

I wanted her as my wife.

Cochran rose from her seat on the couch and I minimized the computer screen. I glanced at her a few times as she made her way across the room, trying not to be obvious that I was watching her. She brushed her finger along the bridge of her nose. *Our sign.* I tried to hide my smile as I saved my design in my online account on the computer, then erased my browser history and closed the window. I couldn't wait to have her in my arms.

I made my way down the hall, pretending to need the latrine. I looked over my shoulder and when I saw no eyes on me, made my way through the door across the hall where Cochran was waiting.

"Have I ever told you that I love a man in uniform?" she whispered, grabbing my arm and pulling me into a vacant room.

I closed the door behind me. "I'll make sure to keep my uniform after this tour." I wrapped her in my arms, holding her as if it were our last day together. I hated the whole situation: the sneaking around, not being able to kiss her whenever I wanted, not being able to cuddle on the couch and watch a movie.

"Good." She smiled as I leaned down and kissed her soft lips enjoying the faint taste of cherry Chapstick.

Taking her hand, I led her to one of the cots and sat in the center, pulling her down to sit on my lap. Her arms wrapped around my neck and she leaned into me. "What were you and Stone laughing about earlier?" I asked, then took a breath of her scent. She always smelled like vanilla ... warm vanilla sugar.

She leaned her head back and gave me a wicked smirk. "I can't tell you. You're my Captain."

"Alys—"

"We were playing Fuck, Marry, Kill," she blurted.

My jaw clenched. I didn't want to hear who she wanted to fuck, but curiosity won. "Who'd you pick?"

After a few beats, she finally spoke. "You can't get mad, Gabe. It was just for shits and giggles."

"All right, I won't. Tell me." I brushed a piece of her hair behind her ear that had fallen from her bun.

"Well, of course, I'd marry you—I love you. And Stone and I both want to kill Major Dick even though he's not bad on the eyes." She paused and took a deep breath before continuing. "Now this is the part you can't get mad at—"

"Just tell me, babe." I knew I couldn't get mad over a silly game, but it was just like when you had a dream and someone pissed you off in it; you'd wake up mad at them for no reason. And that's how I was feeling. I wanted to know who my *competition* was.

"I'd ... I'd fuck Jackson."

My back straightened and my arms wrapped tighter around her. Yeah, I wanted to throttle him even if he was my best friend.

"It's just a game C.H." I smiled. CH stood for Captain Hottie. I knew she used my nickname to lighten the mood. "I only want to fuck you—and *do* only fuck you."

"I know, babe. But my best friend?"

"Just a game, C.H. Just a game."

"I need to come up with my own list." I grinned at her. Two could play this game.

She slapped my arm playfully. "Don't you dare!"

"All right, I won't. But I hope these next six months go by fast. I want Jackson to know you're mine." I brushed my hand under the hem of her army green T-shirt, feeling her smooth belly and needing to feel her soft, warm skin.

She gave a tight smile. "Me too."

"Maybe..." I paused for a moment before continuing to make sure I wanted to suggest this. "Maybe we *should* tell Jackson and Stone? I trust them and they can be our lookout people."

"You want to risk them telling?"

My hands had worked Alyssa's T-shirt from her pants without me knowing. I wanted her and at that moment, I didn't care if my whole crew knew. If someone ran and told Major Dick, I'd deal with it. I'd risk getting kicked out of the army just to be with her and a chance to kick Major Dick's ass. Major Dick wasn't his real name, but he sure as shit earned it, and I'd leave with the respect of everyone in the army because no one liked *Dick*.

"I'd risk anything for you."

"Okay, let's tell them. I trust them. Stone's my best friend too."

"Good." I agreed and began to lift her shirt over her head until there was a knock on the door. We both stilled, me holding my breath.

"Cap, we gotta Dustoff," Jackson called out behind the closed door. While I wanted to spend the rest of the day with Cochran on my lap, we had a MEDIVAC call we had to go to.

"Shit, he already knows," Alyssa whispered, her eyes wide with concern then scurried off my lap.

I watched her, not saying anything while she tucked her shirt into her pants. Jackson knocked on the women's door. He knew I was in there with her.

"How many?" I asked while Alyssa righted herself.

"Two."

"How bad?"

"Urgent. No enemies in the area."

I rushed to the door, swung it open with Alyssa on my heels. "You know nothing." I pointed a finger in his face in warning.

He smiled. "I found you in the shitter. I don't know what you're talking about."

"Good. We'll be right behind you." I grabbed Alyssa's hand and halted her as Jackson continued walking down the hall. "One down and one to go." I smiled and kissed her cherry lips.

"Stone won't be a problem. Tonight I'll show you how happy I am to finally tell people."

"I like the sound of that. But real quick … Since you want to marry me, what shape of diamonds do you like?"

"What?" she asked, scrunching her eyebrows.

"In your game of Fuck, Marry, Kill, what ring would you hope I'd give you?"

She laughed. "You're silly."

"Just tell me. We don't have time for you to question me."

"I don't know. I'd never really given it much thought. I'd like any ring you'd give me."

"All right. Good to know. Let's go so we can get back and tell Jackson and Stone. Then I can take my time tasting you and not have to worry about anyone catching us." I kissed her again before we joined the rest of the crew.

The crew chatted about what was happening in the current episode of *Lost* as we made our way to our coordinates. My thoughts were only of Alyssa. I couldn't wait for tonight so I could take my time making love to her somewhere other than a supply closet.

I stared at her as she laughed with Stone, the desert sand behind her, and I envisioned her in a bikini laying on the beach in Hawaii. I hated Afghanistan. I wanted to be back on American soil with the Pacific Ocean in the distance.

When we finally touched down, the helicopter caused the sand to blow around us. Every day I found sand in places on my body it didn't belong. It felt as if I could never be one hundred percent clean no matter how hard I scrubbed.

The popping of gunfire could be heard in the distance as we made our way from the bird. Heads down, gear in hand, we made it to the soldiers that were covered in crimson blood. After Cochran and Stone had patched up the bullet holes on each soldier with enough gauze so we could transport them back to base, the crew and I strapped them on the gurneys. I faintly heard the gunfire getting closer as we stood.

Pop. Pop. Pop.

"I thought you said dispatch radioed there were no enemy troops in the area?" I asked Jackson.

"That's what the 9-Line said."

Usually dispatch was correct when they'd called in a 9-Line MEDEVAC request for us. They'd tell us where the location was, how many patients, if we needed special equipment ... Nine items to prepare us. Obviously they were wrong this time.

"We need to move. They're getting closer."

The wind kicked up, blowing the rough sand in the air and making it hard to see our own hands in front of our eyes. I fucking hated Afghanistan.

The gunfire got louder.

Pop. Pop. Pop.

"Let's move!"

Jackson radioed base. "Charlie Tango, this is Delta Sky. We have enemy fire and we're being ambushed. Send backup, stat."

My crew and I picked up the two gurneys and began running toward the helicopter. The gunfire was close as we slid one gurney in.

Pop. Pop. Pop.

"Cap!" Jackson yelled.

I looked back seeing enemy troops in the distance, the wind dying down enough to see them crouch and take aim.

Before we could pull our weapons, they fired.

"Get this gurney in!" I snapped, drawing my gun and covering my crew.

Instinct took over as I aimed, firing my gun and praying we didn't get hit with bullets as we stood in the open desert with nothing to hide behind. As we fired back, Cochran and Stone tended to our downed soldiers.

"Heads down, keep firing!" I barked.

Pop. Pop. Pop.

"Watch Cochran's and Stone's six, Woodring!"

Pop.

"Move, move, move!"

Pop. Pop.

We continued to fire. I didn't know how many enemy troops there were. I couldn't see with all the sand in the air, but we kept firing until the wind wasn't blowing and we saw all of the enemies down.

"Everyone good?" I asked. I turned around to see one of my medics down. I couldn't tell who, but my heart stopped.

"Jackson!" I hollered as I ran to the downed medic.

When I reached her, I fell to my knees, flipping her over —Cochran.

"No!" I yelled, my heart pounding so hard that I thought it would beat out of my chest. Alyssa wasn't moving and blood started to seep and stain her uniform.

"Fuck!" Jackson shouted, kneeling beside me.

"No!" I yelled again. This couldn't be happening. This was Alyssa, the love of my life. She was part of my crew. The crew I was trained to protect and the one person I wanted to protect the most was down, her chest covered in dark red blood and not moving.

"Cap, we gotta get her in the bird. More enemies could be coming," Jackson affirmed.

I was numb, unable to move. Alyssa was in my arms still not moving and barely breathing. I held her asking her to open her eyes ...

But she didn't.

"Open your eyes, Cochran." I could feel the tightness in my throat as I fought off the tears that were building. Everything around me didn't matter anymore. I only cared for Alyssa and she was shot—shot on my watch.

"Cap, we gotta move," Jackson persisted.

"Put her in the bird so I can stop the bleeding," Stone begged.

I hesitated for a minute, still looking at Alyssa. The severity of the situation hadn't hit yet.

"Cap—"

"All right!" I picked her body off the ground, placing her inside the helicopter. We piled in and I removed her helmet. Her beautiful blue eyes didn't stare back at me. Her smile wasn't spread across her face like it had been thirty minutes prior.

Tears rolled down my cheeks. No one had seen me cry before. I was a soldier. I was an American hero. I was a fucking captain—I didn't cry. But as my worst fear came crashing down around me, I lost it.

Tears trickled down my cheeks and onto Alyssa as she lay in my arms, her breathing diminishing every second. I didn't care anymore. This was real and she was the love of my life. I wanted to go back to thirty minutes ago and prepare everyone for the ambush. I wanted to be the one in front of the bullet—not Alyssa. I wanted to save her.

We started to fly back to base, the tears still rolling down my face. No one said anything. Stone and Jackson worked on Alyssa while my other crew members tended to the original soldiers the best they could since they weren't medics.

Alyssa started to cough up blood and then before I knew it, she stopped.

"Stay with me, babe," I pleaded, brushing my fingers down her cheek.

I looked up to see Stone's eyes fill with tears as she listened through a stethoscope, then she shook her head at Jackson, advising my gaze.

"No!" This couldn't be happening. Alyssa wasn't dead. We were going to get married. She was going to take my last name. I was going to wake up next to her every morning—I was counting on forever.

But we weren't.

Alyssa died in my arms on the way back to base and worst of all ...

I didn't get to tell her how much I loved her.

*Find out what happens next. One-Click now!

Made in United States
Orlando, FL
03 December 2023

40050206R00189